Praise for *The Texas*
Gold Meda
Writer's So

"*The Texas Gun Club* is an excellent WWII war novel—realistic, well-plotted, many actual events.... [It] describes the successes and failures of command and battle: friendly fire, poor communications, death, destruction, courage, and valor. It has found a place on my bookshelf.... I am looking forward to the author's promised next novel in the series [*Victory Road*]."

Lee Boyland, Reviewer
Military Writers Society of America (January 2010)

"*The Texas Gun Club* is a well-written account of a very real critical World War II battle. Only the characters are fictional. Careful attention to detail in weapons and equipment, as well as period 'soldier slang,' brings [characters] to life as real people that we might have known back in 1939.... *The Texas Gun Club* highlights one great tragic truth of warfare: Because of personal turbulence and logistic screwups, and despite unit lineage that may go back to the Revolution, we almost always fight the first battle with ad hoc organizations. The Salerno landing found the 36th Texas Division executing a difficult maneuver (establishing a lodgment on a distant defended shore) against an experienced, well-led commander (Field Marshal Kesslring), with precious little time and space to sort it out and get it right. A good read for those who would lead."

MG Don Daniel, USA (Ret.)
Former Commander, 49th Armored Division, TXARNG

"*The Texas Gun Club* is an absolutely superb book. The characters are incredibly realistic, as is the action and the storyline of the two cousins dovetailing through history. That it will be a series is refreshing, and I look forward to reading the next excerpt. . . . For a Navy guy, Commander Bowlin has a great handle on the Army. Time for him to get back to the next installment . . . ."

BG Jack Grubbs, USA (Ret.) PhD, PE
Author of *Bad Intentions*

"Bravo Zulu to Mark Bowlin for writing an exceptionally entertaining, interesting, and educational novel. I could hardly put the book down and found the narrative and story line just captivating. . . . I can't wait to read the further adventures of *The Texas Gun Club*, and I'll happily pass along this book as a great read to all those interested in history, Italy, military operations and, of course, just a good yarn!"

RDML Tony Cothron, USN (Ret.)
Former Director of Naval Intelligence

"I found [*The Texas Gun Club*] a fantastic historical fiction that all members of the division should read. Having been a member of the 141st, it gave me a great sense of pride in the regiment and the 36th Division. I actually chose to have my regimental affiliation with the 141st after reading Commander Bowlin's book . . . ."

SGT Casey Mueller, TXARNG

To Al Jones,

Best Wishes,

Mark Bowlin

Victory Road

A Texas Gun Club Novel

December 2014

Commander Mark Bowlin, USN (Ret.)

Victory Road: A Texas Gun Club Novel
Copyright © 2010 by Mark Bowlin

This is a work of fiction.

Manufactured in the United States of America.

For information, please contact:

The P3 Press
16200 North Dallas Parkway, Suite 170
Dallas, Texas 75248
www.thep3press.com
(972) 248-9500

A New Era in Publishing™

ISBN-13: 978-1-933651-90-3
ISBN-10: 1-933651-90-3
LCCN: 2010914022

Author contact information:
Commander Mark Bowlin, USN (Ret.)
www.MarkBowlin.org

Victory Road is dedicated to my wife,
Susan Bowlin—a beautiful, caring, and
extraordinarily tolerant lady.

Acknowledgments

First and foremost, I need to thank Susan and Alex for their support during the writing of *Victory Road*. Their patience and support makes my post-Navy experiment possible.

Many of my friends graciously consented to the use of their names for characters. I have to single out Toni Bernardi Rose; CAPT Doug Grossmann, USN; and CDR Mark Gerschoffer, USN, for special thanks. You'll soon understand why.

Many generous people offered technical advice, editorial suggestions, and help in a multitude of ways. I would like to thank my primary readers, Stan Bowlin and CDR Bob Rose, USN (Ret.); as well as RDML Tony Cothron, USN (Ret.); CDR Rob "Two-Bit" Hoar, USN; Lt Col Frank Chawk III, USMC; Lt Cdr Robert Hawkins, MBE, RN; Capt Fin Jones, USMC (Ret.); SGT Casey Mueller, TXARNG; Cynthia Stillar; Mark Bowling; the Reverend Mike Allen, PhD; Andy and Ginger Eads; Cassie McQueenie-Tankard; James Clay; Wayne Foster; and Jeff Hunt with the Texas Military Forces Museum.

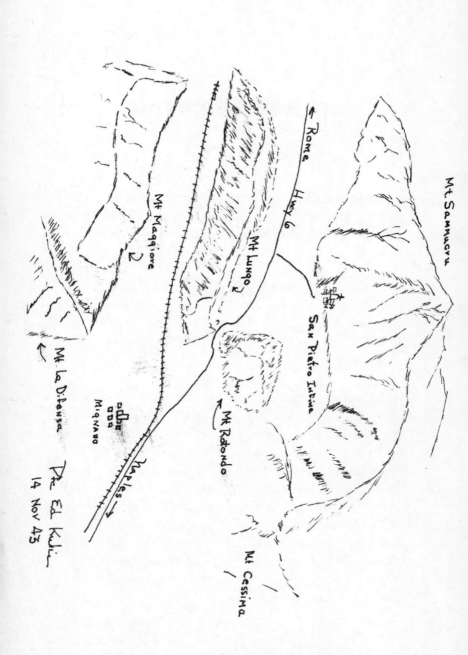

Mt. Sammucro

Rome — Hwy 6

Mt Maggiore

Mt Lungo

San Pietro Infine

Mt La Difensa

Mignano

Mt Rotondo

Naples

Mt Cessima

Pfc Ed Kulik
14 Nov 43

Prologue

The waiter replaced the empty decanter of wine on the table and moved away quickly as if he had something important to attend to, although with the *trattoria* almost empty, he had nothing of consequence to occupy his time. The waiter had family in the *Camorra* who were hard men, but the waiter was not. He was terrified of German soldiers, particularly those who drank.

His only remaining diners were two German officers who wore the uniform of the army, and their arrival had presaged a rapid departure of his few Italian customers who were afraid of being conscripted into labor battalions. Better the *Wehrmacht* than the SS, but it made little difference if they were drunk, and the waiter was certain the two officers had been drinking before they came into the small trattoria. Whether they were drunk before or not was immaterial as they definitely were now. The two German officers alternated between vehement arguments and laughter—both punctuated by pounding on the table. *The only thing worse than Germans in victory*, he thought, *were Germans in defeat.*

They would not pay him for the vast quantity of food and wine that they had consumed, and he knew that he wouldn't complain. It wasn't safe to complain—all of Italy had heard the rumors of the barbaric behavior of their former ally since the surrender of Italy to the Americans and British.

Although the waiter could barely speak proper Italian—his cousins in Livorno claimed they could barely understand his Neapolitan dialect—he could speak almost passable English. The waiter, whose name was Luciano, had worked as a merchant seaman for years before the war, and during his time at sea, he had picked up bits and pieces of many languages. Luciano not only believed that the two men were speaking English, but he suspected that the German officers were speaking in American accents. He had left the sea at the first hint of war, and it had been so long since he had used the language that he wasn't sure. Perhaps they were Dutch or Danish. Regardless, only the occasional word made sense to the waiter, who was not interested in German or Dutch or American gossip in any case. Had he been at least a little more curious, he might have confirmed his suspicion that the men were speaking English, and in American accents—one with a neutral West Coast tone, the other with a southern drawl.

As the waiter moved out of earshot, the thin major poured out the wine for himself and his much larger companion. "I told them it's illegal . . . immoral . . . completely unconscionable." Major Douglas Grossmann was an intelligence officer and had only a passing regard for legalities, morality, and conscience. He was, however, a practical man and would use whatever argument that might hold the promise of success. "It's a drain on our manpower and will have absolutely no effect on the war whatsoever except to brand us all as war criminals. I'll tell you one more thing, Mark . . . it will turn our few remaining supporters in Italy against us and to no beneficial end at all. It is the dumbest goddamned tasking I've ever had." The

Abwehr officer unconsciously started to reach for a pack of cigarettes, but he only had American cigarettes on him and was not in the mood to share with his friend.

"Don't hold back, Doug. Tell me what you really think of the Führer's orders." Captain Mark Gerschoffer laughed at his friend's frustration. Both officers knew that the orders did not come from Adolf Hitler, although they had certainly originated in Berlin. *Total nonsense*, thought Gerschoffer. *Whenever headquarters ordered some questionable action, the orders always seemed to originate from Hitler himself. There weren't enough hours in the day for one man to come up with all the stupidity emanating from Berlin.*

Grossmann broke down, fished for his pack of cigarettes, and offered one to his deputy who declined and lit one of his own—Gerschoffer was addicted to Russian cigarettes, and the Ami tobacco was too smooth for his liking. "I think the Führer is a military genius and is destined to lead us to a new world order based on culture and discipline." Grossmann rolled his eyes as he spoke and then inhaled deeply of his cigarette, "And that's all I have to say on that subject."

"You're a wise man, Doug. I tell that to *all* your friends . . . every morning in the mirror when I shave."

Grossmann laughed at the friendly insult—the mark of true comradeship. He leaned back in his chair and regarded his friend and subordinate fondly. Mark Gerschoffer was one of the bullnecked, thick-bodied variety of German officers, but his size was not just the product of too much beer and too many sausages like many officers. Gerschoffer had been a fullback at the University of Georgia before the war and, appropriately, was the embodiment of a bulldog. Although not particularly tall, he was barrel-chested, muscular, tough, and aggressive. While many Abwehr officers had their reservations about entrusting Grossmann's group of *Auslandsdeutsche* with state secrets, they kept their opinions to themselves in Gerschoffer's presence. Grossmann pointed with his cigarette to the captain's heavy five o'clock shadow, "Since you need to shave at least twice a day, what do you say about me the other time?"

Gerschoffer laughed and thought for a second, "I say that Doug Grossmann is a military genius and is destined to lead me to a new world order of . . . of, what was it? Disciplined culture? Or was it cultured discipline? Failing those, I am supremely confident he will lead me to a new brothel filled with the cream of Europe's whores."

Grossmann slammed his palm down on the table, and then held up his glass, "Yes! To leadership!"

The officers laughed as they clinked glasses and toasted leadership. Grossmann debated leaving the trattoria and finding either a cabaret or a brothel, but tomorrow would be a busy day. He was sober enough to recognize that busy days in his profession usually required clear thinking, so he shook his head and wagged his finger at Gerschoffer.

"You're a bad influence on me. Maybe tomorrow. Let's figure out how to execute these orders and then call it a night."

"Yes sir." Gerschoffer knew the time had come to transition back to being a subordinate. "Tell me what you were told."

Grossmann looked to make sure the waiter was out of earshot. "Our withdrawal from Salerno is going well, and we will eventually hold north of Naples near Monte Cassino. Naples should fall to the enemy in a week or so, and it is Field Marshal Kesselring's assessment that they will probably pause operationally at Naples to let their logistics catch up with them. Then we will fight a delaying action until the Winter Line is prepared at Monte Cassino. Meanwhile, the directive from Berlin is to make Naples as unusable for the Americans and British as possible. The port is to be destroyed, rail lines torn apart, runways demolished, bridges and tunnels blown. We will take all usable industrial equipment, all locomotives, tractors, and trucks. Take electrical generators. Destroy what we can't ship. Destroy the telephone exchanges and the radio stations. Burn whatever petroleum we can't ship north. So, we take what we need, destroy the rest, and make Naples a showcase for other would-be traitors."

"Yes sir. I have no problem with that. It's all standard, but not our mission. The pioneers can do all that. What are we needed for?"

"In addition to making Naples unusable, we are to make it as . . . well, as unpleasant as possible. Terrorize the Italians. Put the squeeze on them and their new allies. Food warehouses are to be emptied or burned. Medical supplies come with us. Make the allies feed and treat these traitors. Again, not our job, but we have a related task. We are to use our knowledge of the Americans and specifically target them when they become the occupiers of this miserable city." He shook his head and looked around the shabby trattoria. "I can't wait to return to Rome."

Gerschoffer poured more wine for himself and his boss. "Me neither. Target them how?"

Grossmann shrugged, "That's up to us to figure out. But I was told that we would be given explosives, time-delayed detonators, and demolitions teams to assist us. So we are to plant time bombs. The location and timing is left to us. I was also told to use my imagination—everything is on the table."

Gerschoffer stared at his boss, momentarily sober, "Time bombs in the city? Are they kidding?"

"No, Mark, it's no joke. And after I complained, the spineless bastards would only give me a verbal. No chance of getting the order in writing. *Ach,* an order's an order. Where do we plant the goddamned things?"

"What's the objective? To kill or terrorize?"

"Yes."

"Oh, Christ. Well, let me think." Gerschoffer leaned back in his chair and scratched the stubble on his chin. "Well, there are going to be two types of Allied soldiers in Naples in two weeks—occupiers and sightseers. Might as well go after both of 'em. I don't mind fightin' the Americans, but I didn't come back to the Fatherland to play dirty tricks on 'em. But as my dear ole southern mama told me many times, 'Any job worth doin' is worth doin' well.'"

"Yes, I'm sure your mother would appreciate the irony." Grossmann smirked but was disquieted at the thought of what his own American mother's reaction would have been. She had died from a British bombing of his hometown of Darmstadt in July, 1940, but before her death had begged her son many times never to fight against her countrymen. Gently holding her burned and wrapped hand on her deathbed, Grossmann had promised her that he would never take up arms against the United States. But the world had changed since 1940. Germany was no longer the triumphant conqueror of Europe but was now fighting for her own survival. He knew that to be true, even if many of his comrades still acted as if the Reich stretched from the Atlantic to the Urals. Grossmann believed that America held the key. If the Americans could be beaten, or at least bogged down, then the Fatherland might destroy the Bolsheviks and survive. Otherwise, apocalypse beckoned—or more appropriately, it would be the *Gotterdammerung* as some Germans were now whispering. *What does my rope of destiny hold,* he wondered.

"I doubt it. She don't have much of a sense of humor anymore. In any case, I don't think I'll tell her." Gerschoffer held similar views to his major on the necessity of America's defeat. He loved the United States and missed Georgia deeply, but he knew that the nation had to be defeated. The lives of his parents and his sisters depended on it. They had moved back to Germany in '38—the year that he graduated from Georgia—in order to work in the family business. His uncle was a Nazi Party functionary who had promised his younger brother that there was plenty of work in Germany for someone with connections, and work had been hard to find in Georgia at the time. The business had indeed flourished, and his parents had taken their profits and relocated to a community of Germans near Posen in the Warthegau territory of what was once, briefly, Poland. They had again been told there was plenty of opportunity in the new *lebensraum* of the Grossdeutsche Reich for someone with connections, but the gathering Bolshevik clouds in the east cast a long shadow on those promises. The Soviets were the true enemy, Gerschoffer believed, but Germany couldn't fight two wars at once. So his philosophy was to stiff-arm the Americans in order to buy time to deal with the Soviets— and pray that they could be dealt with before they crossed the frontiers.

Captain Gerschoffer waved the waiter over again and handed him the empty decanter. Proper planning required more wine, he informed his boss. "As I was saying, two types of Allied soldiers. The occupiers are going to be the military staffs that'll headquarter themselves in Naples while they work on seizing Rome—not that they will, of course."

Grossmann nodded. "Go on. What other military presence can we expect to see in Naples?"

"Once they get the port operational, the majority of supplies will flow through here, as well as through Salerno. The logistics personnel who manage the depots and the depots themselves will be legitimate targets. Also, I would expect the British and Americans to commandeer Italian hospitals for their use—I suppose those ought to be off-limits . . . ."

"Berlin says *nothing* is off-limits."

Gerschoffer stared at his commander and shrugged. "OK. I would imagine that they will also commandeer the Italian military facilities—particularly barracks and headquarters buildings, parade grounds, and training camps for their replacement depots."

Grossmann nodded again. He had come to the same conclusions as Captain Gerschoffer. "Let's plan for the army staff to headquarter on the palace grounds at Caserta. That's where I'd set up shop if I were them."

"Yes sir. I'm not sure it's in our interests to kill Mark Clark though. They might find someone competent to replace him. Besides, I doubt that we can get access to the palace without giving away our intentions."

"Maybe. You're probably right, but we'll look at it anyway. I want to concentrate on barracks and headquarters for the occupiers. Let's also target the buildings along the docks—see if we can kill some of their engineers trying to rehabilitate the port."

"Yes sir. Now, about the sightseers; what do you want to do?"

"Well, let's think through this. Where are the Americans and British going to congregate?"

"The British are less impressed than the Americans with old stuff. They'll head straight for the bars and whorehouses, although some might head for Pompeii. Maybe we can plant bombs in the bus depots. The Americans will sightsee first—cathedrals and museums—and then head to the bars and whorehouses."

Grossmann laughed, "Maybe they'll wait, maybe not. But that gives me an idea. Let's lift the quarantine on those Romanian whores down by the docks as we leave.

We'll have to pay off the Italians to leave them alone. Maybe even set 'em up in a nice house."

Gerschoffer started laughing as well. "Now that's a war crime! Those girls are *nasty*."

"Ugly and diseased, indeed. Yep, just the ticket for a conquering army. Those whores were quarantined in the first place because that particular strain of gonorrhea is cure-resistant—the sulfa drugs won't even touch it. We know from Africa and Sicily that the puritans don't regulate the brothels like we do, so in no time at all, we can take hundreds of soldiers out of action. As virulent as that is, maybe even thousands! They'll either have to divert penicillin from the field hospitals or send the soldiers back to their bases in Africa or Sicily. Either way, we win."

"Through the drip?"

"Through the drip." Grossmann laughed as he reached for the carafe again.

"Talk about unconscionable. What else do you have in mind?"

"Let's leave churches off the list for now, although maybe we'll do them if we have enough time. Starting tomorrow, let's go after the opera house, theaters, cinemas, gelaterias, and open-air markets for a start. I'm gonna think about the hospitals, and if we run out of targets, we'll get the breweries as well."

Gerschoffer shook his head, "That's doin' 'em a favor. The beer's terrible here. How about post offices? I understand the Americans bought up all the stamps in Africa while they were there. Who knew there were so many phila . . . phila . . . what's that word?"

"Philatelist. Well, if they don't get the clap first, we'll kill them too!"

Both officers started laughing and pounding the table again, and the waiter whose comprehension of English was returning with every shouted word shrunk quietly further into the shadows of his restaurant and prayed silently for the Germans to leave.

Chapter One

The tall, lean captain staggered from the blow to his ribs. In years of boxing, including nearly thirty amateur matches, he had never before been hit this hard. He moved back quickly and protected his side before the massive lieutenant could move in on his ribs again. It was notionally a friendly match, but as the captain was finding out, there really wouldn't be such a thing as a friendly boxing match after the captain had made an ill-fated pass at the girlfriend of the lieutenant's cousin.

It was much ado about nothing, the captain had thought. He had drunk too much grappa two nights before and the girl, whose name was Gianina, spoke fluent English and had sharply put him in his place. Even the lieutenant's cousin, a captain himself, was amused when told about the incident and held no ill-will against the boxer.

First Lieutenant Sam Taft was another matter. Taft had taken it upon himself to be the girl's protector from would-be suitors in the absence of his busy cousin, and while he had been friendly enough to the captain since that Friday night, he intended to impart a little lesson on manners. Sam actually liked John Huston, the captain, immensely—after all, they had been drinking together when the incident occurred—but there were limits to friendship. When Sam had finished with the Hollywood boy from Weatherford, he would buy him a drink and the slate would be clean again.

Huston was a very talented boxer, however, and he no intention of losing even a friendly match. He was confident that he would be able to finish off his friend before the remaining round of the three-round match was over. He had speed and experience over the lieutenant, and a quick jab caught Sam below the eye. It had no effect, and Huston ducked just in time to avoid a left hook and then a straight right aimed at his head. It was thrown with deadly force, not friendly at all, and Huston began to suspect that he was being held accountable for his behavior that night. He also began to get angry. *Is he really looking for a fight?*

A sharper jab caught Sam in the face again, and then another one. However, Sam was not without experience either—although he had no equivalent boxing history to his credit. Sam had learned to fight on his father's ranch when he was just a boy. Two of his father's hands, later his when Sam inherited the ranch, had messed around on the rodeo circuit, where they had also learned to box. From them, Sam had learned the fundamentals of boxing and had refined his technique on the boxing team at Texas A&M. He had a love for the sport as well. When he was twelve, he and his father had taken the train from Texas to Chicago to see Jack Dempsey's second fight with Gene Tunney, and even though there were more than a hundred thousand spectators at that fight, Sam and his father were only four rows away from the ring. Although Dempsey had lost the long count match, Dempsey's style was more to his liking than was the cerebral boxer Tunney's. By virtue of his size and demeanor, Sam was a slugger as well. He liked to finish fights with as much economy as possible, and had his last punch connected with Huston, the fight would have been over. As another jab brushed by Sam's cheek, he countered with another hard right to Huston's ribs.

The captain dropped to a knee and glared up at Sam, who calmly moved away. Huston stood up, wiped his brow with his glove, and moved in to finish off the lieutenant. He had had enough, and would not let friendship stand in the way any longer.

"Cap'n Huston!" A signal corps corporal was running hard towards the impromptu ring. "Cap'n!"

Huston looked at Sam who nodded and dropped his guard.

"What?"

"The film's gone! The goddamned film ain't in the warehouse any more."

"Oh, Christ! Did you . . . never mind. Get back there, I'm on my way." Huston turned to his recent opponent, his anger about the match replaced by anger over the missing film. "I gotta go, Sam. Next time you say you want some lessons, I won't take it so easy on you. Apologize to the girl, will ya?"

Sam smiled and nodded, "I will. Do you need some help lookin' for your stuff?"

"No thanks. I'll find it—these idiots couldn't pour piss out of a boot if the instructions were written on the heel. So long. See ya, Jim." With that, Captain Huston bent over gingerly and picked up his uniform shirt and jacket and walked away with the corporal.

Captain Jim Lockridge, the battalion intelligence officer and a friend of Sam and his cousin, had been watching the match. He walked over to Sam stepping over the pegged twine that had served as the boundary of the boxers' ring. Lockridge looked his friend over, saw no appreciable damage, and offered him a towel and a canteen. "You asked Huston for boxin' lessons?"

Sam took the canteen and drank gratefully until it was empty. "Not exactly. I think my words were, 'how 'bout some boxin' lessons?' He must've misunderstood me."

1600 Hours
36th Reconnaissance Troop HQ, Naples

"Let's get started. Where are we at with the replacements?" The commanding officer of the divisional cavalry reconnaissance troop was tired and knew that his officers didn't want a Sunday afternoon meeting, but that was tough. The division would be back on the line very soon, and there weren't enough hours in the week to receive replacement men and officers and get them ready for the inevitable.

Captain Perkin Berger was in temporary command of the 36th Cavalry Reconnaissance Troop (Mechanized), although he hoped it would become a permanent command. He liked the independent nature of the reconnaissance command, and he was forming solid bonds with his officers and his NCOs—even though he was a rifleman and they were cavalry. He missed serving in Able Company with his cousin Sam Taft, and he missed his old platoon, but he could quite honestly say that there was nothing like being in command. He was bivouacked in another section of the sprawling Italian Army base, but one of the benefits of command was his own jeep, and he was able to see his friends in the old battalion as his schedule permitted.

For their part, the cavalrymen of the troop had initially greeted their new commander with a great deal of skepticism and more than a little hostility. Many within the command quietly held the view that if the cavalry community of the Army could not provide an officer quickly to replace Captain Leveque, the previous commanding officer, then an officer within the troop should be promoted and assume command. But those were not the wishes of General Walker, the division commander, and the troop had no remaining officers that were senior enough for command in any case.

Captain Berger was an unknown entity to the troop prior to his arrival, but he had been a very pleasant surprise in the two weeks that he had held command. He had personally talked to every one of his two hundred soldiers in his first week, whether the soldier was a veteran or one of the few replacements that had trickled down to the troop. On his first Saturday in command, the troop had thrown a Texas barbeque, and from his own money Berger had purchased several sides of water buffalo—beef cattle were impossible to come by—which were slow-cooked in hand-dug pits, and the cooking of the briskets had been personally supervised by the new commanding officer. His company cooks had rounded out the meal by providing beans, pork ribs, and cornbread for the soldiers and their dates—some of whom were American USO volunteers, while others were local Italian girls.

His own date was a tall, pretty Italian widow named Gianina, who teased and flirted innocently with his officers and soldiers. Gianina was an art restorer at the Neapolitan National Gallery whose husband, a junior officer, had been killed in the south of France in 1940. She was comfortable around soldiers, and she did what she could to ease the discomfort of the other Italian women present. Very hard times had come to Naples, and decent women could be bought by the relatively rich Americans for the price of a can of meat or vegetables—or for less than a pack of cigarettes. Gianina recognized that many of the women present at the barbeque probably fell into that category, and she pretended not to notice when many of the women scooped their leftovers into a purse, or when some women left with soldiers for short visits to the bushes. She had quite naturally assumed the role of the first lady of the troop, and she quietly ensured that the most shy of the Italian women present left with enough food for themselves and, in many cases, their husbands and children.

The barbeque was a wild success at many levels. A good time was had by all, even if many soldiers regretted the excess the next day when Perkin, before Sunday services, led the troop on a five mile run through the hills surrounding the base. The troopers had fallen in love with Gianina, and they became very protective of her reputation when the inevitable divisional gossip surfaced about their troop commander and his Italian woman. In short order, Perkin was able to win over many of his soldiers—not by paying for the food, but through the force of personality. He had found over the years that there was no substitute for aggressive leadership, and the first step towards being an effective leader was to get to know his soldiers. Although the army disagreed, there was no better way to do that, he believed, than over a cold beer at a barbeque. The army prohibited close fraternization of officers and enlisted, but the 36th Division was a National Guard division in a theater of war, and the usual rules had been bent for so long that many forgotten what they were in the first place. So when the division's military police arrived to shut down the party and the new commander had chatted with them about their hometowns in Texas, joked about old comrades, and given them a gallon jug of iced tea and a tray of brisket and buns to take back to their post, his soldiers were not surprised when the party continued unabated. Two of the MPs came back to the party when they were off duty, and they had been greeted by Perkin and Gianina like long-lost kin.

Personality and a pretty girlfriend only go so far, however, and it was Perkin's professional background that the senior NCOs and officers examined very closely. Feelers were put out by the non-commissioned officers to their counterparts in Able Company, and the news that they got back was reassuring. They learned through the NCO grapevine that Captain Berger was instrumental in holding the southern flank of the beachhead on D-Day at Salerno, and the NCOs of Able Company told a fantastic tale of then-Lieutenant Berger driving a German panzer from the battlefield with a Thompson submachine gun and the tank's own sledgehammer. The troop NCOs were at first skeptical of such a report but it was verified again and again through NCO contacts. The division's senior NCO told his counterparts that the Old Man had personally awarded the Silver Star to Berger just before promoting him. Another Able Company sergeant named Kenton sought out the top sergeant of the troop, and over a few beers at the provisional NCO club, described how his lieutenant had led him and six others on a long-range mission to establish contact with Montgomery's Eighth Army. The master sergeant whistled when Kenton told him the lieutenant had personally killed four German soldiers on the expedition—one with a trench knife. Kenton did not mention the effect the mission had on Captain Berger, nor did he explain that sometimes the officer's im-

pulsive nature got the best of him. The troop would find
that out soon enough, he thought.

First Lieutenant Fenton Mayberry, known as Mabes,
was the company executive officer—the XO. He was sec-
ond-in-command of the company, and most administra-
tive functions of the unit fell on his shoulders. It was to
Mabes that the company commander's question on the
status of replacements was directed.

"Sir, we got two more cavalrymen in last night. Division says that we've received all the replacements that we'll
get for some time, and there are no more troopers for us
in the replacement depot. Our Salerno losses have been
replaced at 85 percent, and division says that is our fair
share, and not to expect any more before we go into combat again." Mayberry was unhappy about the bad news, but
there was little that he or his company commander could
do about it. Losses at Salerno had been more severe than
expected, and there were other units still on the line that
were drawing from the repple-depple, as the replacement
depot was known. Even though the 36th Infantry Division,
the Texas Army, had received notification that it would be
back on the line very soon, it was still a lower priority than
those American divisions that were currently fighting.

"What'd we get?" Perkin was certain that the new soldiers would be of limited value—in his short experience
as company commander, he was becoming aware that the
army was sending the troops that it had, and these were
not necessarily the same as those that were needed.

"Last night? A qualified M-8 driver from Colorado
and a reconnaissance scout from Gonzales."

Perkin was surprised. "Really? Holy smokes . . . I'd
expected a goat-wrangler and a gynecologist." He smiled
inwardly as he watched Mabes blush. The lieutenant was
a very innocent sort, and he had not quite adjusted to Perkin's off-color sense of humor.

"Er . . . yes sir. As for the training, we've gotten most of the replacements up to basic standards, but it'll be a long time before they can match the men they've replaced."

That, Perkin worried, applied as much to him as any other replacement soldier.

Chapter Two

November 8, 1943
1000 Hours
Naples, Italy

The orders were received. The division was to head to assembly areas the next morning to await transport on the long road north. Every mile of that road had been fiercely contested by the German Army, and the Americans and British were relearning a hard lesson about how good the Germans were at defense. Without fail, the Germans blew the bridges over steep mountain ravines and numerous rivers and streams, complicating an advance through a narrow valley that had seen the march of countless armies over the course of countless centuries. While the 36th had been bivouacked near Naples for several weeks of recovery and rehabilitation, the rest of the American VI Corps had continued to push north towards the grand prize of Rome. Those divisions were now exhausted, and the 36th would replace one of them on the line opposite the Germans.

It would be Perkin's last day with Gianina until he could get an opportunity to return to Naples. That would be weeks, certainly—maybe months. Maybe never. He could not tell her he was leaving for the front, but she knew it. She saw it in his face the moment she met Perkin at the museum café that morning. He looked tired and dispirited and lost, which he was. For the first time in the young captain's life, he was not excited about change. He was not restless to leave. He no longer wished to test himself in battle. Perkin wanted to stay with Gianina, and she with him.

That was not an option. They both knew it, and neither wasted time lamenting their separation or asking questions of "what if." Perkin would leave and perhaps not come back, and that was simply a fact that both the soldier and the widow of a soldier accepted. They would make the most of the day and pray for Perkin's safe return to Naples.

"Wait here. I need to get a key from my office and then I have something special to show you." Gianina walked away from Perkin, wiping away a silent tear as she did so.

She was back in a few moments and took Perkin's hand, leading him to the back of the museum and then down a flight of stairs. They walked down a dimly lit corridor. "We're taking some art out of hiding—you should be pleased, it's a vote of confidence in the Allies. It's not all ours. Some of what we have now belongs to museums in Rome or Florence and has been hidden down here for months; we are just the caretakers."

She unlocked a big heavy door and led Perkin into a large room with concrete walls that had nearly a dozen works of art laid out carefully on tables. Some were wrapped and others had been opened since their return from the caves and vaults of Italy. Gianina looked at a long row of light switches and turned on a light over a table at the far side of the room. Two unframed works lay on the table, both wrapped in a heavy cloth but no longer bound. Moving to the larger of the two paintings, Gianina said, "You met me while you and Jim were looking for Caravaggios. We didn't have any then, but we have some now. This is the one that I wanted you to see."

She unfolded the cloth, allowing Perkin to see the painting. It was of a young man standing next to a slightly older woman—based on his clothes and his jaunty feathered hat, Perkin marked the man as a candy-ass or a dandy. The man's right hand, maybe he was just a boy, was held palm-out by the woman while she gazed intently at his face with a slightly mocking look visible in her lips and eyes. The man's other hand rested arrogantly on his hip near the pommel of his sword.

"It's incredible," Perkin said with an excited smile. "What's it called?"

"It's one of two works by Caravaggio named *The Fortune Teller*. This is the first one that he did sometime around 1594 or '95. I love Caravaggio, don't you?" She leaned over and kissed his ear, and then asked, "Tell me, what do you see in the painting?"

Perkin carefully studied the canvas before him. "Well, I ain't an expert on art, but it strikes me as a little odd. If she's supposed to be tellin' his fortune, she ought to be lookin' at his palm. But she ain't. Looks more like she's readin' his face, and maybe she's happy about what she sees. Why's that, d'ya suppose?"

"She's watching his face to see if he notices she's stealing his ring while she tells him how rich and powerful he is to become."

Perkin looked down at the boy's palm and noticed that the fortune teller was carefully sliding a ring off the finger of the dandy. He laughed, "I'll be damned. I hadn't noticed that. I wish I had the time to bring Sam here—he mostly likes paintings of horses, but he'd think this one's a hoot."

"Maybe next time." Gianina put her arms around Perkin's neck and stretched up to kiss him. After a long, lingering kiss, he moved to wrap her up in his arms. She slipped her arms around Perkin's waist, and placed her head on his shoulder and relaxed as he held her tight. Nothing was said, and Gianina held back tears as she wished for the embrace to last forever. Two colleagues walking in the corridor past the closed door were having an animated discussion, and the intrusion into their silence broke the spell of the short moment. She stepped back.

"I have a surprise for you." She looked up at Perkin. Her eyes had dried up and Perkin recognized that her teasing look had returned.

"Another one? This is my lucky day."

"Well, that remains to be seen. I'm going to tell *your* fortune. Give me your hand."

With a grin, Perkin gave her his hand. Gianina looked carefully at his calloused hand, her fingers tracing the lines on his palm. She frowned at one line, shook her head and traced the line again with her finger and then drew her breath in sharply. Gianina shook her head at Perkin with mock sorrow, but her eyes were alight, "Oh darling, it is very short. The lines on your hand tell me one bad story and the calluses tell me of yet more sorrow. You won't like it at all. Perhaps the worst news you could get!"

"What? What is it?"

"Are you sure you want to hear it? It is terrible."

"Bad news can't wait. Let's have it."

"This short line here says that you . . . that you will be celibate for a very long time. Starting tomorrow."

"Oh. I liked his fortune better." Perkin nodded at the boy in the painting. "What else did you see in my lines?"

With a shy grin, Gianina said, "Well these things are never certain, but it looks like the curse of celibacy will lift only when you have returned to Napoli."

Perkin wiped his brow in mock relief. "Whew! Thank goodness. What's the bad news from the calluses?"

Gianina began laughing hard and she nudged Perkin playfully in the ribs, "The calluses tell me you had better be gentle, or you'll hurt yourself!"

They both laughed at Perkin's foretold misfortune, then Gianina asked for his hand again. "Look at me like the boy did," she commanded as she stroked his palm.

"I've no ring to steal, or I'd have already given it to you already." Perkin smiled as the oppression of the impending departure continued to lift.

"No. I'm giving something to you. Look down." So gentle that Perkin could barely feel it, she had placed a rectangular silver locket in his palm.

"What is it?" he asked as he opened the antique locket.

"It's Saint Michael the Archangel. He'll protect you. He's the patron saint of soldiers."

Perkin walked closer to the light and looked at the locket. It was the same general shape as his dog tags but much larger. Instead of a picture inside, there was a painting on a thin ceramic surface which had been cut and filed to fit tightly inside the locket. The painting was small, unbelievably small, yet richly detailed and showed a winged Saint Michael subduing a winged Lucifer—Saint Michael's foot on the back of the prostrate Lucifer's head, one hand holding a sword poised to plunge into his adversary, his other hand holding the chains that shackled Satan. It was incredible imagery with remarkable detail, given its size.

"Oh, Gia . . . it's fantastic. I've never seen anything like it. Where did you find this?"

"The locket is an old family one, but I did the painting . . . well, it is a copy of one by Guido Reni called *The*

Archangel Michael, although I took some liberties with it."
Gianina smiled and then laughed. "Look at the face under
this magnifying glass."

Perkin looked closely at the angel and saw what could
be nothing other than Private Edwin Kulis's tiny bespectacled face resting atop Saint Michael's muscular torso.
Although Perkin could not be sure, the painting so small,
but he thought that Kulis was smiling back at him.

Delighted, Perkin cried, "Is that Kulis?"

"Isn't it divine? I was laughing so hard as I painted the
glasses that I had to do it four times. But you told me that
he saved your life at Paestum and protected you at Paola,
so who better than Eddie as Saint Michael to watch over
you?"

"Who better indeed? I—" Perkin began to thank her,
but Gianina interrupted.

"Do you know why Saint Michael and not Saint
George or Saint Martin? They are also patron saints of
soldiers."

"I have no idea. Why?"

"Your friend, Father Riley, told you that this war is
the war to oppose evil, and Saint Michael will lead God's
army to defeat evil. He will be a good protector for you,"
she said simply.

Patrick Riley was an Irish priest who Perkin had met
in the Italian village of Pisciotta. In addition to being a
Jesuit priest, Riley was also providing information to
his older brother in British military intelligence—an act
which had come to the attention of the Germans. When
Perkin passed through the village of Pisciotta, he stopped
a German patrol that had been sent to arrest the priest. As
Perkin evacuated the priest to a more secure village, one
closer to the American lines, Father Riley had told Perkin
that the war was definable in terms of good and evil, and
it was Riley's contention that Perkin and his soldiers had

been brought to Italy to oppose the incarnation of evil by the Nazis—a notion that Perkin largely rejected, but one which resonated with Gianina. The nature of the war was more complex in Perkin's light than simple black and white notions of good and evil, but he was touched by Gianina's gift.

"I had something made for you as well." Knowing her reaction, Perkin could not keep a grin off of his face although he tried. He reached into his pocket and pulled out a small jewelry box and handed it to the delighted Gianina.

"What's this?" Gianina opened the box. "A cow!? A cow? You give me a cow necklace as a present?"

"It's a longhorn, baby—the universal symbol of Texas. What's wrong, you don't like it?"

"I think . . . ," Gianina sputtered laughingly, "I think that the prediction of your celibacy was off by a day." She put the necklace on and struck a pose for Perkin as she stuck out her tongue. "How does my cow look?"

"Anemic. I reckon Bevo needs some color. Here's the one I meant to give you. The cow was for my daytime girlfriend." From his other pocket, Perkin produced a second box and opened it. Lying inside was another gold necklace, this time with a small square emerald in place of the longhorn.

"Oh Perkin, it is beautiful. *Grazie.*" Gianina put the emerald necklace on without taking off the longhorn. As she modeled them both for Perkin, she exclaimed, "I love it! And I'm not giving back the cow, either. You'll have to give your other girlfriend a pig necklace! Which one do you like better?"

With a grin, Perkin replied, "Depends on where we stand with the prophecy I guess." He gave her another kiss and a hug.

They were interrupted by a knock at the door, and as Gianina answered it, Perkin unwrapped the second painting. He was still staring at it as Gianina walked back to him.

"That was my director. I told him we were looking at *The Fortune Teller* and that I was taking the rest of the day off. We're lucky he likes you; he said . . . oh, Perkin. I didn't want you to see this one."

Perkin had a strained look on his face. "It's OK, sweetheart. This is about Abraham and Isaac?" It was more of a statement than a question. The three foot by four foot canvas showed Abraham as an old bald man with a long beard and a full robe. Abraham was shoving his terrified son facedown onto a rock while looking back towards an angel who was restraining Abraham's hand from cutting Isaac's throat. As he tried to stop Abraham from sacrificing his son, the angel pointed to a ram which seemed to be watching with interest. Despite knowing the story, Perkin felt it wasn't clear from the painting whether Abraham would take the angel's suggestion and sacrifice the ram instead.

Gianina turned Perkin's face from the painting and looked worriedly in his eyes. "You are all right? Yes?" She kissed him on the cheek, stepped back, and explained, "Caravaggio did two depictions of the sacrifice of Isaac. This is the second painting—maybe painted five years after his first—but the action takes place first in this one. In the other painting, which is in America, it's maybe, I don't know, ten seconds later than this. Abraham has just realized he does not have to kill his son. It's more vivid, I think, but less terrifying. I'm sorry that you saw this."

"It's OK. The knife . . . It's OK." Perkin's voice trailed off and he shrugged. Two months before, Perkin had killed a rogue Italian soldier with his trench knife. It was a horrible moment for the then lieutenant—one that he relived frequently in his dreams. More than any other act that he had seen or done in the war, it was his worst memory.

As Gianina wrapped up the Caravaggios, she almost stamped her foot with anger at herself. She had known instinctively that the second painting would disturb Perkin, and she had determined that she would not let him see it. He was getting so much better, she thought—less angry, less moody, and the happy-go-lucky nature that she had suspected existed when she met him was once again the dominant aspect of his personality. His cousin, Sam, had told her that she was a gift to Perkin, "better than fried trout for breakfast," and she was inwardly furious that she might have imperiled what looked to be their last day together.

Perkin seemed to have that sense as well, and he stepped away from the darker side of his nature and smiled gently at her. "Don't worry. It was just a little shock. I'm fine. It's a fantastic work of art about a fantastic story, and maybe someday we can see the other version together in America."

As they walked holding hands down the dark corridor and up the stairs, he said, "Caravaggio should have met Kierkegaard." She shook her head, unfamiliar with the name. "He was a Danish philosopher who wrote a book in the last century called *Fear and Trembling*—I read it my last year in Austin. Kierkegaard used the story of Abraham and Isaac to talk about a lot of things surrounding morality and religion, which were interesting, but the thing that I enjoyed about it was his discussion of faith. He said that Abraham took a leap of faith when he set out to obey God's command to sacrifice his son because he knew that such an order was unreasonable, absurd . . . I don't know, unlikely to come from God. Yet that is the essence of faith: the belief in something that you know intellectually to be unreasonable, absurd, or unlikely, yet you also know in your heart is as certain, as real, as the fact of your hand in mine." As they walked outside into the daylight and towards a bus stop, he stopped and faced Gianina. "Love is like that, I think. Maybe it takes a leap of faith to believe that when the war ends, you and I will be together. It's absurd to think that, yet I do."

1235 Hours
Naples, Italy

Many regard the Neapolitan pizza as the best in the world. Sam certainly thought so, but he had never had anything else. He, Jim Lockridge, and company commander Bill Spaulding had waited for Perkin and Gianina to join them for lunch, after which they all would return to the base together and oversee the final preparations for moving out. With his stomach rumbling, Sam decided he couldn't wait indefinitely, so he gave his cousin five minutes past the appointed time and then ordered pizzas for the table.

Sam seldom ventured far from the company. He despised Naples. The near total destruction of the city and the poverty and misery of the people quickly became oppressive. While anything could be found for a price—anything—Sam felt guilty for spending money on food in the city when so many people around him had neither. The plight of the children of Naples was deeply disturbing to Sam, and he had written home to his wife Maggie that he would buy all the change he could from his soldiers before venturing out so he would have coins to give the kids. There was never enough to go around. With few exceptions, Gianina being one, Sam had little regard for the people of Naples. He understood that times were hard, but he saw little effort to rise above the tough times. Instead, he saw theft and vice on a previously unimaginable scale. Jeeps had to be guarded—taking the rotor was not good enough—supply depots had issued shoot-to-kill directives—and the pimping of female family members was rampant. Despite the best efforts of the Allies, jeeps continued to be taken, stolen American and British supplies were brazenly sold on the black market at inflated prices, and boys gleefully sold their mothers or sisters for cigarettes. Sam knew that most of the crime and vice, particularly the vice, was with the collusion of unscrupulous Allied soldiers, but that endeared him to Naples even less. The whole city was corrupt and corrupting.

"So where are we headed, Jim?" Captain Bill Spaulding, the Able Company commander, knew that there were few options, but speculating on future movements was an obsession for the soldiers.

"North," Jim said teasingly.

"I swear, Jim. I count two professors as close friends, and you both don't know shit sometimes." Both Jim Lockridge and his fellow graduate student at the University of Texas, Perkin, had recently been informed that their written defense of their respective doctoral dissertations, sent from an American encampment in North Africa, had been successful.

"That's not true, Bill. I know a lot. It's Perkin that don't know shit."

"Well, he knows enough to have the prettiest girl in Naples," Sam defended his cousin and stood up to kiss Gianina as she and Perkin arrived.

"Thank you, Sam. You men are terrible to each other. You should not say such things, Jim." Gianina kissed each of the men in turn in the European style and took a chair at the table which the grinning intelligence officer held for her. She sat down a large bag that she had brought from her apartment.

"Gia, there was no offense intended for you—only for Perk. My lord, I like that necklace!"

The Italian girl fingered her emerald necklace and held the stone out for the men to admire. "Perkin gave it to me. Isn't it lovely?"

"That one's nice as well, but I meant the longhorn. It makes me nostalgic." Jim and Perkin had been classmates at the University of Texas.

Sam snorted, "Makes me queasy." Seeing that Gianina didn't understand, Sam said words he would never have uttered to anyone else. "I'm just kidding. It's . . . beautiful. Here, let me pour you a glass of wine."

The lunch progressed with small talk dominating the conversation. Inevitably, the subject drifted to the weather. It had been getting considerably cooler at night, although the daytime was pleasant enough to be outside. The rains were coming though, Gianina warned, and it would get cold in the daytime very soon. It was while they were on the subject of the weather that Gianina reached into her bag and pulled out several heavy, dark brown pullover sweaters and handed one to each of the men, including Perkin.

Bill Spaulding protested for the group. "Gia, thank you, but these must have cost a fortune. We can't take these."

She shook her head and wagged her finger at her friends. "You can't turn down a gift from a Neapolitan. Besides, my landlady and her daughters made them all just for you—I couldn't knit to save my life. She is so grateful to Perkin that she wanted to do something nice for him and his friends. Did he tell you what he did?" The men shook their heads, and while Perkin looked embarrassedly off into the distance, she said, "He paid my rent for a year, and bought a large ham and all sorts of fresh food from the black market for Mrs. Casetti and her girls. We have been busy canning it all for the winter. It may not sound like much, but simple things like rent paid in advance and a few kilos of tomatoes and flour are enough to keep her daughters out of prostitution. We have so little, and you Americans are so generous that she asked me what she could do for Perkin. I said a jumper would be nice. So she made one for each of you. Please accept them. It will get very cold in the mountains this winter, and I don't think that you, you . . . ," she grinned, "cowboys understand what true cold is."

"I don't know what a jumper is, but I sure appreciate the sweater. I hate the cold—I can't remember the last time it froze on the ranch." Sam was delighted with his present. It was hard to find clothes big enough to fit his frame.

"Excuse me, gentlemen." The speaker was Sergeant Jack Younger. The sergeant was Sam's platoon sergeant and a very capable soldier, and he had several Able Company soldiers in tow. As he was in the presence of his company commander, he knocked out a sharp salute that was casually returned by the officers sitting at the table.

"What's up, Sergeant?"

"Sir, me and the boys wanted to know if we could borrow Miss Gianina for a minute. There's supposedly a supply of Mussolini stamps left at the post office yonder that you have to ask for, but we can't seem to find anyone who speaks English. Every time we mention Mussolini, the fella behind the counter starts turnin' red. It'll only take a couple minutes. Please, ma'am?"

"I didn't know you were a pederast, Sergeant," Sam said.

"I ain't, sir!" cried Sergeant Younger. He too started to turn red in the face.

"Sergeant, I think he meant philatelist," intervened Jim Lockridge quickly.

"I'll be happy to help." Gianina stood up and motioned for the officers to sit. She kissed Perkin on the cheek and whispered in his ear, "You stay here and explain to Bear what the difference is. I can't wait to see his face. Finish your lunch and maybe we can go back to my apartment again. Think about that while I'm gone."

The officers sat at the table and watched Gianina and the four soldiers walk the hundred yards to the post office. Knowing that she was being watched, she put a flirtatious swing in her step and turned partly around once to blow a kiss to Perkin.

"My God, Perk," sighed Spaulding. "You don't deserve a girl like that."

The other officers agreed wholeheartedly, and Perkin basked in their jealousy. There was a lengthy discussion of Gianina's beauty and intellect, during which Perkin showed his friends the medallion of Saint Michael she had made for him. After expressing their amazement at its detail, the conversation switched to the distinction between buggery and stamp collecting, and they were still laughing at Sam's mistake when an earsplitting crack followed by a deep rumbling sound emanated from inside the post office. All of the soldiers except Perkin hit the ground and covered their heads. To the combat veterans, it was like being under attack at Salerno again. Perkin slowly came to his feet and stared, disbelieving, at the façade of the stone building. Its large portico had collapsed, and smoke and dust were pouring out of the shattered windows. Screams could be heard from inside the building, and then the walls and the roof began to crumble as though they were tipped dominoes. The screaming abruptly stopped.

"Oh my God . . . Gia!" Perkin shouted, and he began to run towards the collapsing building as he'd never run before.

Chapter Three

November 14, 1943
0820 Hours
1st Battalion HQ, North of Capua, Italy

A collection of rocks in the yard of a farmhouse served as both the chairs and the table for the three soldiers finishing up tin cups of coffee and several sandwiches. It had been difficult for Perkin Berger, Sam Taft, and Bill Spaulding to find a comfortable spot for their second breakfast of the day, but once they had found such a place, they were loath to leave it. Comfort was in as short supply—as was silence, privacy, or air not smelling of wet soldiers. At least it wasn't raining, and the soldiers were grateful for the first dry day in a week.

The coffee was steaming hot, and while they had finished a good hot breakfast only two hours before, they gratefully accepted hot bacon and egg sandwiches from an Able Company soldier serving a rotation on kitchen patrol, or KP as the troops called it. Their bodies could not get enough calories to keep up with the demands of being young and climbing mountains, which is what they had spent the past week doing—except for Perkin.

While Able Company trained in the mountains in Allied hands for small-scale tactical assaults against machine gun emplacements over and over again, Perkin had left his company in the hands of his executive officer and had traveled up to the 3rd Division frontage on the line. With the exception of the terrible morning four days before when he had seen to Gianina's burial, he had spent most of the past week on the front lines—taking a different reconnaissance troop officer with him each time. Twice, he had gone on night patrols as an observer with the troopers of the reconnaissance company of the 3rd Division. One of the patrols was with a sole scout and they got close enough to German lines to hear the muted conversation of the soldiers of the 29th Panzer Grenadiers.

The 3rd Division scout was impressed with the young officer from Texas. Most of his own troop officers, including his platoon officer, had never gone with him on a scouting patrol. It was a routine patrol from his perspective, but he never forgot it was a very lonely job that terrified most soldiers. Crawling in a ditch only yards from the German line, the scout had his senses attuned to see if there was any panic in the officer, and he was pleased to note there was not. The only questionable moment came when two German sentries walked within ten feet of the Americans lying prone in a small depression in the dark. The Texan slowly started to reach for a trench knife that he kept tucked in his leggings, but he stopped when the scout quietly placed a hand on his back. After the patrol was complete, the scout told the officer that he had done a fine job, but they were not out there to kill Germans. He also recommended that the officer move the knife to his belt or strap it across his chest—if it was needed, there was no time to waste by bending over and drawing it. The tall captain nodded seriously, and thanked the soldier as he shook his hand. That patrol had been the night following Gianina's funeral.

After some give and take with the division staff, the reconnaissance troop was bivouacked adjacent to Able Company in the countryside surrounding the town of Capua, but Perkin had not seen much of his old comrades until the night before. Then he had walked over to the Able Company encampment and sat around a small campfire with Bill and Sam, and Bill made questionable hot chocolate from melted candy bars and powdered milk. There was no discussion of Gianina, nor was there any talk of the loss of Sergeant Younger other than Sam's remark that Perkin's old platoon sergeant, Sergeant Kenton, had moved over to his platoon. The soldiers talked some about what Perkin had seen in the 3rd Division sector and, later, they shared already-heard stories about Texas and old comrades. As the fire was dying down, the conversation stopped altogether as each man dwelled on his own thoughts. Both Sam and Bill were thinking about the coming battle, although Sam's wife, Margaret, intruded occasionally into his musings. Perkin's thoughts were elsewhere, and after many minutes of silence he yawned and stood up as he realized how desperately tired he was. Rather than walk back to his company, only a hundred yards away, he walked the ten feet to Sam's tent, crawled inside, and wrapped himself up in one of Sam's blankets. By the time Sam had taken his leggings off and crawled in next to his cousin, Perkin was gently snoring and sleeping better than he had for a week.

"Cap'n, they're about ready to go. Colonel Wranosky is en route from regiment and will be here in a moment." Private Edwin Kulis blinked in a momentary burst of sun through the clouds as he walked through the front door of the occupied farmhouse and delivered the news to the officers resting on the comfortable rocks. His warning of the imminent arrival of the battalion commander was directed to Captain Spaulding, but as he spied Captain Berger, Kulis's scarred face lit up. "Hey, sir!"

Perkin offered a rare smile to his former soldier, "Hey, Eddie. What'cha readin' these days?"

Edwin Kulis was a seventeen-year-old rifleman off of a small farm near Rosebud, Texas. He had fraudulently enlisted while underage to escape the farm and the Depression, and in his opinion, the army was the very best thing to ever happen to him. Although he was short and bookish, he had proven to be quite capable of taking care of himself—the young rifleman had killed five men since landing in Italy two months before.

"I just finished *The Grapes of Wrath*. I traded the Kipling book to Cap'n Huston for it." Kulis shook his head sadly, "I sure felt bad for them Okies."

Perkin nodded, but he allowed himself a small inward smile as he doubted that the Joad family had a worse time in the Depression than the Kulis family. "You hadn't read it before?"

"No sir. It was banned in Rosebud. I saw the movie though, but now I've read the book, I don't think that Henry Fonda's tough enough to be Tom Joad. Do you want it? I already got another one. I'm fixin' to start *The Riddle of the Sands* today if I get the time."

"God no," Perkin shook his head. "I've read it and I don't want to read anything else sad." Perkin stood up and began to trail behind the other officers towards the farmhouse.

"Yes, sir. I'm awful sorry about Miss Gianina, Cap'n. Me and the boys liked her a lot." Kulis again shook his head sadly. He had liked Gianina, and he was concerned for his old comrade. Kulis had a pretty good intuition about Perkin's emotional frailties after Salerno. He had seen the then-lieutenant change dramatically in the span of their four-day mission down the Italian peninsula.

The tall captain nodded, but showed no emotion as he said, "Thanks, Eddie. She thought highly of you, too. You were her favorite." As Perkin stooped to go through the low doorway behind Sam and Bill, he unconsciously touched his Saint Michael medallion under his shirt, then turned back to a furiously blushing Kulis. "Eddie, if we get the chance, I'd like to finish talkin' about books. Ain't pressing—I just want to hear about somethin' other than war. So if not today then when we can find the time."

"Yes sir. I'm doin' a sketch of the Mignano Gap for my journal, so if I don't get grabbed by some off . . . uh, some sergeant, again to dig his jeep outta the mud, I'll be here waitin' for you after your mission briefing." As the captain turned and walked into the villa, Private Kulis found a comfortable spot on the rocks, pulled his journal from his pack, and began to sketch out a map of their objective from memory.

0830 Hours
1st Battalion HQ, North of Capua, Italy

As Sam and the others filed into the house for the mission briefing and took a seat in the crowded downstairs, Sam heard the straining engine of a jeep approaching the front of the farmhouse. *That would be Lieutenant Colonel Wranosky*, he thought, and stood up in anticipation of his battalion commander's arrival.

About as broad as he was high, the thick-set Alabaman was excitable and generally good entertainment for the even-tempered Sam to watch. Today promised to be a good show as the explosive officer stormed into the room, waved his juniors impatiently from attention back into their seats, and tossed his helmet and gloves to his driver.

"Alright boys! We're gettin' close to kick-off. Those dullard sons-a-bitches on the Fifth Army staff have plans for us, and I thought you ought to know about it. So, I've brought y'all here this very fine army morning so I can tell my officers what we're gonna do, and what my expectations are for this comin' battle."

Wranosky gratefully accepted a cup of coffee from his driver, took a deep swallow of the steaming black liquid, and yelped and grimaced in pain as he burned his tongue and throat. As he scowled at his driver through watery eyes and mentally dared his officers to laugh at him, he said hoarsely, "The bottom line, as we all know, is that the easy days are over, and we're goin' back on the line soon. We've replaced our lost equipment, gotten all the new troops we're gonna get, trained all those sons-a-bitches we can, drunk all the grappa, and screwed all the women in this godforsaken country." The colonel replaced his grimace with a broad grin and noted, "Good God Almighty, gentlemen, half the babies born in southern Italy next year are gonna pop out spittin' tobacco, singin' country songs, and wearin' cowboy hats. And as someone who ain't from Texas, I feel right sorry for the poor bastards. Now, since we've done everything else, there's nothin left for us to do but kill Germans and earn our paychecks." After the laughter died down, Wranosky continued, "I've asked my deuce, Jim Lockridge, to kick us off with an overview of our upcoming operation, then share some of his secrets with us as to what them Nazi boys are doing." He sat down in a front row chair that had been reserved for him and nodded at his intelligence officer. "Jim?"

The thin, athletic captain stood up, ran his fingers through his thinning hair as he faced his fellow officers, and nodded in return to his battalion commander. "Good morning, Colonel . . . gentlemen . . . Aggies. For those of you who are new to us, I'm Jim Lockridge, the battalion S-2. As the colonel said, I'm going to give you an update on the battle for Italy so far, tell you of our upcoming mission, called 'Operation Raincoat,' and then talk a little bit about 'them Nazi boys.'"

Lockridge walked to a covered easel and pulled off an old grayish sheet covering a set of maps. The first map shown was of the Italian Peninsula. "Since we came ashore at Salerno on September 9, Fifth Army has covered some hundred miles. Virtually every mile of that journey has been contested by the Germans. So far, the Texas Gun Club took hundreds of casualties in combat at Salerno, and hundreds more soldiers have been removed from duty as a result of injuries from training accidents and illnesses. Particularly bad, from both Africa and Salerno, were the cases of malaria." With a wry grin, Lockridge said, "Compounding this, as Italian payback for leaving behind a slew of t'bacca-chewin' bastards in our wake, we now have over two hundred T-Patchers away from their units today as a result of contracting this persistent form of venereal disease in Naples we've all be hearin' about." To Colonel Wranosky, he said, "There's more than a handful from our battalion that are sick."

"Yeah, I don't know why the docs think that's an excuse to take our boys off the line," Wranosky said. "We're here to fight the Germans, not fuck 'em. But, it's just a matter of time before Clark makes that cesspool off-limits to our boys. Continue." Wranosky shook his head at the thought of Naples.

"Yes sir. Let's begin with Command and Control. When we came ashore at Salerno, we were part of General Clark's Fifth Army assigned to VI Corps. Fifth Army also had X Corps, primarily British, under his command. On Thursday, the 18th, II Corps under Major General Geoffrey Keyes will officially stand up in Fifth Army and will take up the key sector between the British X Corps on the left and our old VI Corps on the right. On Tuesday, we'll move onto the line and relieve 3rd Division. So, we'll remain VI Corps until Thursday, and then the chain of command goes down from Clark to Keyes to our division commander, Major General Walker, to Colonel Jamison at the 141st Infantry Regiment to you, sir. Looking at the map, here are the proposed corps boundaries for Operation Raincoat: X Corps has the western sector from the Tyrrhenian Sea; II Corps is in the middle; VI Corps is to our right and abuts Eighth Army's area of operations on our far right, which then runs eastward to the Adriatic."

Captain Lockridge flipped the map of Italy over, revealing a more detailed map of Italy centered on the area between Rome and Naples. He used his pointer to highlight the central valley running southeast to northwest. "This will be II Corps's sector and where the brunt of the fighting is currently occurring. The coastal road is easily defended on our left. The mountains offer no mobility for us on our left or right, and although all roads may lead to Rome, this is the only one that counts. We'll push through on this road until we get to Rome. Eventually. The Italians call it Highway 6. Our boys call it Victory Road—and that ain't a term of endearment."

"Here's where the Italian campaign stands right now. We're about halfway from Salerno to Rome, and Allied Forces have been in constant combat since September 9. We secured Naples—not in the expected four days, but in four weeks. We've moved past Naples, forced a crossing of the Volturno and now, here are our forward lines in the upper Volturno plain—just shy of ten miles south of Cassino and a little less than a hundred miles southeast of Rome."

"Tomorrow, an operational pause goes into effect. For the first time since Salerno, the offensive shifts into neutral. The front line divisions are exhausted. Some will pause and regroup and reorganize, others will be relieved. The 82nd Airborne leaves us and goes to England for preparations for the cross-channel invasion. The 3rd Division relieved us after Salerno. Now, we'll relieve them. Following the pause, which I expect to last until December 1, comes the resumption of offensive operations across army boundaries, from the Tyrrhenian to the Adriatic. The idea is to push across a broad line. Force the Germans to spread out their reserves, then punch through to Rome. Fifth Army believes that we can be there by Christmas, and once again, the 36th Division is gonna lead the way."

At the murmurings of the assembled officers, Lieutenant Colonel Wranosky stood up and faced the group. "Y'all forget this shit about being in Rome for Christmas. That ain't likely. Clark hasn't brought me into his confidence, so I cain't say why he thinks the replacement of one or two exhausted units with one fresh one changes the equation appreciably." Wranosky looked sad for a nearly imperceptible moment, then his faced hardened and he glared at the assembled officers. "We've got what our British cousins call a long hard slog in front of us. It's gonna take some time to get off this goddamned . . . what'd you call it? Victory Road, right. Then outta the Volturno plain and into the Liri Valley. I don't doubt we'll take Rome, and when we do, I expect the 36th to toss the keys to Clark, but, again, it'll take time. No matter what the Fifth Army staff says, our limited resources in this sideshow theater and this shitty terrain tell me I'm right."

As he sat down again, Wranosky said, "Jim, tell 'em about the Krauts, then we'll cover the corps mission."

"Yes sir. OK, boys, while Fifth Army's been workin' its ass up Victory Road, the Germans have been busy. In the first place, Berlin has decided to defend Italy south of Rome. I suspect that there was some debate about withdrawing to the Alps, but they've obviously decided to hold onto a southern line. It's our belief that Smilin' Albert, better known as Field Marshal Albert Kesselring, has been placed in command of the Italian theater. I think it's an interesting and significant decision on the part of the Germans. Interesting in that Hitler appointed the Luftwaffe officer, Kesselring, over his chief rival for the job, Rommel. Significant, because Kesselring's forte is defense."

"This is a theater of economy for the Germans. Unlike in the east or what we'll face in France, the Germans haven't thrown some hundred divisions here. No, the Germans have only devoted a handful of divisions, about a dozen, to face us, and some of those are in Rome or northern Italy. We learned at Salerno that the mighty, mighty Wehrmacht's no match for us. So, how is it that a handful of units have held up our advance? The simple answer is they take advantage of the terrain, which is easily defensible and constricts maneuver. The Krauts have blown bridges, tunnels, culverts, tore up all the railroads, and mined the roads and the countryside and the river banks. They've stripped the country bare, forced us to feed the Eye-ties, and we've all seen what they've done in Naples. We don't just have to fight an offensive, we have to feed and administer this country.

"With the use of Italian slave labor, the Germans are busy preparing the winter lines. Like we said, they intend to hold us south of Rome, and they've found the ideal place just up the road near the Abbey at Monte Cassino.

There is a deep and fast river running perpendicular to Victory Road that forms the foundation of their main defensive line, which prisoners are referring to as the 'Gustav Line.' By the way," Lockridge said seriously, "I really hope that we're no longer the spearhead before we get to that river—the Rapido River. It's gonna be a heartbreaker. But in the meantime, we've got at least two minor lines to cross: the Barbara Line and the Bernhardt Line. Both will be breached. They're just to delay us until the Gustav Line is complete.

"What can we expect there? In the smaller lines, prepared defenses: mines, concertina wire, interlaced machine gun positions, anti-tank guns, anti-aircraft guns, pre-registered artillery. Up in the mountains: machine gun nest after machine gun nest, booby traps, deliberate rockslides over paths, mines, and more mines. When we get to the Gustav Line, it will be far worse. More of the same, plus concrete bunkers and excellent observation of the battlefield from the Abbey at Monte Cassino and the mountains. In addition to that, prisoners are talking about plans to place Panther turrets in fixed fortifications as anti-tank guns and the use of concealed Mark II flame-thrower turrets. Prisoners are also talking about destroying the highway and flooding the valley plain through destruction of dams and diversion of the river. The mud we've seen to date is a primer for what's to come."

"But before we get to the main line, we have to get into the Liri Valley, and unfortunately, we have to make it through this bottleneck here . . ." Lockridge flipped the map over again to reveal a yet more detailed map. " . . . called the Mignano Gap. I know y'all have looked at these maps before, but here's a refresher on the topography: Highway 6 runs through the bottleneck into the Liri Valley, which leads us to Rome. But the Mignano Gap is a wicked constriction of our maneuver between two mountain complexes. I know you Aggies out there might have trouble following this, so think about it this way: A bird's eye view of our area of operations is like lookin' down on a plate with a strip of bacon in the middle. That's the valley floor where Highway 6 runs. On either side of the bacon, there are two cat head biscuits. Those are the mountain complexes. To top it off, the whole damn plate is covered in sorghum molasses. That's this sticky Italian mud we've come to know. . . ."

Sam leaned over to Perkin and whispered, "Damn. I'm gettin' hungry again." Perkin grinned as Sam's stomach growled.

"The mountain complex on our left is the Camino hill mass. It's about six miles by four miles with the short, steep side fronting our valley. It actually consists of several peaks—Mount Camino, Mount Maggiore, Mount La Rementea, and Mount La Difensa. Camino's the tallest peak on the left flank at 963 meters above sea level—nearly 3,200 feet. By the way, Difensa's been used by the Italian war college as a case study in insurmountable geographic features. I hope they'll have to rewrite their lecture when we're done with it."

"Directly north of the Camino biscuit—" Lockridge smirked as Sam's stomach growled loudly again, "—is our piece of bacon. The Mignano Gap. It's a small, flat corridor between Mounts Camino, on the left, and Sammucro, on the right, through which most of Fifth Army will march on its way to Rome. Two miles at the narrowest, three miles at its widest, it's split in half by this here hill: Mount Lungo, 1,000 feet up. Against the base of the northern biscuit, Mount Sammucro, elevation 3,800 feet, is the village of San Pietro."

Lockridge continued, "OK, to the corps mission. Our mission is to breach the German defenses in the Mignano Gap, force an opening into the Liri Valley, and set the

stage for operations against the Gustav Line and follow-
on operations for the taking of Rome. Corps assets for
this mission: the 36th Division, the 1st Special Service
Force, and the 1st and 3rd Ranger Battalions. The other
division to be assigned to II Corps is the 3rd Division.
They're coming off the line for refit and rehab and will
not be available for this operation. I've heard an Italian
force of at least brigade size will participate, possibly in
our sector, but that's unconfirmed."

Several officers present laughed at this last announce-
ment. "Who cleans up after them?" an officer called out
from the back. The laughter and comments died off as
Wranosky turned around and glared.

Lockridge continued, "Looking at the map, we unlock
the gates to the Liri Valley in a left-to-right sequence. The
first step is the taking of the Camino Hill Mass by both
the British X Corps and us. The navy will stage a demonstration along the coast, suggesting a behind-the-lines
landing at either Gaeta or Formia. It's hoped that this
will draw down German forces to the coast. Meanwhile,
X Corps will launch an assault against the southernmost
peak, Mount Camino, again hoping to draw down forces
to the south. After that's been achieved, II Corps assaults
La Difensa, Remetanea, and Maggiore. When the hill
mass has been cleared, X Corps relieves II Corps and as-
sumes control of the entire massif. The southern gate to
the Liri Valley will be in our control, and we can then shift
to the northern gate: Mount Sammucro."

Lockridge paused long enough to take a sip of coffee from a white china teacup, a prized possession of the
owners of the farmhouse. He cleared his throat and resumed, "The 1st Special Service Force will be attached
to the 36th, and they and the 142nd Regimental Combat Team will lead the assault against the II Corps targets—"

"Excuse me, sir," interrupted Second Lieutenant Frank McCarter, an Able Company platoon leader. "What's the 1st Special Service Force?"

Lieutenant Colonel Wranosky stood up and answered for Captain Lockridge. "They're a combined American-Canadian, uh . . . I don't know . . . commando brigade—three very small regiments and a service battalion. All told, about the size of a standard infantry battalion. They were formed last year, and they're under the command of an American colonel named Frederick. Highly trained mountain fighters, according to their supporters. Canucks and criminals, according to others. Although I'll never understand the fascination with these so-called special forces, I'm glad to have the additional troops under General Walker's command. Go ahead, Jim."

"Right, sir. OK, initially, the 142nd gets the hot work on the mountainside to the left. The 143rd will be on the right, and we'll be in the center. The 143rd holds the right flank, and on order moves against German positions on Mount Sammucro. We, the 141st, will conduct diversionary attacks against German positions on Mount Lungo and in the vicinity of San Pietro during this period, and it's our job to defend the corridor against German counterattacks. That's the good news. The bad news is that once Fifth Army's advance resumes, we're likely out front—"

Wranosky interrupted again with a rare check of his intelligence officer, "It ain't bad news, Jim. Ain't good news, neither. It's just our mission, plain and simple." Wranosky stood once more and faced his junior officers. "You boys listen up. We all know that there are good missions and bad missions, but in the end, it don't matter. We do what Uncle Sam tells us, good or bad." Wranosky frowned as he thought for a moment, then brightened and grinned, "Let's keep this all in perspective: we cain't go home and we cain't stay here. We're stuck in three damn feet of mud, and we got icy mountains on either side of us and a cold wet winter to come. Keepin' with the Deuce's breakfast theme, it'd be like a 15,000 strong Donner Party, and that's a party I don't plan to attend. And it ain't like we have a choice, but if we did, it would look like . . . well, we either go back to the armpit of Europe and the poxiest damned whores in the whole drippin' history of venereal disease, or we go forward and face the Wehrmacht. I don't know 'bout y'all, but . . . well, let me put it this way: I ain't afraid of the Germans."

1010 Hours
CINC Southwest Headquarters, Monte Soratte, Italy

"No sir. I'm not asking for special treatment, but—" Major Douglas Grossmann seethed as he was cut off by the disagreeable colonel staring at him with disdain.

"Enough, Major. I know your objections. You'll have your orders tonight." With that, the colonel put on his overcoat, returned Grossmann's automatic salute, and walked out of the conference room.

Douglas Grossmann looked around the empty conference room and shook his head at the stupidity of the orders he'd just received. He looked at the rich mahogany panels on the wall then stared dumbly at the leather portfolio he'd brought into the room. This day was to have been the highlight of his career, but he'd just been notified that his death warrant would arrive that evening.

The liaison staff of the Wehrmacht had already had extensive quarters in Rome as it had been a busy war for the Italy-based Germans. Long before the Tripartite Pact of 1940 formally introduced the world to the Axis Powers, German officers had been available to the Italian military staff as advisors. Once the war began, German officers also served to coordinate the activities of the two militaries. Many of those officers who rotated through Rome over the years referred to themselves jokingly as "the fire brigade," as they had helped Italy through one military catastrophe after another. It was a clear pattern: Mussolini would embark on a military adventure without consultations with the Führer and then would get bogged down and require assistance. The European side of the Axis, however, wasn't an arrangement between equals. Despite the Führer's apparent regard for Mussolini, Germany was clearly the senior partner. As the junior partner was expected to follow the German lead, the Italians were forced to navigate the rocky course between catastrophes of their own making and those initiated by Germany.

Major Douglas Grossmann had been stationed in Italy for nearly two years before Italy's armistice with the Allies had necessitated a military occupation of the unfortunate country. While he enjoyed the comforts of Rome and was eternally grateful to be in the Eternal City instead of on the Eastern Front, he candidly admitted to himself from time to time that he had not contributed much to the war effort. Still, what contributions he had made seemed completely unappreciated.

The Abwehr high command had always been uncertain where to best use a man of Grossmann's pedigree and talents. He had excelled in his intelligence training and was a natural linguist with the gift of impartial judgment—an invaluable trait to one in the business of human intelligence—and had never outwardly given the high command cause to doubt his loyalty. Yet Grossmann had extensive ties to America, including an American mother. He had spent more of his life in Coronado, California than he had in the Fatherland. Though his German accent was impeccable, he sometimes used English phrases in casual conversation. More concerning was a very American attitude to authority, an attitude that had no comfortable home in the Third Reich.

Grossmann was aware of at least one occasion when he had come to the attention of Admiral Wilhelm Canaris, the head of German military intelligence. In late 1939, the suggestion had been made to Canaris that perhaps Grossmann, then a lieutenant, was a good candidate to go to Eire and Ulster to bring Teutonic order to a faltering collaboration with the Irish Republican Army. When Grossmann's supervisor asked him his thoughts on the potential IRA project, Grossmann's caustic reply in English was, "Those fucking retards? The goddamned Taigs are so infiltrated that you might as well hand me over to MI6 now!" Those comments had been reported back, verbatim, to Canaris. While the Admiral disapproved of the vulgarity, he agreed with the assessment and the plan had been shelved.

That still left the question of what to do with the officer. During the dull months of the Sitzkrieg and the exhilarating days of the spring campaign in France in 1940, Grossmann was assigned to the Anglo-American directorate and was later posted in occupied Paris. The nomadic officer had found another home.

Grossmann loved France. He was fluent in French, and it was easy living. Above all things, he liked the French women—they were less resentful than he expected they would be and to top it off, the food and the wine were superb. Being stationed in France was like living a vacation, and even his military duties were enjoyable.

Following the British evacuation at Dunkirk, he spent many hours interrogating captured British soldiers. He had been trained to impersonate several British accents, and he would sit down with select British officers or NCOs, offer them a cigarette, and tell them in an Etonian accent—or sometimes, a Welsh accent—that his name was Neville Drinkwater or Lee Llewellyn. His British uniform was authentic, his accent and vernacular perfect, and he was so believable that when he broke the news that Churchill had surrendered, some of the prisoners began weeping. He would state officiously that he was in personnel administration and he had been sent to prepare them for repatriation. By the terms of the agreement, he would tell them, Britain would keep a small standing army, and he needed to know which prisoners were regular army and desired further service. He also needed some other information: name, service number, unit, date of commission or rank, commanding officer, and next of kin in Britain. Sometimes it worked, and he would sit with those soldiers and share a cigarette and talk about units or weapons or senior officers. It was mostly low-level information, but it added up. Sometimes it didn't work, and while once posing as Captain Drinkwater, he was nearly beaten unconscious by an irate lieutenant from the Royal Scots before the guards could rescue him. On a different occasion, another soldier from the Royal Scots confided in Grossmann that he believed the Germans had summarily executed twenty Jocks who had surrendered at Dunkirk, and would Sergeant Llewellyn ensure that information made it home? That was an interesting tidbit of data that Grossmann quietly researched and found to be valid. He tucked away the pertinent information, including the names of the responsible officers, for a rainy day.

He talked to the occasional Canadian prisoners, sometimes pretending to be a Canadian officer and using a similar story about Britain's surrender. Other times, he told them he was American, assigned to the US diplomatic mission in France, and that the United States was representing Canadian interests through its embassy. This was frequently successful as the Canadians appreciated hearing a familiar accent, and they responded to his apparent sympathy and outrage for their plight. He quit using that cover when a recently captured Canadian major dryly noted that, as Canada maintained diplomatic relations with Vichy France, American representation was hardly necessary.

Grossmann was also assigned analytical duties which he enjoyed as well. In assessment after assessment, he answered the questions posed to him by his superiors: Yes, England will fight alone if necessary. No, they will not accept a peace with Germany that recognizes her continental hegemony, particularly if Poland and France aren't restored. Well, Mr. Churchill is different from Mr. Chamberlain because he has an American mother. America? No, the Americans are not soft, and they will fight if forced into it. The Führer thinks America won't be able to threaten us until 1970 or 1980? I wouldn't question the Führer's judgment, but American industrial potential is unfathomable—they are pure capitalists with unlimited resources.

As Hitler's attention turned from cross-channel operations to the Soviet Union following the failure of the Luftwaffe in the Battle of Britain, Grossmann had felt the tectonic shift within the intelligence community. Great Britain was a concern, obviously—in particular the Royal Navy—but the English were defeated even if they were too foolish to recognize the fact. They could make trouble in peripheral sideshows, but Russia was to be the big top.

Grossmann spoke no Slavic languages, found Slavic literature tedious and the names unintelligible, and unlike most hard-charging Abwehr officers in early 1941, Grossmann didn't volunteer for service in Africa, the Bal-

kans, or for Operation Barbarossa.* Certainly he would
have gone with minimal complaint to any of those theaters if ordered, but outside of the carnal prospect of the
tall and beautiful women along the Dalmatian Coast in
friendly Croatia, the simple truth was that he wasn't interested. France would work just fine for Grossmann as long
as he was allowed to remain.

His time in France ended with the declaration of war
against the United States on December 11, 1941. In con-
trast to the delighted exclamations of his colleagues to the
news, Grossmann sat silent, dumbfounded. War with the
United States was not totally unexpected, but it was still
a harsh slap across his face. There was no question where
his loyalties lay, but the Führer's declaration left him pro-
foundly distressed. That night, Grossmann sought release
in the bars of Paris. Although the thought had crossed
his mind that his throat might be cut by a newly inspired
Frenchman if he got too drunk, he nevertheless drank
himself to near unconsciousness. As it worked out, his
throat wasn't cut, and he was carried back to his quarters by two good-natured artillery lieutenants on leave in
Paris while he loudly sang a slurred and obscene version
of the Horst Wessel song. The next day, nursing a mil-
lennial hangover, he reflected on the changing fortunes
of the Reich. Even if the Führer couldn't recognize the
consequences of his decision, Grossmann knew it sig-
naled the beginning of the end for Hitler's empire. *Why
in God's name had the Führer declared war on America?* As
Grossmann understood the terms of the Tripartite Pact,
Germany was only obligated to come to Japan's defense
if Japan was attacked by the United States, not the other
way around. *Insanity,* he thought.

---

* The Afrika Korps was stood up by General Rommel on 17 February 1941;
Germany attacked Yugoslavia and Greece on 6 April 1941; and Operation Barbarossa was the invasion of the Soviet Union beginning 22 June 1941.

Two days after the declaration of war, Grossmann received orders to Rome. He never had an adequate explanation for the transfer, but suspected that someone in his chain of command wanted him far away from the American diplomatic mission in Vichy. Perhaps they thought he would defect or be turned as an agent, but as he thought, bitterly, *What good am I if I don't have access to the Americans?* After a few weeks leave with his father in Darmstadt, he was transferred to Abwehr I, the branch of German military intelligence responsible for human intelligence collection, and ordered to assume command of the Rome Abwehr office. It, too, was a great posting.

Grossmann found that Italian women were more beautiful, but less rewarding as lovers than the French women. He was always something of a forbidden fruit to the French ladies, which added tension and excitement to his numerous affairs, but he found to his surprise that being an ally was hardly advantageous in Rome. He had much greater salacious fortune posing as an American trapped in Rome, and he was astonished at the number of Italian women who would offer him sanctuary, which of course he always declined and never reported. The food was more to his liking than in Paris, but he found the Italian wines execrable after the complex Bordeaux and the likeable Burgundies he had access to in Paris. He had once been given a case of the incredible '29 Chateau Latour simply for interceding with the military police in Paris on behalf of a merchant who was accused of profiteering. While the corruption in Rome was worse, and bribery more common, he couldn't be bought with a case of Italian wine.

It was in Rome that he met Antoniette Bernardi and Mark Gerschoffer. Gerschoffer was to become Grossmann's best friend in the whole of the German Army. Bernardi was to become his most successful agent. When he was introduced to Bernardi by his predecessor in the Rome station, the normally smooth Grossmann was dumbstruck. Without question, she was the most beautiful woman that Grossmann had ever met. Bernardi was short, just five feet, three inches tall, but she had a self-assured bearing that made her seem taller. She was beautiful: light olive tint to her skin, coal-black hair, black eyes, and a stunning, winsome, smile. They sat down alone together at a café after the introductions were made, and Grossmann was already half-convinced that he would do anything for this woman. Lie, cheat, steal, kill—whatever she needed. She was so caring, so personable, seemingly so fragile and so empathetic, that in minutes he was telling her his life story. She asked logical, piercing, questions in such a kind, yet seductive manner that Grossmann talked on and on about his life. It was, he realized later, an almost hypnotic experience where he could barely recall what he had said. It was while he was telling her of his mother's death that he brought himself up short. A look of greedy amusement had flitted so quickly through those dark eyes, to be instantly replaced by warm sympathy, that he almost doubted what he had seen. But the perceptive Grossmann had seen enough to know that he was getting a rare glimpse into the true nature of Antoniette Bernardi, and he quickly changed the subject.

Later, as he reviewed her file, Grossmann discovered that Bernardi was just seventeen. He'd marked her as a decade older. His predecessor, a lugubrious captain by the name of von Wietershiem, told Grossmann about her that night over several schnapps.

"Antoniette will be your best agent," he said. "She's a dedicated fascist. Admires the Führer very much. I think she is the best we are running in all of Italy already. But, I must warn you, sir, she is unlike anyone I've met before. She has no innocence of youth, but she's not a hard story—her doting father's quite wealthy, in fact. She exudes compassion, yet has none." Wietershiem pulled out a silver cigarette case emboldened with the family coat of arms from his uniform breast pocket, offered a cigarette to Grossmann, and said sardonically, "I don't know how God could have created such a beautiful creature, yet in His greatness neglected to give it a soul. She's without modesty, entirely without scruples . . . a heart as cold as a witch's caress." He shook his head as he lit Grossmann's cigarette. "I'm heading east to join my uncle's staff, so I hope there is a God. If there is, for God's sake, don't try to seduce her yourself. I don't think that she would let you, she's too professional, but it might be worse if she did. Either way, she would dangle your desire before you for an eternity—until you either kill her or yourself in despair." Grossmann had laughed at the time, but later thought over and heeded Wietershiem's advice.

They worked well as a team. The analytical Grossmann would develop the targets, following leads from other intelligence, looking for weaknesses to exploit. Bernardi would seduce the target, apply her amazing empathy, and ask the most pertinent yet innocuous questions. She had explained to Grossmann once that most self-important men don't listen to a beautiful girl's questions, they just answer them.

Only a few of her targets ever suspected they were being interrogated. Even then, the more lovelorn simply banished the suspicion and continued to talk. Others broke off the affair with various excuses, and if inconsequential, they were allowed to drift away. However, if they had continuing value to the Reich, Grossmann would attempt to overtly recruit their services. Sometimes with resounding success, sometimes with devastating failure. Of the latter group, Bernardi had lured one, a colonel of the *Carabinieri* to a final rendezvous in a moonlit park in Rome known for discrete assignations. As Grossmann walked up to the couple sitting on a bench in a remote corner of the park, Bernardi stood up and walked away without a word. Grossmann had taken her place on the bench, informed her confused lover in Italian that he was Major Wolff of the Gestapo, and then asked the man to consider working on behalf of the Third Reich. The Gestapo, he felt, was more awe-inspiring than the Abwehr. But the Carabinieri official was intimidated neither by the offices of the Gestapo nor the smallish Grossmann, and when the Italian officer contemptuously shook his head and stood to leave, Captain Gerschoffer stepped out of the shadows behind the bench and drove an ice pick into his spine. It was a regrettable outcome, as the colonel had close ties to the court of King Victor Emmanuel, but Grossmann had accurately predicted that the Carabinieri officer could not be bought or coerced, so he had offered only a token bribe and a half-hearted threat. It was the first killing that he had personally witnessed, even after all the years of war, and the first that he felt directly responsible for, yet he was surprised that he was unmoved by the officer's murder.

Still, it was much more rewarding, personally and professionally, to turn a potential adversary into an ally. He enjoyed the mental challenge of preparing for each target—knowing whether to appeal to greed or patriotism, or whether to resort to good old-fashioned blackmail, or, if necessary, to terminate a liability like the Carabinieri officer. As far as methods went, as long as it was successful, he preferred blackmail—as chief of the Rome office, he had a budget to adhere to, and he hated to part with funds in order to buy information.

For many months, Bernardi had been the regular lover of an Italian priest assigned to the Vatican Curia. The man was well-connected within the Church hierarchy and was an insatiable gossip, making him extraordinarily valuable to Major Grossmann.

The priest also had an established record of seducing teenage girls—Bernardi, for once, had to dress and act her young age—and surprisingly, the priest was one of her most accomplished lovers. Grossmann had set up a nice apartment just under a mile from the Vatican for Bernardi's liaisons. The priest, after changing into street clothes, would meet her once a week after dark. Most of the information she collected was banal and trivial, mere pillow talk consisting of gossip about Vatican leadership, but it proved accumulative in value as Grossmann developed a working and predictive model of Vatican politics over the months.

The priest had been mildly surprised by Bernardi's knowledge of the personalities and the workings of the Holy See, and two or three times, he had been disquieted by the directness of his lover's questions, but blinded by lust and ego, he overlooked the alarms sounded by his conscience and his considerable intellect. It was over two bottles of wine and a shared bath with the exquisitely beautiful girl that the priest awoke to the nature and danger of his relationship with Antoniette Bernardi. He had been gossiping about Monsignor Hugh O'Flaherty, one of his superiors in the Vatican Curia, and he mentioned his suspicions that the Irishman was sympathetic to the plight of captured Allied servicemen. It was likely, he said, that O'Flaherty was helping downed American and British pilots to hide in the Italian countryside or even escape back to Allied lines. This was interesting enough to Bernardi, and she had heard and reported these kinds of rumors from the priest before, but his next revelation—that one of O'Flaherty's fellow Irishmen in Rome was rumored to have a brother in British intelligence—caused her to drop her carefully constructed guard. In the candlelight of the bathroom, the priest saw the tiniest flicker of triumph and greed in her black eyes, and it was a momentary glimpse into hell.

He bolted upright in the bath, explaining lamely that in his haste to see Bernardi he had neglected some vital task and had to leave immediately. Bernardi could read his panic and knew that she had made some inexplicable error, but she smoothly offered her understanding. While the priest got dressed in the bedroom she placed a discrete phone call to the apartment next door.

When the priest opened the door from the bedroom, he was surprised and concerned to find Bernardi was gone and two men were waiting for him. The larger of the two men—the much larger of the two men—walked swiftly to the priest and punched him hard in the solar plexus. The priest dropped without a sound and writhed on the floor in agony, trying to catch his breath, while the large man pulled over two chairs from the small dining room.

Grossmann had watched with some amusement. He had always been struck by the fact that despite the Italians' volatile and argumentative nature, their arguments seldom came to blows. He had never seen an Italian fistfight, and this Italian didn't know how to take a punch.

When the priest had recovered sufficiently to push himself onto his hands and knees, Grossmann knelt next to him and said sternly in perfect Italian, "Not a word, Father! We're going to help you to that chair, and then we're going to discuss your rape of my niece. If you say a word that is not in response to a question, my little brother will break your neck before you have time to beg forgiveness for your sins."

As Captain Gerschoffer helped the stricken priest to his feet, the Italian began to stammer that it wasn't rape, that she was quite willing. His explanation was cut short as Gerschoffer hit him hard again. This time, Gerschoffer kicked the feet out from under the breathless man, pinning the wheezing priest's head to the floor with his boot.

"Now?" Gerschoffer asked in his German-accented Italian.

"I don't know. What do you think?" Grossmann switched to German, knowing that the priest could speak it as well.

"I say we kill this rapist now, then go to the cabaret. I don't want to be late for the show."

"You surprise me, brother. Do you think that catching a song and dance number is more important than this man's life?" Grossmann asked with a smile.

"No, of course not. I didn't say that. I think a song and dance *and* a drink and perhaps a sandwich is more important than this man's life. I'm getting hungry. Let me finish it now."

The priest closed his eyes and began mumbling, his chest heaving in and out. Gerschoffer put more pressure on his skull, but Grossmann stopped him with a hand on the captain's arm. "No, he's praying. Let's see if his prayers will be answered. Lift him up."

When the Italian was set in the chair, Grossmann brought his face to within a few inches from the unfortunate priest's, looked him in the eyes and said in Italian, "Father, we're discussing whether to let you live. I understand if you might believe you have a vested interest in this discussion, and therefore a voice in the discussion, but I assure you that this decision is mine and mine alone. I value my brother's opinion greatly, but, still, I decide. So, I ask some questions, you provide some answers. Do you understand?"

The priest nodded and Grossmann continued, "Good. First: introductions. I am *Sturmbannfuhrer* Karl Wolff, Junior, of the SS. This is my brother, *Hauptsturmfuhrer* Peter Wolff, also of the SS. Second, about my niece. Well, you might have guessed it, but she's not really my niece. That term is more of a . . . a . . . what's the word I'm looking for?"

"A metaphor?" Gerschoffer suggested helpfully.

"No, but it's a figurative term . . . damn. What's the word? Oh, well. Sorry, Father, I'm a little shocked by your behavior, and I can't seem to think straight . . . but let me try to explain. Her father is a prominent member of the Fascist Party. We are National Socialists. That makes us like brothers, so in a figurative sense it was like you were raping my fourteen-year-old niece. Yes, yes, I know. She looks much older, but she's really just a child. So, leaving your vows aside for a moment—and that's really a matter between you, your conscience, and the Pope, as far as we're concerned—as far as the law is concerned, rape it was."

The priest dropped his head and began to weep.

"No, Father. You need to stay with me here. I need you to focus before I ask you a few questions." Grossmann pulled a chair over next to the priest and sat down. He looked at Gerschoffer and asked, "Brother, would you hand me that folder there please?"

Grossmann took a dark brown leather folder from Captain Gerschoffer and opened it to reveal several sheets of paper and several enlarged photographs. Grossmann pulled the photos out and glanced at the first picture in the stack.

"Wow. Peter, what do you make of this?" He handed the photo back to the large captain.

"I'm sorry. It's a terrible picture. I needed a larger lens or something, but you *can* see his face." Gerschoffer smirked as he looked at the large black-and-white photograph.

"Yes, true. But I meant the picture itself, not the artistry of the photographer . . . you know, the act that's being captured."

"Oh, the act. Well . . . that act's illegal in Italy."

"You know, I think you're right . . . and it should be. It looks quite painful and degrading." Grossmann showed the picture to the priest, who groaned and looked away. "Father, sodomy is both a sin and a violation of secular law. How you can live with yourself is beyond me. Here, look at this one. It's tough to make out, but do we think that's blood on the sheets? Hard to guess what a court might think, this being in black and white, but it almost looks like blood on my niece's thighs as well. A thousand times out of a thousand times, they would never think of chocolate sauce, you dog. What about this one? *Ach*, pictures are only a snapshot in time, but I can't tell if she's crying out in pain or crying out in ecstasy. While the possibilities might say something about you as a man, I fear that either option is a losing proposition for a priest. Here's my favorite! If you don't mind, may I say that I admire this greatly? I've never been good with knots, you see. Oh . . . here's one more you need to look at."

Grossmann placed another picture into the trembling hands of the priest, who dropped it as if it were on fire.

"Yes, yes. You know that lady, don't you? So do we. That's your mother, isn't it? I've seldom enjoyed a journey to Siena as much as the one I took with my brother here. See there? The quality of this picture, the artistry of this photographer? I don't like to brag, but I took *this* picture. See this one? That's my brother standing there with your mama."

It was a picture of a beaming Gerschoffer in the uniform of an SS lieutenant standing with his arm around an elderly, smiling lady at a flower stand. The next picture was a close up of their faces close together, smiling broadly for the camera, with the death's head insignia on Gerschoffer's hat clearly visible.

"Oh! And here's another one! I hadn't meant to show you this, but since I have it out, why not? It's very expressionistic, don't you think? Maybe it's more in line with what the Americans are now calling 'film noir,' but I go back to an older time. I call this picture *Der müde Tod*, which is, of course, taken from Fritz Lang's very fine film of the same name—is he a Jew?" Grossmann asked of Gerschoffer, who shrugged. "They make such marvelous films. Anyway, it translates to *The Weary Death*. It's hard to see in the darkness, but I fancy my brother looks tired of killing. I thought of naming it first *Thanatus*, which was, I don't know, too classical, too Greek. Then I thought of *Shiva*, but the duality of essence in the name doesn't capture my brother's singularity as a destroyer. As a man of the cloth, you must be philosophical. What are your thoughts?"

It was a stark black-and-white photo showing the un-mistakable profile of a German soldier, his body partly emerged from the shadows under a dim streetlight. The soldier's face could not be made out, it was in the shadow of his helmet, but the outlined physique in the photo was clearly Gerschoffer's. An SS dagger held in his right hand pointed downward, leading the eyes to a highly polished jackboot resting on a corpse—the face of whom was also lost in the shadows. As the priest's eyes followed the shape of the body under the jackboot, he saw an arm twisted in an impossibly awkward angle and the legs and shoes of a woman showing from beneath a torn black dress—the modest dress of an older woman. The priest looked mute-ly in horror at the picture, and then raised his face, tears streaming down his cheeks, towards Grossmann.

"No thoughts on the name? But you will admit, yes, a fine picture?" said Grossmann. "Truthfully, I think it's my best work, and it was taken under the most unusual of circumstances. As I said, I don't wish to brag, but like the Führer, I'm a bit of an artist. Where was this, Peter? I don't remember . . . Paris? Stalingrad?"

With a casualness that made the priest's blood run cold, Gerschoffer shrugged again and said, "Paris, Stalingrad, Siena. What's the fucking difference?"

"What's the fucking difference, indeed. Well said, Peter! Father, are you paying attention? You're shaking so. Would . . . would you like some tea? No? Well, please listen carefully then. This is the point where I resolve your immediate future as well as that of your mother. From time to time, I will ask you some questions about the state of affairs within the Holy See, and you will, to the best of your ability, answer truthfully. On some subjects, such as, say, Father O'Flaherty, when I ask for amplifying information that might require some research on your part, you will find the answers we seek. I will not ask you to put your life on the line, nor will I compromise your position in the Vatican Curia, nor, hopefully, will the rape of my niece need to be discussed again—you won't see her again, by the way. I just need a little information, just a little bit, really, so my government might make informed decisions on its relationship with the Holy See. That's all we want. Now, I know that you like to gossip, but I'm going to ask one more thing. Just one more. Will you be discrete about this conversation, including in the confessional, or will our next visit to Siena be more wearisome than the last?"

A year of work about to be pissed away. Grossmann's thoughts swam as he sat alone in the Abwehr conference room. *Wasted time.*

The Italian had been a prime source. He had identified an Irish priest named Riley in the Jesuit Curia in Rome as a suspected conduit to British intelligence. Inquiries to Abwehr contacts in Dublin had recently provided information that largely substantiated the claim, and the Abwehr high command was excited to exploit the intelligence. In September, just days after the Allied landings, Captain Gerschoffer had been ordered to arrest the priest in the no-man's-land of southern Italy. The Abwehr team had been captured by a patrol led by then-lieutenant Berger of the 141st Infantry in the village of Pisciotta, and the priest had been safely evacuated to Allied lines. It was a disappointing operation, and had Major Grossmann not been undercover in the Allied encampment at the time, he might well have been scapegoated for the failure to capture the Irishman.

Not all had been for naught, however. An analysis of the personalities of the Holy See had been prepared, and separate lists of clergy sympathetic and hostile to the Third Reich were complete. Not surprisingly, the latter list was more far extensive than the former—but the list of those who were sympathetic to Germany included names that reached high into the Vatican hierarchy.

A separate but related thread of intelligence reporting derived from the priest concerned Monsignor Hugh O'Flaherty. The Irishman, in contravention of Vatican policy, had taken an active role in the protection of escaped Allied prisoners of war and was believed to have helped hundreds of escaped POWs and downed airman back to Allied lines or into sympathetic Italian homes.

It was in the collection against and analysis of O'Flaherty's operations that Major Grossmann felt he had made the greatest contribution to the war, and he was making preparations to present his findings to the Abwehr high command. Then, with the high command's approval, he and Captain Gerschoffer would personally infiltrate the O'Flaherty network by posing as downed airmen. He hoped to prove his theory that O'Flaherty was an agent of British intelligence, and that Father Patrick Riley had been the Monsignor's handler.

Today was the day, in fact, that he had scheduled his briefing with his superiors. It was all prepared: the list of sympathetic priests within the Holy See and recommendations for further recruitment and exploitation; a network diagram showing links between the Irishmen and British military intelligence—although the link with O'Flaherty was highlighted as speculative; a plan for infiltration by Gerschoffer and Grossmann; and a final plan to roll up the Vatican operation. He had even made recommendations of a strategic nature on how the Foreign Office should demarche the Vatican and what demands should be made of Pope Pius. Grossmann noted that it could even be the basis for a complete revision of the Concordat of 1933.

It was brilliant work, and Grossmann knew it. But instead of finding a conference room full of invited officers when he arrived that morning to conduct his briefing, there was only a sole colonel of the Abwehr—a disagreeable prick from the admiral's staff—who had never cared for Grossmann or his *Auslandsdeutsche.*

"Herr Major," the colonel had said upon his entrance to the briefing room. "Your meeting is canceled. Your operation against the Holy See is being held in abeyance indefinitely. You and your group of . . . Yankee doodles . . . will receive new orders immediately. Is there any part of this that you do not understand?"

"Yes sir." Instantly angry, Grossmann replied curtly, "I don't understand a goddamned thing."

"Yes . . . ," the colonel sighed. "Americans require explanations. Well, Admiral Canaris has authorized me to inform you that the Abwehr has become aware that General Wolff of the SS has been ordered by the Führer to develop contingency plans to arrest Pius XII. Naturally, should the SS proceed with the execution of these orders, they will damage our position throughout the world of

Catholicism beyond repair. The SS can't possibly complete these orders with the finesse required and they, likely as not, will kill His Holiness in the process. In short order, we may face religious insurrection from France to Croatia, and the Führer will be furious and looking for someone to hold accountable."

"Therefore, the Admiral has decided to extricate the Abwehr for the time being. In other words: let the SS take the blame. You are to place your analysis of Monsignor O'Flaherty in the Abwehr vault here in Rome, and it is the Admiral's verbal orders that your intelligence is not to be shared with the SS under any circumstances. Also, your agents are forbidden to contact your sources in the Vatican in the services of the Third Reich until this can be sorted out. In short, the Vatican is now the problem of the SS—perhaps someday we'll come in and clean up their mess, but don't hold your breath."

Grossmann was puzzled, "You know about . . . ."

"Yes, Major. Of course the admiral is aware of your work. As you have a classical flair, no doubt Juvenal comes to mind: '*Quis custodiet ipsos custodes.*' Well, in your case, we watch our own watchmen. Did you really think we would let a handful of Yankees run about German intelligence without close monitoring? Oh, the admiral did tell me to say, and I quote, 'Good work, but I'll execute them myself if either he or the gorilla pose as General Wolff's sons again.' Unquote. There. I've said it. Now I have a train north to catch."

"Sir!" Grossmann was stunned. "What . . . what happens next? With us? What are my orders?"

The colonel opened a cigarette case, took out a cigarette with tobacco-stained fingers, and tapped the cigarette impatiently on the case's incongruously painted image of Betty Boop. He lit the cigarette with an American steel Zippo lighter, and after he had inhaled deeply, he said with consideration in his voice, "Your orders will arrive shortly, but let me take a moment to explain. You have a certain skill—limited, yes, but of value to the Abwehr. Since your utility in Rome has expired, you are being sent to where you might better serve the Fatherland. You, your Neanderthal captain, and your Roman whore—if she will go—are to establish collection operations against the American Fifth Army in the Naples-Caserta-Monte Cassino area of operations. Specifically, you are to provide usable intelligence on American leadership, units, disposition, and movements. You will be provided the proper uniforms, weapons, and identification, and you'll be briefed this evening by Abwehr communications specialists on radio and courier options and procedures."

Grossmann was shaking his head as he tried to organize his thoughts. "This isn't like when I was among Fifth Army in September. They have counterintelligence networks established now. Procedures for security. What do I do about support? Where do we stay? I can't exactly throw together a shelter half with Gerschoffer at a 45th Division encampment or walk in demanding staff billeting. What about rations, money? Transportation?"

The colonel was growing tired of the questions and replied rather sharply, "Your support needs will be met by our contract people in the Camorra.* The same people who assisted you with the explosives operation in September will set you up in various safe houses in Naples, provide you with a stolen American jeep, food—whatever you need."

Grossmann ran his hand through his hair and groaned, "Oh, Jesus! Do you really think they haven't been bought off by the Americans? They'll sell me out to American counterintelligence for a can of Spam. Is that all you think my life is worth?"

---

* The Camorra is the (loosely) organized crime of Naples.

The colonel stared hard at Grossmann, all trace of sympathy gone. "I suppose we value you more than, what were your words? 'A song, a dance, and a drink.' You would be wise to remember the Fatherland has lost more than a million men on the Eastern Front this year alone. Good soldiers who died fighting at Stalingrad and Kursk. What makes you special?"

Chapter Four

November 29, 1943
0620 Hours
Mount La Difensa, Italy

The scout's unfocused eyes stared unceasingly towards the heavens. His Thompson submachine gun had slid thirty yards down the mountainside, and his helmet was nowhere to be seen. The scout's body lay twisted among the sharp granite rocks of the eastern slope of Mount La Difensa, one leg thrown sharply over the other, an arm obviously broken. His neck was bent over at a right angle and his ear was resting on his shoulder, giving the man a quizzical look in death.

As the morning light came slowly to the northeast slope of Mount La Difensa, Perkin had been able to finally locate his lost soldier. Had the light come any later, he might have made the same misstep in the dark—as it was, Perkin was bleeding from several minor scrapes from falls. The scout wasn't far from Perkin, but twelve feet below him, and the young captain was grateful that the dead man seemed to be looking elsewhere. Perkin was tired and didn't want to be judged by the dead.

The unfortunate scout, a corporal named Alberto Garcia from Gonzales, Texas, was his second dead scout on this mission. His first, a farm boy from Michigan, had not even made it to the line of departure when his jeep slid in the Italian mud and rolled over in a ditch. The driver had been thrown from the jeep and knocked unconscious, but the scout had been pushed into the ooze of the ditch by the weight of the jeep and had drowned in the road-side mud before anyone had noticed the upturned vehicle. Casualties from accidents were nearly keeping pace with combat casualties, and Perkin, as the troop commander, had to keep a constant stream of paperwork flowing to higher headquarters reporting illnesses and injuries. He was saddened by both soldiers' deaths, but he was becoming more calloused and accepting of the unfairness of wartime life, and he tried to recall personal details of both soldiers for the letters to parents that he needed to write. *Thank God they were both single*, he thought.

Perkin watched a low-hanging bank of clouds work its way over the Liri Valley to the north and decided that he would remain tucked behind some rocks until the clouds were upon him. Only then would he move to his dead scout and collect a dog tag from Corporal Garcia before skirting up the mountainside as quickly as he could in the covering fog.

It was a questionable call to personally go out to find Garcia, and if that had been the only issue, he would not have left the encampment. As the company commander, he should have sent another scout, or multiple scouts. If he had felt it required an officer, he should have sent a platoon leader. He was a troop commander, for now at least, and it was not his role in the war to personally lead scouting missions, let alone conduct a solitary reconnaissance. But he wasn't entirely alone—he had scouts working possible traversing routes lower down the mountain. The upper route that he was taking along the rock-strewn goat path was the one that he believed the mission planners would ultimately choose. It was, as the line went, the road less traveled. *That's not right,* he thought, *how did that poem go?* As the cloud approached, Perkin thought about Frost's last words from "The Road Not Taken," which if he remembered right was from a collection appropriately entitled *Mountain Intervals*: "I took the one less traveled by, and that has made all the difference." Taking that as a sign, Perkin became a little more optimistic about the road, or rather the goat path less traveled, and a little less concerned about his presence on the mountainside.

The mission that the reconnaissance company was supporting was too important, too time-critical, in Perkin's mind for him to leave it to anyone else. Within ninety-six hours, two of the small regiments of the 1st Special Service Force would be working its way along this mountain slope in an attempt to attack German positions on Mount La Difensa from behind. It looked suicidal from the goat path, but as attacking through the front door had led to severe losses for the 3rd Division and the 142nd Regiment during previous efforts, it looked like the back door was the only way into the German mountaintop bastion on Mount La Difensa. Perhaps the American-Canadian force could replicate General Wolfe's feat at Quebec, but Perkin nevertheless cast a skeptical eye on the rocks above him. The last third of the mountain to its peak was a nearly vertical cliff. It would be challenging beyond description. When the cloud arrived, he would take a closer look at the cliff's base.

From his position about halfway up the mountain slope, Perkin turned about and looked down in the emerging light onto the Mignano Gap and the present and future battlefields. It was an incredible vantage, and the vehicles and people below looked like ants scurrying about with purpose below his feet. The view was one he felt every general officer in the theater should see before ordering troops to further action in the Italian theater. Victory Road emerged from the wide Volturno plain on his right and ran through the Mignano Gap to emerge in the Liri Valley to his left. The Mignano Gap was going to be a ballbuster, Perkin knew. It was if the entirety of the Fifth Army were to be squeezed through a soda straw, and the narrow bottleneck of some two miles was ringed by experienced German artillery and manned by the best defensive fighters in the world. It was an imminently defensible position, and moving through the gap would be expensive. *It would be worse,* he thought, *maybe impossible, if they didn't get control of this mountain. Then that one. Then that one. Damn.*

As he waited patiently for the large cloud to provide him cover, his thoughts ran to Gianina again. Perkin was deeply saddened by her death, but he was finding himself able to put it in perspective: People were dying all around him. He, himself, would most likely die in this war, and perhaps the only way to cope with the war's unfairness and savagery was to accept the inevitability of death in it for him and the others he cared for. Acknowledge death's position in life, acknowledge that those he loved would die, and acknowledge that senescence would have no role in his own destiny. Acknowledge death and move on—a harsh philosophy for a harsh time.

Gianina's death was tragic, but to Perkin there was only a little more to it than that. *It was,* he thought, *meaningless.* As with the death of millions of civilians in the war so far, Perkin believed that it had no value: Her death had not advanced the war nor inspired others to greatness.

She wasn't killed saving a life or feeding the poor or driving the Nazis from her homeland. She was buying a goddamned postage stamp. Her death was simply the random confluence of time and space. Five minutes earlier at the post office and she would still be alive. A different café that afternoon, and she would still be alive.

Perkin sighed softly and then thought, as he did often, of the men who had ordered the bombing of Naples. He could understand, if not excuse, the destruction of the port, the bridges, and the infrastructure. But what value to the German army was there in the murder of civilians in the bombing of a post office? None. It didn't drive Italy out of the war again. It didn't slow down the Allied advance. If anything, it stiffened Allied resolve, and it validated Italy's decision to switch sides. The bombing was an act of pique—childish pique—and misplaced revenge for wounded pride.

Perkin unconsciously touched his medallion of Saint Michael as he contemplated misplaced revenge, and then the medallion took his thoughts momentarily to his friend, Father Riley. Would Riley tell him now that revenge would serve no good purpose? That the cost to his soul would be paid out over eternity? Perkin suspected that the priest would say something along those lines, as he had many months before, but Perkin didn't care. He could, he would, kill those responsible if given the chance, but how to get that chance? Perkin had puzzled over that question since her death. As he watched the dark cloud come closer—there was rain or sleet in the clouds, and he would get wet once more—he asked himself again if he could find the men responsible and kill them, avenge her death, would that be childish pique or misplaced revenge? Or just old-fashioned Texas justice? To Perkin's academic mind, it was a fascinating collection of questions, no less fascinating since he was the central figure in his musings, and he mentally ran through the variables and consequences of revenge over and again—consequences ranging from court-martial to damnation and variables such as what he would do if he could only find the men who planted the bombs and not the officers who issued the orders.

That had been a troublesome variable for Perkin. Was it fair to blame the soldiers who were only following orders? Why wasn't it? He was held to a code of conduct that prohibited waging war against civilians, why should the enemy not be held to the same standard? As the quest for vengeance was seldom logical or consistent, Perkin put his code of conduct aside for the moment and had decided that he'd kill them, too—although he doubted that he would ever find either the decision-makers or the soldiers ordered to do the dirty work. Jim Lockridge had told him that Fifth Army intelligence was investigating the matter, but it likely would not be clarified or resolved until after the war . . . and then only if the Allies won.

Perkin knew his friends were afraid that he was coming unhinged by Gianina's death and the trauma of the war. He was both amused and touched by Sam, Jim, and Bill's evident concern for his well-being, particularly their avoidance of any talk of war or death. Difficult to do in their present circumstances, but they tried. Perhaps they thought he was headed for a section eight, a mental breakdown and discharge, or perhaps they thought he was going to be prone to shell-shock or battle fatigue or even suicide. Nothing could be further from the truth—even if he had pulled his pistol a few nights after her death and contemplated the easy relief of oblivion. Shaking his head at his weakness, the pistol, a captured Luger, was soon holstered. That was the night he had achieved his reckoning with death, and Perkin's mental state was steadily reaching a somewhat somber equilibrium with life.

It was time to move. The cloud had come abreast of Perkin, and the leading edge would envelop him in moments. It was the only safe way to move in daylight when outside the protection of the tree line. Gunners in the valley below, German and American, viewed the mountainside as fair game, and freely fired at any movement. Most importantly, his presence on the mountainside should not indicate Allied interest in that particular route, although there were signs that reconnaissance parties had moved along this goat path before. One recent and mucky set of footprints heading towards the German side of things suggested the owner of the prints was unfamiliar with the pratfalls of country life.

Perkin slid over the rocks and dropped the last few feet to where his soldier lay. The path curved around this drop, but that would have been difficult for his soldier to follow in the dark. Perkin closed the eyes of the dead soldier, took one of the dog tags from around the scout's neck, and then debated moving the body. He hated the thought of leaving his soldier behind, but he didn't think he could carry the dead man down the mountain by himself. Perkin likewise felt uncomfortable about leaving his soldier in an awkward position, exposed to the wind and the rain and the carrion-eaters, but he couldn't bury the body and he wanted to minimize his time and footprints on the mountain. He'd make sure the body was recovered after the battle.

Perkin left his soldier with no words spoken to the dead man, no prayer for Garcia's salvation, and he resumed his movement across and up the mountain. He wanted to get to an area where the cliff dropped from the mountain peak and joined with the mountain's slope to the base of the mountain in the valley. Before the cloud cover arrived, Perkin had identified an area where a shallow approach to the cliff's base was broad enough to support at least a company of soldiers. He knew little of mountain climbing, but to his layman's eye the cliff looked as good there as anywhere else to launch an assault. He would make a recommendation that the Forcemen consider this spot for their ascent, but before he left he wanted to look for signs of mines or booby traps at the base of the cliff.

There were none, and no signs of Germans other than garbage thrown off the cliff from its summit. Perkin reached the base of the cliff and looked up. It was less strictly vertical than it had appeared from his earlier position, and the hard granite wall that reached up into the clouds was creviced and splintered as though it had been ripped apart by giant claws. Perkin's opinion of the site was affirmed when he saw sufficient outcroppings and cracks for hand and footholds to convince him that he could climb to the unseen summit without ropes.

Time again to leave. The cloud cover wouldn't remain for long, and the garbage indicated there were German sentries at the summit, whether they expected an assault or not. Perkin suddenly stiffened as he heard what sounded like boots on gravel. The fog was visually disorienting, but it also oddly distorted sounds. Perkin could occasionally hear distant gun fire—the loud booms echoing through the mountains as German and British gunners traded artillery fire in the X Corps sector—but unless it was directed at him, it was not of concern. The boots on the gravel were a concern, however, and Perkin flushed as he realized he had no easy egress from his position. It was likely a German patrol.

Although Perkin was uncertain of the orientation of the sounds, he assumed the patrol was moving towards the Allied lines under the cloud cover, and he decided to let the patrol pass him by, then move down the mountain through the cover of trees and traverse back to the encampment below the goat path. Perkin moved as quietly away from the cliff as he could, and crouched behind a boulder as the noise grew closer.

It was not a German patrol, but an Allied one. Two men, actually, both wearing American uniforms and carrying Thompson submachine guns. One was short and trim, the other heavyset and more muscular. The two men walked to virtually the same spot that Perkin had stood just moments before. The muscular soldier handed his weapon to the other and climbed the first ten feet of the cliff before working his way down. He nodded to the other soldier and gave him a thumbs-up.

The two soldiers turned to leave and Perkin recognized one of the men. He wasn't American, but a Canadian officer named Rose. Perkin had met the Canadian lieutenant months before in the Eighth Army headquarters near Nicastro in southernmost Italy. Perkin bent over, picked up a small pebble and tossed it at Rose, but missed and hit the other man on the cheek. Both men started and whipped around, their weapons ready.

With a large smile on his face, Perkin walked out from behind his rocks, his Thompson held above his head. He walked over to the two men, put his finger to his lips, then pointed upwards. He silently shook hands with Rose, whose pleased smile had replaced the shock on his face, and with a gesture of his head, Perkin indicated down the mountain. Rose nodded in agreement.

Perkin stopped in the cover of some trees before they reached Corporal Garcia's body and whispered, "The uniform's an improvement, but your arrowhead's pointed the wrong way. Good to see you again." Rose was wearing the uniform of the 1st Special Service Force, whose unit patch was an upright red spearhead with USA and Canada embroidered into the spear tip.

"Yanks a lot . . . it's a spearhead for Christ's sake. Oh. Goodness gracious, they made you a captain . . . in that case, you can call it whatever you want. Sir." Rose grinned. In the same low whisper, "This is Sergeant Whitely, of your army."

Sergeant Whitely nodded, then mumbled to Lieutenant Rose in an Appalachian accent, "Sir, we need to get off this here mountain. The fog sure ain't gonna last."

Without further discussion, the sergeant took the point. When they got to the dead scout, Perkin handed his Thompson to Rose and picked Garcia's stiffening body up and hefted him over his shoulders in a fireman's carry. He didn't want to carry the dead man, but he had help now if he needed it.

1549 Hours
1st Battalion HQ, Near Mignano, Italy

"Tell him, Bob! Tell him what you told me."

"Yes sir! Just a second!"

Lieutenant Rose was feeling a little overwhelmed. He had not had a great deal of exposure to Captain Berger, just a few hours in Nicastro and a few hours more on Mount La Difensa, but Perkin had struck the Canadian as a thoughtful, albeit slightly irreverent, professional. Now, the tall Texan was now highly animated and almost jumping up and down with excitement—all over a remark made in passing once they were off the mountainside and safely behind enemy lines.

After they had left Garcia's body at a 36th Division field hospital, Rose had explained that he and Whitely were on the mountain for the very same reason as Perkin. Even though the 36th Division Reconnaissance Troop was conducting the initial reconnaissance, the 1st Special Service Force wanted an early look at the terrain, and Rose had been tasked with the job. When Perkin asked how Rose came to be a Forceman, he was told that Rose had submitted his request to transfer from the Eighth Army staff while Montgomery was still in Sicily. Rose had recently been assigned to the Canadian-American force as the brigade's assistant intelligence officer.

The Canadian lieutenant was excited to be at the tactical level again because, as he explained to Perkin, "The Eighth Army is too goddamned slow for my taste." He had not been in combat personally since the 1st Canadian Division landed in Sicily. When he had learned that the Force was being transferred from the Aleutians to Europe, he requested reassignment and had been "stashed" at the Fifth Army headquarters in Caserta. It was an offhand remark about the German booby traps on the palace grounds that caught Perkin's attention and led to Rose being brought to the 1st Battalion headquarters.

"Tell him, Bob!" The "him" in question was the battalion intelligence officer, Jim Lockridge, who was irritated that he was pulled away from work by Perkin.

"Tell me what, Perkin? We're moving out soon, you know; I don't have much time. Who are you, Lieutenant?"

"Rose, sir. First Special Service Force. I'm Canadian."

"Nice to meet you. What do you boys need?"

Rose fidgeted, wondering if he had said too much to Perkin, then decided in for a penny, in for a pound. "Sir . . . ."

"Call me Jim."

"Thank you. I go by Bob. I was explaining to Perkin that I was down at Caserta waiting for the Force to arrive in-theater, and I was assigned to catalogue German booby traps found in Caserta and Naples. Some were being sent to England and America for exploitation—see how they work and all—and some were being retained as evidence should there be a criminal prosecution after the war."

Lockridge looked hard at the Canadian, and then over at Perkin who could barely contain himself. This was related to the bombing of the post office. He felt the hair stand up on his arm as his excitement mounted as well, and Lockridge unconsciously ran his finger around the neck of the sweater that had been given to him by Gianina that day. Perkin wasn't the only American who wanted revenge.

"Tell him about the squid, Bob!" Then, too impatient for Lieutenant Rose's story to unfold, Perkin blurted, "There's a squid officer who filed a report about the German intelligence officers who were involved."

"Really?" Lockridge asked. To Rose, he said, "What's a naval officer have to do with it?"

Rose couldn't fathom the reason for the Americans' excitement, but he would have had to be devoid of senses not to feel it. But Rose wasn't one easily given to sentimental flights, and he stared momentarily at the two Allied officers with his pale blue eyes before saying, "I don't know your interest in this, but I'd appreciate it if you keep this on the down-low. I'll track you sons-a-bitches down if my name comes out in print somewhere in a way that ties me to this. Understood?"

As they both nodded, Rose thought over his words carefully. He shouldn't have said anything in the first place, but Lockridge was an intelligence officer, and Perkin, Rose felt, had earned some trust by carrying down Garcia's body. Rose had been extremely impressed that Perkin had refused help in carrying down the scout, and that he been able to maintain his balance on the mountain with a dead man draped around his shoulders. The Canadian reflected that he would have likely sent a party to reclaim the body after the fighting had made it safe to do so.

"While I was at Caserta and working on this project, I met this naval intelligence officer—a lieutenant commander—who was killing time at Caserta. I think he'd been in Naples too long and needed some time away from the Neapolitans. Don't ask me his name; it's not important. He's been on the mainland since before either the Fifth or Eighth Army landed, and he was providing intelligence back to Allied headquarters on landing sites, beach conditions, enemy movements, and so on. This fellow had been in Naples and had given the Fifth Army a realistic appreciation of the damage to the port by both Allied bombing and German demolitions. His reports saved lives before landing, and time after we took Naples. Same thing."

Rose lit a cigarette, offered one to Perkin and Lockridge, who both declined, then said, "I had met him at the headquarters and struck up a conversation. Later we went to the officer's club for a drink. I think he'd already had a drop or two of whisky before I talked to him that evening, so take this for what it's worth. But he told me that his contact in Naples was the Camorra, the Neapolitan mob. Before coming to Europe, he'd made contact with the mob in New York, including in prison, and the mob had made his contacts possible in Naples." Rose gave a short laugh, then snorted. "I'll say this for you Yanks, you're in no short supply of patriotism. Even your criminals wear the stars and stripes on their sleeves. So, this fellow landed in southern Italy by submarine, made his way to Naples, met up with the Camorra, which provided him with a safe house, logistical support, and contract help. I guess he carried some gold with him, but most was done on the word of an Italian mob boss in prison in far northern New York—almost in frozen frog country."

"Excuse me?" asked Perkin.

"Quebec—"

"Wait just a second," interrupted Jim. "Are you telling us that this squid met with Lucky Luciano? Is that the *capo* you're talking about?"

Rose shrugged, "I dunno . . . I think so. Hell, I don't know who he is. Anyway, back to my story and then I need a lift back to my unit. So, the naval gentleman is a few sheets to the wind and tells me that he's heard of a German intelligence unit comprised of American or Anglo-German officers, and that they were involved in the civilian bombing campaign."

Perkin's face was lit up, and he had a fire burning in his eyes that Jim hadn't seen for months. The American intelligence officer whistled, then said, "Boy, I'd like to talk to him. Can you set it up?"

Rose shook his head, "Look fellas, I shouldn't have said anything in the first place. No telling what this was classified. But go to Caserta and ask your G-2 for the naval intelligence officer. There's only one. Now, Perkin, take me back to the Force headquarters."

Chapter Five

November 30, 1943
0600 Hours
Mount Rotondo, Italy

"Tell me again why the Rangers are doing this." Sam shook his head in disbelief.

"Because General Keyes ordered it.* That's why." Perkin was a little testy. He had not had much sleep in the past forty-eight hours, and the Ranger mission, which was just commencing, worried him deeply. It was a mission that should have been assigned to his troop and not assault forces.

"Thanks. Next time I need a lesson in army stupidity, I'll come to you for advice."

Perkin heard the asperity in Sam's voice, then offered a grin as he said, "Speakin' of stupid, Bear, how many Aggies does it take to screw in a light bulb?"

---

* Lieutenant General Geoffrey Keyes was the American II Corps commander.

Sam, who couldn't resist an Aggie joke, said, "Fifty. One to hold the light bulb, and forty-nine to turn the room."

Perkin laughed and said, "Naw. That's just Aggie propaganda. The truth is no one knows. It's never been done before."

Sam grinned and replied, "You know that there are four kinds of Aggies? Us that can count, and them that cain't." Sam's grin widened as he watched Perkin work through the joke, and then he started laughing—a deep belly laugh that had several nearby soldiers grinning even though they hadn't heard the joke.

Sam and Perkin, in company with Captain Spaulding and Captain Lockridge, were occupying a set of foxholes on Mount Rotondo, a small hill at the southeastern edge of the valley. The hill had changed hands several times between the Germans and the Americans, and the foxholes that they were occupying might have been dug by either army over the course of the last month. Given that they were near the northern crest of the hill and with a view of San Pietro, Sam guessed that they had been dug by soldiers of the 3rd Infantry Division. Whoever had dug them didn't dig deep enough for Sam's frame, and unless he curled up in a tight ball, the majority of his body remained exposed.

Sam's regiment, the 141st Infantry Regiment of the 36th Division, was assigned as the reserve force for the attacking Rangers, and his battalion, the 1st Battalion of the 141st Infantry Regiment, was the regimental reserve. That translated to Sam that it was unlikely that he would be in combat that day, and along with Lieutenant Colonel Wranosky and a few other officers from the battalion and regimental staffs, they had climbed Monte Rotondo to observe the Ranger operations.

It was Captain Waller Finley-Jones, the British liaison officer to the 141st, who answered Sam's question.

"General Keyes ordered the reconnaissance, but it comes from Clark himself. Clark is desirous that Jerry not know from where the strike is coming, so VI Corps to our right will conduct a series of limited-objective attacks in their sector, and X Corps to our left will do the same. This is one of a couple of limted-objective attacks that will occur in II Corps area. The idea is to force Jerry into spreading his forces around, so that when we ultimately move against him in the next week, he does not possess a preponderance of mass in any single area. Your corps commander suspects that San Pietro might be lightly held and accordingly obliged the Rangers to conduct a reconnaissance in force against it."

Perkin looked his Welsh friend and asked, "What if it's lightly defended? Do we take and hold it?"

"No. We are only conducting a limited attack, a demonstration if you prefer, and then we withdraw." The British officer was cool and reserved, which to his friends indicated a concern seldom witnessed. Finley-Jones was normally so cheerful and friendly that the consensus was that he would make a good Texan. Today, he seemed like a British officer.

Sam looked at the geometry of the valley in front of him, and his heart dropped. Two months before, he and Jim Lockridge had been on another hilltop and had witnessed the destruction of a battalion of Texans. The Texans had marched through a more open valley than the one he now saw and were caught in the open by German artillery gunners high in the surrounding mountains. This seemed even worse. Mount Lungo to the west, Mount Sammucro to the east, and Mount Rotondo to the south formed a small triangle with San Pietro near the northern apex. The Germans held two of the three sides of the triangle.

"Jim, does that remind you—" Sam didn't want to finish the remainder of his question.

"Yes. It does." The intelligence officer had been thinking the same thought. "But the Rangers won't cross the
open ground like last time. I'm sure they'll work their way
through to village along the base of Sammucro."

The officers nodded. That seemed the way to do it,
although the order itself made little sense to Sam. *Why
conduct a reconnaissance in force when you know where the
enemy is?*

0630 Hours
Caserta, Italy

The tall soldier rolled out of bed and grasped at his
uniform hanging in a small wardrobe. His head ached
from so much wine the night before, and he was a little
bewildered and not at all certain where he was. Then he
remembered. He was in Antoniette's apartment.

Captain Ronald Ebbins looked around in the dim
light of the room and he saw the tousled sheets on the
bed, the heavy quilt pulled over to his side, but she was not
there. Ebbins had only heard a few days before that Bernardi was in Caserta. He'd last seen her in Naples in early
October, when she had informed him that she intended
to spend a few months on the Isle of Capri in isolation
from the war. She'd then dropped out of contact, and he
assumed that he would never see her again. For Ebbins,
it was a major disappointment. He had never known a
woman like Antoniette Bernardi.

Words failed Ebbins when he thought of the young
Italian lady. He had never before felt love—it was difficult for a narcissist to love others—but Antoniette was
different. She was so empathetic. So understanding. So
kind and loving and appreciative that Ebbins had genuinely missed her. That she looked great on his arm was

just icing on the cake as far as Ebbins was concerned, and he reveled in the jealous glances that others cast his way. When he received her note a few days before stating that she longed for his company, and would it be possible to meet at her uncle's apartment in Caserta, he had managed to find an excuse to visit the Fifth Army's headquarters.

She loved him. Of that, he was certain. The joy in her face lit the whole room when he walked through the apartment's door. When he swept her up in his arms, he kissed the softest lips he'd ever known. Although she had already prepared a dinner for him, she insisted they visit the bedroom first. Their love-making was frantic—the exercise of passion by two lovers separated by duty and war and reunited by fortune—and she had cried in his arms over their lost time. Even the dinner afterwards was magnificent. Only the wine was questionable—a slight bitter taste—but she insisted that he finish his glass to see if it improved. It did not, and she opened another bottle— a fine Bordeaux that must have cost a small fortune—and they drank that bottle together in the bath. It was her idea, and such an idea, thought Ebbins.

They relaxed for over an hour in a steaming bath. What a luxury! Few houses in Italy that had seen the war still had running water, let alone hot water. Ebbins had not been warm or dry in the past month, and for the first time since he arrived in Italy, he felt truly safe. Maybe for the first time in his life, he felt loved. He had a beautiful, loving woman who was rich and, apparently, was a gourmet cook. Perhaps he would not return to south Texas after the war, but would remain with this incredible woman who loved him so. He was a banker—he could work anywhere.

Where is she? The thought brought Ebbins out of his reverie, and he recalled that she occasionally liked a morning walk. It was unlike her in so many respects that he thought once again that Antoniette Bernardi was still something of a mystery. He went into the bathroom and relieved himself—the first working toilet he had seen for weeks—and washed his face and combed his hair. Ebbins put on his overcoat and walked out to see if he could find the love of his life.

0648 Hours
Caserta, Italy

"I don't have much time, Douglas, he'll wake soon." Bernardi sat at a small café table across from Douglas Grossmann, who was wearing the uniform of a major assigned to the Fifth Army staff.

Out of habit, Grossmann looked around to see if anyone was within listening distance. The café was empty, and the café owner was in the back preparing *cornetti* for the morning. Grossmann had seated himself so he could keep an eye on the door to Bernardi's apartment building, and if Ebbins appeared, he could duck out a back door without being seen.

"May I first say how lovely you look?" Grossmann smirked inwardly.

"Don't flatter me, Douglas; it won't get you into my bed. Give me one of your cigarettes." After Grossmann had lit her cigarette, she inhaled deeply and said in her low, husky voice, "They don't intend to begin the offensive through the valley for another week. He doesn't know precisely, but he said that they are bedeviled—he didn't use that word but I don't remember exactly—they are bedeviled by the mountains. Their strategy is to clear the mountains first in the west, then come up through the valley. The silly bastard actually used my breasts to describe how they would do it."

Allowing himself a salacious grin, Grossmann said, "You'd best show me how he did it."

"Do you want to see my breasts or do you want to know how General Clark will sequence his offensive?"

Grossmann laughed, the friendliest laugh he'd had for weeks. "It's been awhile so I'd rather see breasts. General Clark can wait."

With something approaching a genuine smile herself, Bernardi leaned forward at the table and unbuttoned the top two buttons on her blouse. "If it furthers the cause, look closely. This one here is Camino. The British will take it first, starting this week. Then the Americans from Texas will take this one here next week." She reached over, took Grossmann's hand and gently kissed his index finger. She used it to draw a line up her cleavage. "Then, they go here. Everything else is incidental and is to confuse you. The landings at Gaeta . . . ," she said, moving his hand to cup her left breast, " . . . are not for real, um, they're decoys. No, that's not the word he used. A 'feint.' Yes, a feint. You know, they think they'll be in Rome by Christmas."

Bernardi took Grossmann's hand off her breast, seductively kissed his palm, leaned back in her chair, and smiled mischievously at Grossmann. His wide eyes amused her, and she knew that should she ever desire to destroy him, Grossmann was hers for the taking. No matter how he might truly feel about her.

"Douglas?"

"Yes, my dear?" His heart was slowing down again, and he had restored his normal calm.

"Will they be in Rome by Christmas?"

"No. Not this Christmas, my dear."

"How long do I need to stay with this fool? Until next Christmas? I can't bear to be with him much longer. He grunts and thrusts and squeals like a pig for thirty seconds, then rolls over and begs me to tell him what a man he is." She stamped her foot in feigned frustration and exclaimed, "I miss my priest so! You know I'll do anything for Il Duce and the Führer, but really . . . can't you make him go away?"

"You want me to kill him because he's boorish?"

"Yes. Would you please?"

Grossmann suppressed a shiver, thought briefly of the contribution this woman was making to the Fatherland and said, "OK then. When he has served his purpose, yes. I promise."

"Good. Then I will tell you one last thing, Douglas." Her eyes were alight. She had been saving the best for last. "From a gentleman friend at Fifth Army headquarters: The Allies are moving stocks of poison gas into the Italian theater."

"What? Are you certain?" This was a shock. Unlike the Great War, no chemical weapons had been used so far in the war. This could signal a major change of strategy by the Allies and might be the most important information he had gathered in his entire career.

"Yes, yes! Into the port of Bari. You know of Bari?" When Grossmann nodded, she continued, "An American freighter at berth 29 is full of mustard gas. My gentleman friend says not to tell anyone, *allora*, but in case the Krauts—I hate that word—in case the Krauts use it first, then the Allies can respond in kind. Do you think it important?"

"Oh, I think it will raise some eyebrows. How did you get that information?"

"Your 'fortified' wine and a hot bath seem to lead to self-importance and loquaciousness."

"I shall remember that. Thank you for the information, my dear." Grossmann could barely sit still. The information on the Fifth Army offensive was good, and would likely help validate intelligence analyses already made.

But the information on the mustard gas was earth-shattering—it might go to the Führer himself, if it was valid. *Would the high command risk a few bombers to find out?*

"You're welcome. Don't forget to kill Ebbins, and by the way, don't forget to kill Taft, either."

"I haven't forgotten. Ah, I see the good captain coming out now. I must go. *Ciao.*"

0655 Hours
Mount Rotondo, Italy

"Oh dear God." Perkin was watching the deployment of the 3rd Ranger Battalion with dread. They had emerged from the morning fog marching in attack formation from the eastern edge of the valley on their way to San Pietro. "Why don't they just have the flags and drums out?"

"It's like Gettysburg," said Captain Lockridge.

"Balaclava," said Captain Finley-Jones. "'*C'est magnifique, mais ce n'est pas la guerre.*'"

"There ain't nothin' magnificent about it, Waller. I saw how that movie ends." Sam's knowledge of the battle of Balaclava was limited to the 1936 movie *The Charge of the Light Brigade.* Perkin had been enamored with Olivia de Havilland and had dragged his cousin to see it several times before Sam refused to go any more.

"Yes. That was a terrible film was it not? It's a dangerous thing—fictionalizing history." Finley-Jones shook his head sadly.

"Well, it wouldn't pay to speculate on that," Sam said absently. He sighted his battalion commander, who was walking to the edge of the small hill's summit. "Colonel Wranosky! Ain't there something we can do?"

The battalion commander looked over at Sam when he heard his name. A shake of his head and the look at his grim face was answer enough for Sam. Wranosky turned his gaze back to the Rangers just as the first German artillery boomed out from the mountain behind San Pietro.

"I didn't think it was a bad movie. Ah, Christ. Here it goes," Perk said to Sam, and they both held their breath as they waited for the rounds to arrive. It was a miss. A plume of smoke appeared to the left of a company of Rangers, which, to a man, dove into the mud. Seconds later, the entire German artillery corps opened fire, the valley quickly filled with smoke, and the watchers from above lost sight of the Rangers below.

American counter-battery fire began almost immediately, and in the midst of thunderous explosions, Lieutenant Colonel Wranosky called the small cadre of officers over to him.

"We might as well head back to our units. This position's likely to be shelled before long, and we cain't do them boys any good anyway. Here's what's gonna happen: Those Rangers are gonna push their way up to the edge of San Pietro, then come back and report the enemy's there in force, and if we want it, we're gonna have to destroy the damn place first."

Wranosky pointed to a long, low, rectangular hill in the center of the valley. "See that there hill? That's Mount Lungo. They got artillery there, and heavy mortars and all sorts of nasty shit to control this valley. It makes sense, don't it? Nobody takes San Pietro until Lungo's fallen. That's our job tomorrow."

1000 hours
36th Division HQ, Mignano, Italy

The division had commandeered a barn for a temporary headquarters, and a coal-burning heater in a corner gave Perkin the first warmth he had felt for days. He had been ordered to report at 1000, presumably for a staff meeting, and he was surprised to find that there was no meeting scheduled.

An orderly spied him standing by the heater, approached him, and said, "Mornin' Cap'n Berger. The G-3 needs to talk to you, sir. He'll be here in a moment. Give me your canteen cup, and I'll fill it with somethin' hot for you."

As the soldier filled Perkin's cup from a large enamel pot, Perkin looked around the barn. Like almost every structure he had seen in Italy, it was made from stone and mortar. It even had a stone floor, which had been washed and scrubbed by the soldiers until it was army clean. But the smell of animals would forever permeate the structure, and the smell triggered a brief childhood memory of playing on his Uncle Raymond's ranch with Sam.

A Dutch door opened, and Lieutenant Colonel Fred Walker, Jr., strode into the barn. He nodded to Perkin then headed straight for the coffee. Perkin studied the division's G-3 and tried to divine his intent. He could not, but he noted, not for the first time, that the operations officer was very young to be a lieutenant colonel. Walker was, in fact, the same age as Perkin, and they had determined once that they had likely played together as two-year-olds at Camp Greene when their fathers served together during the Great War. At the time of Salerno, Walker had been a battalion commander, and his battalion had fought with great distinction in the British X Corps sector with the Rangers.

Lieutenant Colonel Walker filled his cup, topped off Perkin's without asking, and motioned with his head to two chairs set against a wall of the barn. He was considerably shorter than Perkin, with very alert and intense eyes set over a hawkish nose. His shoes and leggings were covered with mud, and Perkin surmised that he had been out to the battlefield to see conditions for himself.

Walker gestured at the orderly who handed him a folder, then walked away. Without opening the folder, Walker said, "Perkin, I've some bad news for you."

"The war's over?" Perkin looked innocently at the operations officer.

"What? Uh, no. The adjutant has informed me that Captain Leveque's convalescence in Oran is complete, and he is fit for duty. He just debarked from a troopship in Naples, and you will turn over your command to him upon his return. Sorry."

"Oh. Shit. Sorry, sir. I was hoping for some more time," Perkin was indeed sorry—the troop was just now engaging in combat, and he was finally comfortable in his role as the commander. But at a different, deeper, level, Perkin was in fact ambivalent about the news. Being a reconnaissance company commander had been interesting and educational, and he had enjoyed command immensely, but there was something limiting about the job that Perkin couldn't explain.

Walker studied the Texan for a moment and continued, "So, that leaves us with the question of what's next for you. The adjutant is noting in your records that you were a company commander in combat. So, professionally, that box is checked for you. We'll put you in line for a rifle company command if you want, but the division commander . . . well, my father asked me to discuss other options with you."

"I'm a rifleman at heart, sir. What other options are there?" Perkin was dreading the news. Walker might kind-heartedly intend to do him a professional favor by broadening his horizons in supply or communications or a myriad of other occupations that he ought to know if he were to stay in the army after the war.

"Well, here's how I see it, Perkin. You're not just a rifleman. You're a rifleman with a PhD. That puts you into a very select group of one as far as I know, and you're a rifleman who seems to do pretty well on his own or in small groups." Walker strummed his fingers on the folder and smiled at Perkin, "That's not to say that your performance as a platoon leader and troop commander wasn't good. Both were above par. But as we've had this discussion before, just a few days ago in fact: I recognize your desire to be out front, to conduct the patrols yourself, but that's not the job of the troop commander—at least not in a static maneuver environment like this. No, the troop commander's job is to manage the application of limited resources against the mountain of reconnaissance requirements that this division has. You've done that and done it well. You are both a good leader and a good manager, and you have demonstrated courage and ingenuity . . . but we get the sense that you're bored. Am I right?

At the slight nod of Perkin's head, Walker said kindly, "So, regardless of Captain Leveque's return, maybe a reconnaissance troop isn't the best place for you in any case. Perhaps there's a more active role for you in this war, where we can better use your talents. Before we talk about that, I want to share something with you."

Walker opened the folder, and flipped through several pages until he came to a handwritten letter. "My dad received a note from a British intelligence officer, a Lieutenant Colonel Russ, about you two months ago. Russ was impressed enough with your patrol down the peninsula to write this: 'My dearest general, I wish to convey my gratitude for the assistance of one of your officers, Lieutenant Perkin Berger of the 141st Infantry. The information that he provided Eighth Army greatly facilitated our advance to the Salerno area of operations, and his analyses of lines of communication, enemy dispositions, and indigenous personnel proved unerringly accurate. As a firm ally of the United States, I would respectfully like to proffer an unsolicited recommendation, namely, that Lieutenant Berger would make a fine intelligence officer. He has a keen sense of observation, demonstrated analytical skills, and an impressive memory. I'm an old foot soldier myself, so I can say without insult that his skills are wasted in the infantry. Hoping that I've not been too presumptuous, yours sincerely, Michael Russ.'"

Lieutenant Colonel Walker looked hard at Perkin, then said, "While I personally think that the infantry is where we want our best officers, there may be something to Russ's assessment of your qualifications. I think that the intelligence boys would love to get their hands on you. I don't know, with the right recommendations, maybe you could get a transfer to the OSS.* You've heard of them?"

Perkin nodded but said nothing.

"I don't know how you get in, but we could make inquiries through Fifth Army if you like." It was more of a question than a statement.

Perkin thought about the offer. Intelligence was a good fit for him. He knew it, and had thought about it many times. It was, however, a divergence from what he had planned. He'd hoped to have a rifle battalion of his own by 1945 or 1946, if the war went on long enough, and he didn't know if he could make it back to the infantry while the war was still on. There was one other thing that bothered him, and he said, "Sir, I really appreciate you and your father looking out for me, and the OSS appeals to me—I would like very much to be in intelligence—but I want to stay with the division. My cousin and my friends are here, and I can't leave them. I've been with the 36th for four years now, and I wanna be with the gun club at the war's end."

---

* The Office of Strategic Services. The forerunner to the modern CIA, the OSS was created by executive order in June 1942.

Walker nodded. It was a sincere answer, and he'd seen more than one Texan rebel past insubordination to the verge of mutiny upon receiving orders outside of the division. "Well, there's not much in this line in the division that we can give you. You're too senior for the intelligence platoon. There are intelligence billets on the staffs at battalion, regiment, and division levels, and at corps and army echelons as well. What would you think of those?"

Perkin took a deep breath, and he felt his face flush as he thought through what he intended to say to the colonel. *You pays your pennies, you takes your chances*, he thought. Perkin said, "May I defer an answer for a little while, sir, while I think about it? But, um, this opens the door to something I've been thinking about. Do you have a couple more minutes for me, sir?"

Chapter Six

December 1, 1943
2235 Hours
South of Mount Lungo, Italy

Sam Taft hated night operations. His vision, which was so spectacular in daylight, seemed worthless to him at nighttime. His eyes strained in the darkness as he looked first to his left and then to his right. He couldn't see a thing—although, he reflected gratefully, neither could the Germans. Flares rose into the sky from the mountains and elsewhere in the valley as sentries reacted to noises in the dark, but that helped Sam no more than the occasional burst of light coming from the artillery tubes on the mountains.

War is a process of action and counter-action, adaptation and counter-adaptation, and unsuccessful action had already been taken against Mount Lungo weeks before as the 3rd Division's advance in this sector ground to a halt. As the Wehrmacht never seemed content to rest on its laurels, it had spent the intervening days improving its position in the bottleneck of the Mignano Gap, even as German engineers and forced Italian labor built the main German defenses less than ten miles further up Victory Road.

When Sam had reviewed the aerial imagery of the Mignano Gap, he saw that Mount Lungo was a two-mile-long oval in the valley, a grave-shaped bump that rose more than five hundred feet from the valley floor. It effectively split the narrow valley in half as it ran to the northwest, the railway running to its west and Highway 6 to its east. The aerial reconnaissance photos that Jim Lockridge had shown to the platoon suggested that the hill complex was smooth and without fault, but as Sam had known, of course, it wasn't. Mount Lungo was covered with boulders and shrubs and rifts with little gullies, although most of its trees were long shattered by artillery fire. The rocks and shrubs would give the attacking force cover as they climbed up the hillside, but it would also give great cover to the defenders of Mount Lungo.

Mount Lungo wasn't Sam's immediate concern, although it might be later in the week. Able Company was taking the right flank of the battalion's assault on Mount Lungo, and as such wasn't expected to fight much on Lungo itself. Highway 6 had a small but sharp bend around a spur of Mount Rotondo that was considerably lower in elevation than Mount Rotondo proper. The spur, a small hill, lay right in the middle of the two small mountains—Rotondo and Lungo. It had been heavily wooded before the warring armies established it as a no-man's-land, but weeks of back and forth artillery duels had left it shredded and cratered and reduced its tree cover by half.

Able Company would take the little hill and the stretch of Highway 6 that skirted around it. The rest of the battalion would focus on the southern end of Mount Lungo. When the division controlled the mountains on either side, Clark's army would move up the stretch of Victory Road that Able Company had taken.

Sam's immediate objective was a small farmhouse set only a few yards off of Highway 6. It was the gatekeeper to the valley beyond, and he was to kill or capture the German soldiers that occupied the house. B.G.E. Beams's 2nd Platoon would assault a German pillbox on the slope of Mount Lungo to his left, while Frank McCarter's 3rd Platoon would be held in reserve. Once he had taken the farmhouse, he would move through the German defenses and take the little hill.

Two days before, Perkin's scouts had established a covert observation post on the little spur dropping off of Mount Rotondo. From their vantage, they were able to observe German movement along Victory Road and along the slopes of Mount Lungo. During the day, the reconnaissance team had observed enemy activity in and out of the farmhouse, its barn, the smokehouse, and an outhouse. The Germans had clearly mined the perimeter of the farmhouse, but had left a safe path to the highway on the farm's front, and a pathway through the back that was used by German patrols en route to observing the Americans. It was from the rear of the farm that Sam would make his approach.

As a man of the land himself, Sam felt a deep sympathy for the owners of the farm. The farmhouse was little more than a stone hut, and the rest of the buildings were equally shabby, but the hut likely contained the entirety of the owners' possessions. Sam's country nose detected the scent of pigs mixed with the scents of cattle and draft horses, but he suspected that the horses were now impressed into the German army and the cattle and pigs were likely long-since served on the German dinner table.

More sadly, the owners had probably been forced into slave labor on the Gustav line. If they lived to return, they would find their little home and all of their belongings destroyed.

As he waited for H-Hour, the time the attack was to begin, Sam thought of his own house and his ranch in south Texas. No foreign army would occupy his home, at least not while he and Margaret still breathed, and he wondered if the peasants who lived there had resisted.

The thought led to a shiver, and then Sam tried unsuccessfully to suppress another. In addition to an underlying apprehension, there was also a gentle misting rain leading to a trickle of ice-cold water down the back of Sam's neck. No matter how he fixed his collar or tilted his helmet, he seemed unable to stem the flow down his back, and he resigned himself to another night of misery. At least the excitement would take his mind off of it once the fighting started—*maybe for good*, he thought wryly. Sam couldn't remember the last time he'd been warm and dry, and despite constant foot inspections, his medics were dealing with the first cases of trench foot in the platoon. That would soon get worse, Sam knew.

"Sir?" A nearly imperceptible whisper reached Sam, and he was silently joined by one of Perkin's scouts—a trooper named McNamee from Luling, Texas.

Sam started, and whispered, "Here." Even though he felt his senses were as finely attuned as possible, he had not seen or heard the soldier approach. Sergeant Kenton, who was laying in the tree line next to Sam, also started. Embarrassed, Kenton leaned in to hear the scout's report.

The soldier knelt next to Sam. In a soft voice that barely made it to soldiers' ears, he said, "Four Krauts in the house, sir. The back of the house faces us, and there's an MG-42 set in the back left window yonder. I seen it set up yesterday in the daylight, and there's a feller in there smokin' now. He thinks he's set back far enough no one could see him, but he ain't. He's got a good arc of fire from there, sir, and can cover your whole approach. There were three on security walkin' the perimeter, and they's regular as clockwork, sir. I just kilt one on the left side of the house. Had no choice, sir, but he'll be missed 'fore long. There's one coverin' the front between the highway and the house, and he'll come around to the far right corner shortly to have a smoke with the feller patrolling the far side. Jes' up the road towards the hilltop, about four hundred meters to our left, there's a pillbox set in a little cut in the road, but they won't have a direct line of fire onto you 'til you cross the highway. We've passed that info to your company commander. There ain't nothin' to your right. These bubbas are the end of the line, sir. So, unless they reinforce straight down from the hilltop or along the highway, you should be golden for a little while."

Sam thought for a second and asked, "Anything else I need to know?"

"No sir." The trooper paused, then offered, "If you want, I'll get the guard when he comes back this way. No offense, sir, but I reckon I'm a little quieter than all y'all boys would be." McNamee was regarded as the top scout in the troop and therefore had low expectations of others.

"No. We'll do it. Good work, thank you." Sam's heart warmed to the trooper for the offer, and he was grateful for the information, but this was his platoon's mission.

"You're welcome, L.T. Cap'n Berger tolt me to take care of y'all. When this kicks off, I'm gonna redeploy my team on the far side of this here little hill and we'll start recon of the valley before us. I'll let Cap'n Spaulding know what we're gonna do, and I'll make sure we give your company a heads up when the counterattack is comin.'"

Sam wished the soldier good luck and told Sergeant Kenton to make the final preparation for the assault. Private Fratelli would take out the guard, and he wanted to be sure that Able's opening shots were through the window where the machine gun was. He thought about the scouts' mission and he shivered again. He shook off his musings about being behind enemy lines for days at a time and focused on the scout's last words. Every Allied advance in the war had been met by a German counterattack. They never passively gave ground, and they inevitably punched back hard. Sam didn't know whether forewarned was forearmed in the case of the Wehrmacht, but at least he thought Able Company had a good plan to secure the right flank of the battalion attack on Mount Lungo.

The assault on Mount Lungo was a limited-objective operation. They were to secure, at a minimum, the southern half of the hill mass and eliminate the German artillery that was pounding the Allied lines. That artillery was only a drop in the bucket, Sam knew, but it was the southernmost artillery that the Germans could bring to bear. More importantly, the battalion assault at Mount Lungo was to suggest to the Germans that the main assault was coming up the middle of the valley from the beginning, while the primary objective was to secure the Camino hill mass and unlock the southern gate. Finally, as Bill Spaulding had pointed out the day before, controlling at least a mile of the hill mass eliminated a small salient into the II Corps line and would allow the Allies to protect the flanks of the eventual force that would move against the village of San Pietro.

The night before the assault on Mount Lungo, Spaulding had brought all of his officers together, and they had been joined by Perkin. After going through a rundown of platoon responsibilities, communications, and a myriad of other concerns, Spaulding had led the officers to a campfire in the lee of a small hill. Against the backdrop of counter-battery dueling between German and Texan artillery, Spaulding cleared his throat and said with a smile, "Well, boys. Here we are again. We haven't been in combat for two months, but tomorrow's our time. Although he's here with us now, I'm sorry that we've lost Perkin to division. I was looking forward to him climbin' on another tank, or maybe a *nebelwerfer* this time with the Able Company hammer, but so be it. Instead, he's toolin' about behind enemy lines lookin' for Jerry when any damn fool could tell him that the Krauts are just up the road and waitin' for us. Anyway, Able Company's been joined by two fine new officers, Robert 'Two-Bit' Hoar and B.G.E. Beams, and thank God, they're both Texans."

Spaulding faced the young officers and looked them over as he had many times since they joined the company. Two-Bit Hoar was fresh from Trinity University in Waxahachie. The religious Hoar was deeply embarrassed by his nickname, but had struck up an incongruous friendship with the profane B.G.E. Beams, who had been a Houston policeman before the war. Together with Frank McCarter, the three second lieutenants were as close as triplets.

"I know this is your first time in action, but you boys are going to do just fine tomorrow. Remember to lead by example. Be aggressive: savage in battle, compassionate in victory. No, check that. Screw compassion. Just be savage in battle." Spaulding looked around and found Sam. "Damn it, Sam, these speeches are gettin' too long. Y'all put your cups out for a Texas roister."

The officers thrust their cups into a small circle while Sam pulled out a bottle of T.W. Samuel's bourbon from his pack and poured a healthy Texas-sized shot into each cup. As he had done on the eve of the Battle of Salerno, Bill served as the master of ceremonies.

Spaulding pulled a wad of tobacco from his cheek and threw it on the ground. He cleared his throat and said, "You new boys ain't done this before, so follow our lead."

The cups were put into a tight circle, clinking against each other, with each wrist held outward at a right angle. Spaulding offered the first toast in the ritual in a deep voice: "To God."

The soldiers repeated the toast, but instead of taking a drink they lifted their cups to their ears and listened to the silent bourbon for a moment.

The hands were placed back in the center of the circle, still held at that odd angle, and Spaulding gave the second toast: "To country." The young officers repeated the toast and the movement of the drink to their ears and back.

"To Texas!" Once again, the officers repeated the toast and cups moved back and forth in the silence of the circle.

The final toast of the roister was always unique, usually improvised, but Spaulding had one in mind—at the request of Perkin. Spaulding looked each of his officers in the eyes and said, "I want to remind you that drinking to a roister is legally and morally binding, so no goin' back. OK, when we get in there tomorrow, I want you to wear those sons-a-bitches out. Make them pay for taking us away from home, for killing our friends and countrymen, for bein' animals to the people of this poor country. We're gonna make them suffer for what they've done. Gentlemen, to revenge! Revenge for our boys lost at Paestum, revenge for our Rangers, and revenge for Gianina and those boys in Naples."

"To revenge!" Everyone seconded the toast and instead of lifting the cup to their ears, they clinked their cups together and finished the toast with a loud, rolling "Roiiiiissssster!" and each man slammed back his shot. When his eyes were done watering, B.G.E. Beams had exclaimed, "By God, that's a great toast! B.G.E. stands for 'Bourbon Guzzler Extraordinaire!' Let's do another one!"

Wanting clear heads for the next day, Bill Spaulding had vetoed a second round, although the thought appealed to him, and Sam was carefully husbanding his bourbon in any case. As the meeting broke up, Sam stayed to talk to Bill and Perkin, and Sam heard Hoar say to Beams as they walked away, "When he says wear them out, is he talking about spanking?"

When the second lieutenants had cleared the area, Sam, Bill, and Perkin had another quiet round of drinks. It was then that Perkin told his comrades of his conversation with Lieutenant Colonel Walker. Sam and Bill's consensus was that Perkin would be an excellent intelligence officer, and it had been Captain Spaulding's recommendation that Perkin see if he could get a battalion S-2 position.

"Unlike the regiment or division staffs," Spaulding said, "you're the intel bubba in charge as a captain. Now, whether it's a good fit for you or not is gonna depend a lot on your battalion commander and the executive officer. At least in this battalion, Jim has a lot of personal freedom in what he does, and he has more of an impact on this battalion's operations than any other officer that I know of. Wranosky trusts him completely, and I don't know of many captains with as much authority as Jim."

Sam agreed but noted, "Here's the flip side to that coin: You get the wrong pair, and it could be just as limiting as any other job in the army. I ain't sayin' it's a crap shoot, Perk, but it might be. Now, are you sure that you want to step away from the infantry? Going to a battalion job ain't exactly a rear echelon dream billet, but it may not carry the same respect with a post-war selection board as a rifle company command."

Perkin had replied, "Yeah, I've given that some thought, and I honestly can't claim to know whether the regular army's gonna be looking for guard officers when this is all over. If the Depression's not truly over and we go down to an army of a hundred thousand again, there won't be a job for me in uniform. If, as I suspect, we're somewheres 'tween here and there, maybe there will be. I don't know, but I'm thinkin' maybe I'll take my chances in the intelligence line. Speakin' of which, I'm gonna be out of touch for a few days."

To Sam and Bill's great consternation, Perkin then explained where he was heading. He then shook their hands and wished them well in their upcoming battle. As he handed the stunned Sam a deadman's letter addressed to his grandfather, he simply said, "So long," and departed the little encampment.

When Perkin had left and Captain Spaulding had bedded down, Sam stayed up late thinking, and he decided that Perkin would be the death of him. He was so like how Old Perkin had described Perk's father—an idealistic risk-taker—but Perkin seemed to have been blessed with either very good luck or a very diligent guardian angel. Sam said a long prayer for his cousin, then walked back to his pack and pulled out a coarse green woolen blanket. He wouldn't go to sleep for awhile anyways, and he wanted to enjoy the rare campfire.

It was later on, as that campfire was dying down and the artillery fire had dropped off, that Sam heard Hoar and Beams singing a cowboy's lament in fine tenor voices, and the song moved him to tears.

I met an old man at a roadside cantina
Somewhere in New Mexico.
He said, Sit down, son, and I'll tell you a story
About this one-horse rodeo.

Well, a long time ago I was born down in Texas,
But here's where I'll make my last stand.

My pa was a farmer, but I was cut different.
I never could work the hard land.

Oh but I was a hero, and I was a cowboy,
Out on the range I would ride like the wind.
I pray that some day, the good Lord will take me
And let me go back there again
To ride on the range with my friends.

I fell in love with a young senorita
When I was just barely a man.
She stole my heart, but I still had to leave her
And go chase that old wild wind.

Oh but I was a hero, and I was a cowboy,
Out on the range I would ride like the wind.
I pray that some day, the good Lord, He will take me,
And let me go back there again
To ride on the range with my friends.

I said I don't know how I made it this far.
My good friends have all passed away.
So I took all I had and I bought this cantina,
And here's where I'll spend my last days.

Oh but I was a hero, and I was a cowboy,
Out on the range I would ride like the wind,
But I know that some day, the good Lord, He will take me,
And let me go back there again
To ride on the range with my friends.
Yippee ki-yi-yay, git along little dogies!

It was a fine song, Sam had reflected, and it made him
terribly homesick—even after the mood was broken when

a passing soldier called out in the dark, "Hey! Did that senorita have big tits?"

Beams' answer led to scattered laughter among the company soldiers that were still awake: "You bet, partner! B.G.E. stands for Big Goddamned Enchiladas!"

As the laughter died away, and the encampment became as quiet as it could be with thousands of soldiers nearby, Sam tried to remember the words to the song. Sam may have been a cowboy, but he had no notions of being a hero—he wasn't Perkin. Sam had been commended for his role in the defense of a little bridge at Mount San Chirico, but to Sam, the medals held little value. Fighting was a ticket home, and the war meant little more to Sam than that. Finish this battle and move on to the next one, then the one after that, until there were no more battles to fight. Then he could go home to Texas and Margaret. *One day*, Sam thought, *maybe the good Lord will take me, and let me go back there again.*

Sam looked at his watch—a Rolex Viceroy and a present from Margaret. At the time, Sam had been upset at the extravagant gift. Although money had never been an issue for Sam, he thought it a waste when he already had an Army A-11. But unlike his army watch, the Rolex kept perfect time, and more importantly, it was a constant reminder of Margaret. In time, he came to value the watch greatly. In civilian life, Sam had seldom even carried a watch as he had a highly developed internal clock and could generally tell the time within two or three minutes without looking at a timepiece. Now his internal clock was telling him it was about time, and he struggled to find enough light from a distant flare to see his watch.

Suddenly, a white flash and then a deep booming behind Sam indicated the Allied artillery had opened up, and Sam knew that the northern half of Mount Lungo would explode in seconds.

Sam said to Kenton, "Get ready," and he raised a small Very pistol over his head and pulled the trigger. A flash of light, a trail of smoke, and a brilliant red light flared above their heads. Sam had given the signal for the battalion attack to commence.

"Fire!" Sam bellowed at the top of his lungs. A split second later, his soldiers did just that. The first German casualties were the German sentry and his smoking companion, who were killed at a distance of twenty yards by Private Fratelli and his BAR.* There was no more need for silence now.

A Browning .30 caliber machine gun from the company's weapons platoon opened fire immediately upon Sam's order, and Sam watched, fascinated, as the tracer rounds worked quickly into the window that the scout had indicated. As the gunner continued to pour round after round into the shattered window, the riflemen of the platoon opened fire at every other window and door of the house. Two designated riflemen ran forward along what Sam hoped was the safe route through the minefield towards the house. Sam watched in the surreal light of the red flare as they dropped to the earth and covered their heads. The artillery rounds had ripped directly overhead. While the shells had not been close to Sam's position, the noise, light, and the movement of the ground had spooked the two soldiers.

"Get up, goddammit!" Sergeant Kenton was already on his feet. He ran to the edge of the minefield, where he shouted again, "Get going! Move!"

One soldier leapt to his feet, took one step, and decided he wasn't going alone. He turned back and pulled

---

* Browning Automatic Rifle. Each rifle squad generally had one BAR—a 30.06 caliber automatic rifle configured with a 20-round box magazine and frequently used as a light machine gun.

the other soldier up by the shoulder of his coat. Both soldiers sprinted to the wall of the farmhouse, one soldier slamming hard into the stone. Sam watched as each of his men tossed a grenade through the farmhouse's two windows, and he held his breath as they ducked below the sill. Two sharp blasts came from the grenades, and the soldiers moved quickly to the back door of the house. One soldier kicked it open and the second soldier tossed in another grenade. Again, they took shelter as the grenade's explosion threw shrapnel and debris out of the opening.

As they had planned, Sergeant Kenton and Private Kulis sprinted down the trail and into the house. Sam heard one shot from within the hut. After a few more seconds, Sergeant Kenton called out, "All clear!"

As Sam ran up to the house, he was gratified to see several soldiers immediately start taping off the area of the suspected minefield while several other soldiers moved quickly to establish a perimeter around the house.

One of the grenades had shattered and ignited a kerosene lantern, used for light as the house had no electricity, and the fire was spreading across the floor and up a tarp the Germans had been using as a blackout curtain.

Sam had no time to lose; he spun around and headed outside. Before he left, he took in the utter devastation inside the little building. As the scout had told him only a few minutes before, there were exactly four German soldiers in the house. All dead. A field radio was crackling on a table, and the soldiers' meager belongings, packs, and supplies were shredded and smoldering in the kitchen. Sam stopped momentarily and looked at the soldiers' packs, which had oddly remained neatly stacked in a corner. No sooner had the thought crossed Sam's mind that a squared-away sergeant must have been in charge in the farmhouse, that he saw an *unterfeldwebel* lying face down in the doorway of the far room. His smoking tunic was nearly torn from his body, and a bullet hole sat neatly in the back of his head. The sergeant was stretched out as if he had been crawling to the machine gun in the window. As Sam walked outside, he saw a shattered bisque doll on the floor and thought of the people who lived in the charnel house. He said, "Kenton, see if we can put the fire out. I don't want to give the Kraut gunners a bright reference point. Don't risk anyone for it, though, and then get out."

Sergeant Kenton looked doubtful for a second, shrugged inwardly, and said to two soldiers standing in the doorway, "See if there's a pump or a cistern. Start bringing buckets in. You two," he said to Kulis and another watching soldier, "bring over the mattress off the bed. Soak it in water and try to smother the flames." Kenton reached up and yanked the tarp off the window frame and carefully threw the burning tarp out of the shattered window and onto the sodden ground. The house was mostly stone, so it wouldn't burn down—although whether it would survive the night was an open question.

As Sam moved off to help prepare the defenses, he heard a loud explosion to his left. It must have been a satchel charge thrown into the pillbox up the road. After the echoes had died, Sam heard a distant wolf howl from up the road, and the war cry, "B.G.E. stands for Bunker Got Exploded! Goddamn, this is fun!"

Sam shook his head. This wasn't his notion of a good time. He motioned for his radio operator, a soldier from Houston named Mark Christian. "Get Cap'n Spaulding. Let him know we've taken the house, no casualties, and we're preparing to move to our next objective." Sam's first skirmish in the valley of death had taken five minutes and was a victory with no casualties.

2240 Hours
Mount Cesima, Italy

When the artillery began their hot work, Perkin was sitting on the turret of a brand new M8 armored car, on a road near the crest of Mount Cesima. He was leaving the American lines shortly, but he wanted to watch the beginning of Sam's battle and see if he could divine any sort of outcome. That he might be able to do so was unlikely in the extreme, and he intellectually prepared himself that it would look terrible from his vantage regardless of how the battle progressed, but he felt that he owed it to the company and the battalion to be their witness.

Although both sides were using blackout procedures, there was enough light over the battlefield from reflected fires for Perkin to be able to make out the dim shape of Mount Lungo. The artillery tubes were behind Perkin on Mount Cesima and down in the valley, and he resisted the temptation to turn and look for the flashes from the 105 and 155 millimeter howitzers that were supporting the battalion assault. Instead, he wanted to watch for the round's impact, and he wasn't disappointed. The rounds landed nearly simultaneously and were dead on target on the northern half of the hill mass.

Mount Lungo looked as though a torch had been suddenly set to it. Dozens of flashes indicated the artillery strikes—most were brief bursts of light that seemed out of synch with the explosions that Perkin heard, but several others led to secondary explosions. At least four distant vehicles were furiously burning within seconds of the barrage beginning, and a high column of flame indicated to Perkin that the gunners had found a small fuel depot.

Through the deep booming of the howitzers and the sharper cracks of exploding rounds, Perkin could hear a machine gun—an American machine gun—chattering away down in the valley. He hoped that it was being put to good use, and not for the first time since turning over his command that morning to Captain Leveque, he questioned his sanity in volunteering for this mission. He desperately wanted to be with Sam and the company.

"Cap'n Berger? Cap'n?"

Perkin realized the sergeant commanding the M8 had been trying to get his attention for some time.

"It's time?"

"Yes sir."

It was a bumpy ten-minute ride along a mountaintop road to yet another ridge. This one was, in fact, a saddle ridge that connected the mountains Sammucro and Cesima. Perkin had been there only once before, when the 3rd Infantry Division had held the sector. In peacetime, the ridge would have held the most splendid of vistas—a grand view of Mount Sammucro's majestic slope to San Pietro and the valley floor below. But on this day, the ridge was covered with concertina wire, stone and wood embattlements, and machine guns facing the unseen threat through the night.

A small collection of men greeted Perkin when he dismounted from the M8. Some were familiar faces, such as the intelligence officer from the 143rd Regiment, which controlled this sector. He was a portly major with an untrimmed mustache and an irreverent view of the war and its sensibilities.

"Well, howdy, Perkin. I understand you're leading a one man assault on Saint Pedro. Is that right?" The officer, whose name was Harlan MacMahon, had a wide grin that was heard by Perkin, if not clearly seen.

"What? Well, don't that beat all? I thought the general sent me here to arrange tomorrow's tee times." Perkin offered the major his hand, which was firmly grasped.

The intelligence officer took Perkin to the ridge, and in the fading light of a distant flare, he pointed off into the valley and said, "Listen carefully because I'm gonna tell you something important about this valley. And you can quote me on this." The major paused for dramatic effect and said, "I could hit a golf ball a thousand yards from up here."

"Straight down don't count, Harlan."

"The hell it don't, Perk. And you best not call me by my first name, or people will think we're friends or something."

"I don't have any choice. I can't bring myself to pronounce your name like you do." The major's ancestors had come to Texas from Ireland with a two century-long layover in France, and he pronounced his name Mac-ma-hone.

The major laughed again, then pulled Perkin over to a young captain—one of the unfamiliar faces.

"Perkin, this is Henry Waskow. He's in command of B Company, and he'll explain to you about how we're thinkin' of getting you over to St. Petersburg or whatever it's called. Henry, this here's my friend, Perkin Berger. We used to play golf together in Austin, and I beat him every time."

"He cheated every time, Henry, so none of those count. Nice to meet you. What are your thoughts on this?" Perkin was getting anxious to leave. The longer he stayed and chatted with an old friend, the harder it was going to be to begin his mission.

Misunderstanding the question, the young captain said, "Well, I don't play golf, but I've had enough exposure to the major to think you might be onto something there." But Captain Waskow was anxious to move on as well, so his foray into the familiar conversation was brief. He looked at Perkin and said, "I understand that you're gonna scout out San Pietro, and that you want our help in gettin' down off of this ridge. Is that right?"

"Yeah, that's about it."

"OK. We have two ways that we can get you into the valley. Over to our left . . ." The officer faced the valley from the saddle ridge and indicated to the south, ". . . there's a path that we use that will get you into the trees quickly. It's a shepherd's path, and there are several cutbacks that herders have left into the rock. Eventually, what you'll want is a lateral trail that follows about three hundred yards beneath us around to the olive groves on Mount Sammucro. The trail is exposed but still the best way across on the mountainside. To our right, we've got another ingress/egress point. It's closer to Mount Sammucro, but pretty darn steep gettin' down to that lateral trail. You'd have to rappel down for part of it, and you don't want to leave here in the daytime. I can have a couple of boys help you with the ropes and all, but unless you're a mountain climber, I'd recommend the longer, safer route."

Major MacMahon jumped in. "You can't get there all the way tonight. So you're gonna have to find a spot in the rocks and stay immobile in the day unless there's heavy fog, and even then, I'd be damned cautious about moving around here. That lateral trail will take you above the village, and then it's like what we talked about earlier, Perk. As I showed you on the aerial photos, your best bet is to move beyond Pietro and come in above the town and down the ravines on the backside of the village. In effect, you'll hook around the town, and that gives you the best chance of getting past their defenses, which are all pointin' this way. Then you can scout out those defenses from other angles. And if there ain't any Germans there like some folks think, then you can stroll in and have an espresso and a cornetti and put it on the general's tab."

Chapter Seven

December 2, 1943
0015 Hours
Caserta, Italy

"You are so good at what you do, and so brave. I don't understand how you men face the war every day like you do." Antoniette Bernardi rolled over, letting the sheet slip down her side, and she whispered the words in the tall captain's ears.

"We all have our burden to bear in this war, and I won't give up until we've won." Captain Ronald Ebbins was feeling noble and somehow connected to bravery. His division was back in battle, and while it was truly life-or-death for those fighting, Ebbins had not fired his carbine since landing in Italy some months before. The irony and hypocrisy of his statement to Bernardi was lost on him, however, and he continued to bask in her praise.

Ebbins had volunteered to be a courier back to Fifth Army headquarters again, and Ebbins felt no remorse about leaving his comrades behind while he lay in bed with a beautiful girl. A nice dinner at Caserta's most exclusive restaurant had cost him a pretty penny, but Bernardi was worth it all. She had been delightful company, telling Ebbins about Rome and Florence, and they had danced to the music of a wonderful jazz quartet until curfew was upon them. The wonderful evening had been capped off at Bernardi's apartment where they shared a bottle of wine—although if Ebbins had been more alert, he might have noticed that she drank very little of the bottle herself.

"You are soon going into battle yourself, my love?" Bernardi asked, her eyes seeming to glow with pride for her warrior.

"As soon as I get back. I didn't want to come here— other than to see you, of course. My regiment obviously needs me. I pretty much run all of its operations . . . but I had to come down to meet with General Clark." Ebbin's lie was told as much by habit as design, and he knew that Bernardi knew he was a mere captain. She seemed to know a lot about the American military, but she never seemed to challenge him on the small white lies. It didn't matter what he said—she was obviously in love with him.

"Yes, I know. You told me. Maybe the fight will be over when you get back? I don't want you to get hurt." Sympathy for the warrior.

"No." True remorse. "We only have one battalion in the fight now, and they're really just a diversion on that little island of a hill in the middle of the valley while we get ready for next week."

"Isn't that an uneven fight? One, what did you call it? Battalion . . . against the German Army?"

"Well, yeah, that would be uneven, but war don't work like that, sweetheart." He said condescendingly. "This battalion's pretty tough, well commanded. They'll do fine, but I gotta get back tomorrow morning and make sure they're OK."

"You're so brave. I'm so proud of you."

She leaned over and kissed Ebbins, an act that she found repulsive but nevertheless made her appear convincingly passionate. But rather than respond, Ebbins mused absently, "But that's Taft's battalion. Maybe he'll get his this time."

"Oh, I don't worry about him any more. Not with you around. Nor his cousin either. Would you like some more wine?" Bernardi had run afoul of Sam Taft in the village of Ogliastro Cilento after the division had landed at Salerno, and she had been exhorting Major Grossman to kill the lieutenant. Taft, for his part, was completely unaware of her lingering animus. So greatly did she desire to hurt Sam that she had told Grossmann that he should kill Perkin Berger if the opportunity presented itself.

"Oh, I didn't know you had met ol' Pickin' Boogers." Ebbins' smile disappeared and at the thought of Perkin, his irritation began to mount.

"I haven't. He was just pointed out to me in the village, as the rude man's cousin." Bernardi smoothly answered.

"Well, he's likely one problem we'll probably never have to deal with again. I shouldn't tell you this, but who the hell would you tell anyway? Pickin' Boogers volunteered for a reconnaissance mission to scout out that village. San whatever. I doubt he'll make it back alive. What a showboat."

Antoniette Bernardi agreed that it sounded like an ostentatious act, somehow selfish, and she poured another glass of wine for Ebbins. She wanted him to fall asleep quickly so she could pass the information to Major Grossmann that night. While some might bide their time, when it came to revenge Bernardi felt that it was best to seize the day.

0555 Hours
Mount Rotondo Spur, Italy

The first counterattacks had been by the book. The artillery came first. Concentrated fire from unseen artillery tubes thousands of yards away, unerringly accurate. *And why not?* Sam thought. *The Germans had weeks to prepare for this moment.*

A barrage was laid down between the Germans' outpost positions further into the valley and the advanced defensive positions that the 1st Battalion was in the process of overrunning. Then the barrage had been worked forward towards the American lines. The Germans had decided that the advanced positions were lost, and they intended to make the Americans pay a price for taking them.

Although the barrage came in the dead of night, it had no longer seemed like nightfall in the valley of death— from the sharp white lights of the high explosive rounds and the fires on Mount Lungo reflecting light onto the battlefield, the night had become a grey twilight of flashes and shadows. Sam and his platoon had been working slowly across the mined highway and its ditches towards the spur when the first rounds landed six hundred yards in front of them, on the other side of the little hill. The next salvo was four hundred yards on its far slope, then two hundred yards and onto the crest, then a hundred yards away on its near slope. To Sam's left, he could see a similar advance of fires along the path of Victory Road as it curved around the spur and turned into the valley.

When the barrage started, all Sam could see at first was the flash of light into the sky as the first rounds fell on the far side of the hill, but the noise and thunder of the explosions told him the rounds were striking uncomfortably close. But as the barrage rolled forward and struck onto the crest, the impending doom was evident—to stay meant certain destruction from the artillery. To run meant possible death and dismemberment from mines. It was the most terrifying choice Sam could imagine.

For an infinitesimally small moment, Sam stood in place, then he decided. "Move! To the hillside! Go!"

Sam's soldiers had been deployed in a skirmish line as they approached Highway 6. One squad was to head to the left and form the link to the 2nd Platoon, and the other two squads were to occupy the hill. They had been moving slowly across a very narrow distance, as the road and its ditches were surely mined.

Out of the corner of his eye, Sam saw Sergeant Kenton grabbing soldiers and pushing them forward to the hill. At a sprint, the two squads with Sam crossed the highway. They had made it across the highway and almost to the hill when a soldier on the platoon's left had stepped on a mine. A small squib charge detonated and the main charge and hundreds of steel balls were ejected from the mine's casing. A second later, the main charge detonated and a circle of death and destruction spread out instantly from the mine. Six soldiers were brought to the ground, and screams for medics and help pierced through the ringing in Sam's ears.

Then the artillery arrived. The rounds began to drop screaming onto the position on the other side of the road. Had they frozen there, dropped to the ground, his platoon might have been wiped out in a heartbeat. As it was, white-hot shrapnel whizzed through the night air. Most passed over Sam's soldiers, but some found targets, and more soldiers fell.

Sam and his sergeants urged the soldiers forward towards the relative safety of the hill. Some men had dropped to the ground and covered up. Others sprinted forward through the mined ditches to the slope of the hill. Yet others stood in place, terrified of moving in the minefield, terrified of the other nameless horrors awaiting them in the darkness.

The noise and the violence of the artillery added to the confusion of the moment, and calls and screams for help disoriented Sam and the other soldiers. But he felt that they had to keep moving—to stay put was death. Fortunately, the artillery was only close to them for an excruciatingly terrifying moment as the small rolling barrage moved like a wave across the battlefield. By the time the German gunners had adjusted their fire again and were beginning to target the small farmhouse, Sam had most of the platoon working its way up the small hill.

It was a good decision. After the artillery followed the infantry. Small-scale thrusts designed to determine the disposition of the attacking force—how far they had advanced, what units were engaged—but not to retake the lost ground. The main counterattack would come later.

As the dawn broke tentatively over the peak of Mount La Difensa, Sam was wondering when that main counterattack would come, and where the *schwerpunkt*—the focal point—of the attack might be.

Sam and his platoon were the dead end of the right flank of the battalion's main line of resistance. As the attack was a limited-objective attack, and those objectives had been met, they were going no further. Sam and his soldiers would dig into the mud and the rock of the little hill and wait for the Germans to come to them. If the Germans did not come, all the better, but they would. But where? Straight up Highway 6 in the center of the line, or one of the flanks?

The Germans would let him know in due course, but in the meanwhile, Sam and his soldiers were busy. Fighting positions were frantically being dug on both the far slope of the hill and on the American side. If they had to give ground, they would have prepared positions to fall back on.

Captain Spaulding had allocated two machine guns—M1919 .30 caliber Brownings—for Sam's sector, and he had just finished siting those. He was pleased with his defenses on the little hill—overlapping machine guns covered the approaches to the hill from the valley, riflemen were dug in across the hill, and mortarmen sited behind them. Even a small minefield had been laid on the slope of Mount Rotondo to protect his flanks.

Meanwhile soldiers from Frank McCarter's platoon were busy assisting engineers with removing German mines along the highway and around the remains of the farmhouse—it had been destroyed by the night's artillery—and on the spur hill as well. Even more engineers were busy digging pits on the spur and along Highway 6, and anti-tank guns were being moved in as quickly as possible. The next attack might not be a small thrust but a full-scale counterattack formed around an armored battle group.

"Sam!" Sam turned, and saw Captain Spaulding walking up the hill from behind, his radioman in trail.

"Hey, Bill! How y'all?"

"Fair to middlin'. How y'all doin'?"

"Can't complain—no one listens anymore."

The two officers met and shook hands. Although they had each known that the other had survived the evening's events, the pleasure of seeing each other alive and intact was evident.

"Where do we stand, Bear?"

"We're about done with the first round, and we'll keep diggin' in. I reckon our biggest threat is infiltration along the base of Rotondo, but the engineers got us some mines in there, and I've posted a sniper along that way. Maybe armor'll come check us out too from down in the valley."

Captain Spaulding nodded, then asked, "Casualties?"

"Yes sir. Two dead, eight more wounded. The dead were Thorn and McKean—the two boys who led the assault on the house. One of 'em tripped a mine going across the highway and it got both of 'em. Four of the wounded were evacuated; the rest are OK. Here's the list." Sam handed him a piece of paper torn from a small green notebook. "We were demining the road and the ditches when the barrage found us, and I thought we'd be better off riskin' mines than artillery in the open, so I ran 'em across. I don't know what to say other than I'm awful sorry about that, Bill."

"Sam, I did the same thing. Those are the breaks." Spaulding shook his head sadly. He had known Thorn and McKean for two years.

Captain Spaulding talked about defensive positions for several more minutes, and he and Sam coordinated their responses as best as possible to the anticipated counterattack. After spitting a long stream of tobacco juice onto a rock, Spaulding looked at his watch and said, "I need to be heading back. I want to stay close to Beams for a while and watch him. He's got them boys wound up, and if as much as a rabbit hops across the highway, Beams's platoon is gonna blow off ol' Peter Cottontail's balls faster than Kulis can find a whore."

It was an odd thing. Sam felt terrible about the loss of his soldiers, and he appreciated the magnitude of the moment, yet he wasn't going to let the losses become oppressive. He had lost soldiers at Salerno, and knew he would lose many more before the war ended. So Sam jumped at the chance for lightness and smiled at Captain Spaulding's comment about Lieutenant Beams and his soldiers. Beams was a high-energy officer, and his enthusiasm trickled down to the troops. Then Sam laughed and said, "Bunny Gets Emasculated?" Sam wasn't particularly good with word games so he laughed even harder at his own wit.

On a day when humor was at a premium, Sam's laughter was infectious and Spaulding joined in. "More like Beams Gets Excited!"

"Bill, ya gotta tell me . . . what's his real name?"

The company commander grinned and said, "I can't. He swore me to secrecy. Only the company clerk and I know."

"Yeah, that little shit won't tell me either. Come on . . . I might die on this hill, and I'd hate to go to the great beyond not knowing."

Spaulding looked around to make sure no one was listening in and said in a conspiratorial whisper, "Well, seein' as you're the next in command, maybe you ought to know. Branf—"

"Sorry to interrupt, Cap'n, but Colonel Wranosky wants a word." Captain Spaulding's radioman was either unaware of the momentous news he was disrupting, or he didn't care. He seemed completely unconcerned as he handed the captain the radio handset.

When Spaulding returned, the laughter was gone, but at least was not replaced by grim discontent. As he stuffed more tobacco into his cheek, he said, "Come with me. Wranosky's comin' over to take a look at us and chat."

"Any the word on what's next?"

"We'll find out in a few moments."

0625 Hours
1st Battalion HQ, South of Mount Lungo, Italy

Sam and Bill jogged through a cleared mine lane to the shelter of the destroyed farmhouse. The home was gone and the ruins still smoldering, but the smokehouse only twenty yards away was largely intact. It had become the 1st

Battalion command post, and when the two officers walked in, they were greeted with the pleasing smell of smoked meats. Sam looked to the rafters hopefully, but the hams and sausages had long been taken by the Germans.

"Lieutenant Taft, how are you this fine army morning?" Lieutenant Colonel Wranosky had his jacket drawn up tight around his neck, and his helmet pulled as low as it would go. He looked cheerful despite his shivering.

"Outstanding, sir. How are you?" Sam had long ago learned never to tell the truth to that question when asked by a senior officer.

"Well, my feet are burnin' but every other part of me is cold and wet, and my piles won't let me sit down for more than a minute, but standing's worse. Other than those minor inconveniences, though, I'm pretty damned outstanding, too!" said Wranosky with a grin. He loved his junior officers, and had a particularly warm spot in his heart for those who had been with him on the beach at Paestum.

"Well, I'm glad to see the weather agrees with you, sir." Sam laughed. He nodded to the other officers gathered around the battalion commander; most belonged to Wranosky's staff. Sam moved over next to Jim Lockridge and nudged him shoulder to shoulder. "Hey there, bubba."

"Hey, Bear."

Colonel Wranosky cleared his throat and said, "Alright boys, listen up. We've met our objectives. We hold the southern end of Mount Lungo, the highway entrance into the valley, and now we have all of Mount Rotondo. Congratulations, everyone . . . It went as well as could be expected. Now, we tried to push past our objectives on Lungo, but they're dug in like ticks on a coon dog— and we can't take the whole thing with two companies, so we're ordered to wait. No surprise there. Colonel Jamison says that Fifth Army is sending us an Italian brigade to clear Lungo, and when they arrive, we'll withdraw to Rotondo. 'Til then, we're gonna hold what we've taken. Everybody understand so far?" When the assembled officers nodded their assent, Wranosky said, "I'm gonna let Jim tell ya what we think's gonna happen."

Jim Lockridge stepped out into the circle and looked around at his friends and colleagues. "What we've seen so far are a series of small counterthrusts. The main counterattack obviously hasn't happened yet, but if it's gonna come, I suspect it'll come sooner rather than later. They really only have a few choices here.

"One: they sit back and let us keep it without challenge other than makin' us miserable by artillery fires. They're just fightin' a holdin' action until the winter line is done. We know it, they know it, they know we know it. So don't let us advance further, but hold us here as best they can for now. Two: a full-up counterattack with a battalion-sized armored task force. There's two problems here: the mud's so damn bad they'll be digging their tracks out until next summer; the other problem is we changed the geometry. They have to come at us from the valley now while under observation and fire—just like the Rangers went across the other day. They'll pay a big price if they try it. Three: somethin' in between one and two. Shell the shit out of us, particularly on Lungo, and follow up with small-scale infantry thrusts not unlike what we've seen so far. That's where I'm putting my money."

Colonel Wranosky nodded. "Time will tell. You'd think these sons-a-bitches would see the writin' on the wall and just give up. For the life of me, I cain't figure out what they gain by prolongin' this. But givin' up ain't the German way. Alright . . . Jim, Bill, and Sam, stay here for a moment. Everyone else, back to work."

When the other officers had departed the smokehouse, Wranosky put his hands on his hips and looked at

Sam, "Any word on that idiot cousin of yours?" He smiled briefly to take the sting out of the words.

"No sir. He was supposed to have left last night. He didn't think he'd make it across in daylight, so he's gonna lay low somewheres in the rocks."

"I swear, I don't know what the Old Man was thinkin'. It's a stupid idea, and I *know* it came from Perkin himself. Jim, next time you hear of somethin' this dumb, you come and get me." Wranosky shook his head trying to think of options, but he didn't voice his full thoughts. He didn't want to tell Sam that he thought Perkin was on a dead-man's mission. "All right, Bill, since you obviously didn't train Professor Numbnuts well enough, I'm putting this on you. Figure out a way to support Berger without puttin' anyone else at risk. No officers or NCOs leave us, but if you feel you can release a sniper team for the day, I'll let you do it. Jim, you coordinate anything you have to with the 143rd to make it happen. I admire the size of his balls, but what a dumb son of a bitch!"

0645 Hours
Mount Rotondo Spur, Italy

The meeting had just broken up, and Sam and Bill Lockridge were walking back to the spur of Mount Rotondo when the first artillery arrived in support of the counterattack. It was the most brutal and punishing barrage that the soldiers had yet seen.

The German gunners focused on the soldiers of the 1/141st that were deployed on the southern half of Mount Lungo, and it seemed as if the artillery would destroy the little mountain. Great plumes of smoke and mud went skyward in the drizzling rain, and it was apparent that the Germans had brought more to bear than just the smaller field guns. The barrage was horrific, and for a moment Sam and Bill stopped and stared at the devastation that was being wrought on their friends only hundreds of yards away.

"Good luck!" Bill shouted as he broke out of his trance and started running back to his command post.

"You, too!" Sam replied as he sprinted past a bulldozer that was knocking over stumps of trees. The engineers had started building a road to the crest of the spur to allow anti-tank guns and armor to be brought forward. He ran back towards his own command post, a muddy water-filled foxhole on the spur, and he spied Sergeant Kenton walking through the deployed platoon. Kenton had not been idle in Sam's brief absence. He had taken advantage of the growing daylight to make improvements of their defensive positions and ensure the soldiers were ready to go. They were.

"Anything?" Sam was referring to movement in the valley before them.

"No sir. How do you reckon this is gonna unfold?" Bill Kenton was one of the few soldiers in the regiment as large as Sam. He was covered in wet mud up to his eyebrows from digging his foxhole.

"Well, I'm hopin' they'll run away after seein' you. I dunno. Looks like they're gonna try and retake all of Lungo. That'll make our position here uncomfortable. Of course, if they were to take our position, it'd put the boys on Lungo in a bad spot. Battalion says we're to dig in and hold our ground."

"OK, we're good to—"

It was then that they heard a distant whoosh, whoosh, whoosh of rockets from far off on the other side of the valley. The soldiers had never heard the sound in combat but knew of it from training films and the passed-down lore of other soldiers. It was the sound of *nebelwerfers*—

multi-barrel electrically-launched mortar rockets. Reports from soldiers in Sicily, who had been on the receiving end before, indicated that the attacks were terrifying.

A long silence followed the sound of the launch-ers before small explosions were heard. Once again, the rounds detonated elsewhere. Not on Mount Lungo, but in the valley as it constricted to the gap between Lungo and the spur. Not high explosives or the greatly-feared incendiary rounds, but smoke. Dozens of rounds from the nebelwerfers began to fill the bowl of the little valley with a choking, acrid smoke.

Sam looked back at Sergeant Kenton, whose face had turned grim. They nodded silently, then began to walk in opposite directions along the ragged line of their deployed troops. The message they called out was remarkably simi-lar: "Get ready boys! They're gonna try and force the gap with armor. Bazooka teams get ready! Gunners get ready! Riflemen . . . get ready, boys!"

0645 Hours
Mount Sammucro, Italy

Perkin shifted uncomfortably in his little den of rocks. He had thought it impossible that an adult man could have slid into the narrow entrance of the cave, but his Italian escort had shown him otherwise. By taking off his pack and helmet and pushing himself on his stomach, feet first up the mountain, even a tall and lanky American could fit. It was a comically awkward feat, and one that Perkin didn't think he could replicate again without help. He was somewhat cramped in his little cave with his pack, helmet and Thompson taking up space, but at least the floor itself was relatively smooth. even if the little cave was too small for Perkin to roll onto his back or side.

The Italian was a former goat herder whose herd had been confiscated by German soldiers. When he had shown up at the regimental headquarters of the 143rd Infantry a week before, bearing a note in English that said, *The Americans will pay for your goats*, a sympathetic Italian-American sergeant had explained that although the US Army could not reimburse him for animals now being eaten by the enemy, perhaps there was some work for the herder. The sergeant had first fed the Italian and then taken him to a fellow NCO on the intelligence staff of the 143rd Infantry Regiment. After a translated discussion of the mountain with Major MacMahon, the herder had been offered a job as a mountain guide for the American Army—an offer which he willingly took.

Perkin had been astounded by the nimbleness of his guide, but the Italian had been working on that very mountain for nearly forty years. His balance and footing were as sure as his daily charges. His guide was less impressed with Perkin's nimbleness, but he had led a few Americans into the mountains, and he found that none of them were very sure-footed in the loose scree of Mount Sammucro. He was not surprised. Even his cousins in San Pietro could not keep up with him on the mountain, and they had been raised on its very slope.

So he had patiently guided Perkin down a narrow pathway from the saddle ridge and along multiple cutbacks, many of which had been improved over the years by the herder. His Italian commands, given in what Perkin recognized as the Neapolitan dialect, were purposely kept simple. Follow me. Step there. Slowly. Hold here.

If it had not been for the war, the herder could have walked along the trails to San Pietro in less than an hour, even at night, but the American could not. The mountainside was too steep, the paths too uneven, and the rock too unstable for a novice to safely keep such a pace. Perkin was in no rush—he knew that as the paths approached German positions, the trails would be mined and pickets would be in place. Consequently, Perkin was only able to make it to Mount Sammucro proper, still more than a mile from the village, before the herder had led him off the path, up the mountainside, and through the rocks to his cave.

After Perkin had shimmied and been pushed backwards into the cave, the herder had stacked a few rocks in front of the slit of an entrance, grinned a toothless grin at Perkin, and mumbled a few instructions before he left. Within his limited vocabulary of Italian and relying on Spanish cognates, Perkin came to the understanding that his guide had taken many naps in the cave over the years, that it was good shelter from a storm, and would the *signore* please not defecate in his cave. Perkin was less certain about his understanding of a portion of the instructions the herder told him about vipers. When the herder left, he had turned on his flashlight and anxiously looked around the cave. There were no adders in the cave that he could see, and he felt sure he had seen the entirety of the cave. It was only about seven or eight feet deep, about three feet wide, and no more than fourteen or fifteen inches tall. That the dimensions of his cave were similar to a coffin's did not escape Perkin, and he worried needlessly about the inexorable weight of the mountain pressing down on his cave.

Compounding his worry was the battle. He could hear fighting in the valley, and he assumed it was Sam's fight. The sounds were the now-familiar noises of combat: the chatter of American machine guns and the much faster ripping noise of the German MG-42. The sharper sounds of individual rifle fire punctuated the silence between the deep booms and explosions of artillery—and Perkin took the rifle fire as an indication of a counterattack. Buttressing that argument was a sound that Perkin had never heard before except on army films: a distant whoosh, whoosh, whoosh, whoosh, whoosh, whoosh— each sound separated by a second. The last droning noise was followed shortly thereafter by multiple explosions. It was Perkin's guess that the noise was the sound of a nebelwerfer attack.

There were many versions of the nebelwerfer, nicknamed "screaming meemies" by American soldiers in Africa and Sicily, but Perkin guessed that he was hearing the six-barrelled variant. In an intelligence assessment he had read, the German Army referred to the nebelwerfer as a chemical mortar, but it actually fired a rocket-propelled payload which, in addition to high explosive, could be smoke, gas, or incendiary rounds—the latter being something that made all soldiers nervous. Perkin was tempted to crawl out from the cave and see for himself, but any movement on the mountainside would be suicidal without the cover of fog.

In rapid succession, Perkin heard several more launches of the rockets, and he counted a total of thirty-six before they fell silent. There must be at least a battery of nebelwerfers, he decided, and if the Germans were smart, they would quickly pack up and move before firing again. The propellant was known to leave a grayish trail of smoke in the air, and Perkin prayed for American counter-battery fire to be swift and sure. At least half of his prayer was answered as the 36th Division's field artillery opened fire almost instantly, but the results were unknown to Perkin.

The sounds of combat continued, and despite his anxiety for Sam and the battalion, he yawned. Perkin had been running on a deficit of sleep since the death of Gianina. It was not just the pain of his loss that led to sleepless nights—though he missed her deeply—but so much of his routine consisted of meetings and the routine administration of the troop in the daytime, while the darkness of night provided cover for many of the troop's missions. Two to four hours' sleep per day had been his norm, and he was simply running out of energy. Unable to stay awake any longer just to listen to unseen artillery duels, he lay his head on his crossed arms and fell asleep.

0705 Hours
Mount Rotondo Spur, Italy

They heard the squeal of the tracks even before the sound of the diesel engines reached them. The smoke was still swirling through the valley, but it was not as effective as a good fog. Sam could see shapes moving in the distance—two pairs of tanks moving in a single file along the highway with infantry in company—before the smoke blew back into his position.

His end of the valley was so narrow—only a few hundred yards separated the bases of Mounts Lungo and Rotondo—that Sam knew it was impossible for this fight to pass him by. The tanks would either roll towards him first, in which case he would have to take on the German tanks directly, or they would turn to his left and try to bull through the rest of the battalion on Lungo. In that case, their flank would be exposed to him.

When the artillery shifted onto the spur, Sam thought he knew what the answer would be: the Germans would clear the spur first and try to envelop the troops on Lungo. In the midst of the shelling of Mount Lungo, heavy 155 millimeter high-explosive rounds came crashing down suddenly onto Sam's little hillock. There was no chance to yell a warning to his troops—it was on them that quickly. Sam had been on the receiving end of artillery before—at Salerno—and a sudden flashback of the experience made the blood drain from his face and his body go cold.

Dozens of the remaining trees on the spur shattered and splintered as the first rounds detonated in the tree tops. A small piece of white-hot shrapnel screeched by Sam's head and buried itself into the mud of Sam's foxhole. He stared mutely at it as he crouched low in the watery foxhole. As the fragment sizzled and smoked in the mud, he was insanely tempted to touch it, to pick it up and save it as a memento. It would still be there later, he thought. Sensing that the artillery was shifting again, Sam pulled himself from the mud and ran down towards the tree line. Behind him, he heard Sergeant Kenton calling out to the platoon, "Stay down, goddammit! Stay down."

Sam saw what he needed to see. He turned and sprinted back to Kenton. "Platoon of rifles approaching. Three hundred to five hundred yards out and on either side of the highway. Armor right behind lead element. Bazooka team sprints out in the smoke. Kill the lead tank and sprint back."

Sam waved his radioman over. While he waited impatiently for him to raise the company commander, he squatted and looked out into the smoke. Nothing. He could see nothing, but they had to be close. His ears were ringing so badly that they were nearly worthless, and when the radioman handed him the handset, he yelled unnecessarily into it.

"Hammer Six, Hammer One. Lead armor and infantry three hundred yards out. Infantry dispersed on either side of the highway—some using the tracks for cover. I saw four Panzer IVs, must be more behind 'em. We're gonna take out the lead tank. Can you get me fires one hundred yards northwest of my tree line and then work it forwards towards San Pietro? Put the call in now. Gotta go. Hammer One out."

Sergeant Kenton had been listening, and by the time Sam had handed back the handset, he was squatting next to a bazooka team giving them instructions. Kenton looked at Sam and nodded. Sam nodded back and watched as Kenton and two soldiers ran into the smoke.

When they were gone from sight, he ran to the nearest machine gun team. "When they come back, start firing into the smoke."

"I can't see nothing out there, sir!" The machine gunner was a young soldier from Uvalde who was uncertain of what was going on. What is called the fog of war had descended to his level, and he was confused. His brown eyes were wide as he looked up at Sam.

"I know. Rifles are working their way up. Criss-cross into the smoke and work your way back into the valley."

It all came together in one moment. Sam heard the whoosh of the rocket and an explosion as it found its target. Immediately, gunfire erupted from the German panzer grenadiers, but they were firing into the smoke. Three figures came running full bore out of the smoke as if they were being chased by Death himself, and Sam turned and dropped his arm. Two American M1919 machine guns opened fired and worked back and forth across the valley floor. In response, a German MG-42 opened up and began firing blindly into the smoke—the rounds going wildly over Sam's head. Then the American artillery arrived.

It was much closer to Sam's position than he had expected, and the shock of the exploding rounds sent the Texans ducking for cover yet again. But true to Sam's request, the division's artillery put forth a rolling barrage reminiscent of the Great War that walked forwards down the valley. If the smoke hadn't been so thick, the Texans would have been treated to the horrific show of a lifetime as the 105 and 155 millimeter rounds being fired by the Texans made the no-man's-land of the valley a living hell for the panzer grenadiers crouching low in the open.

One hundred yards to Sam's left, two 57-millimeter anti-tank guns jumped simultaneously as a gap in the smoke revealed that a German panzer had closed almost to the Lungo-Rotondo gap. The fog of war had affected both sides, and the German tankers had moved much farther through the valley than they intended. They paid a stiff price as the panzer exploded—the force lifted the turret off the chassis only to slam back down with a loud clang.

Sam's soldiers began to fire blindly into the smoke as well. They aimed low and hoped for targets. Sam waited until each man had fired at least a clip, then he gave the order to cease fire. It was good for the troops to have shot at something, and it gave him a brief moment to identify those soldiers who hesitated or were shy. There weren't many.

When the firing stopped, Sam strained to hear if the Germans were firing. They were not. It was another unique experience for Sam in the war. He had fought another battle, in daytime and in fairly close quarters, yet had less vision onto the battlefield than he would have had at night. There were no flashes of explosions or muzzles to guide his senses. Though he had only briefly seen the enemy, it seemed less frightening in retrospect than a night battle simply because of the benefit of a little light.

Sam refought the battle in his mind and wondered if the Germans saw the battle the same way he did—had they continued to push through with such a small attack, he was not sure what they would have gained. The excellent American artillery made it difficult for infantry to survive in the valley, and even though the Texans were in a hastily prepared defense, they would butcher the tankers without infantry support. In Sam's opinion, the little hillock wasn't worth the effort to retake it. Sam wondered if it would be worth the effort to defend it.

The stalemate in no-man's-land would continue.

1000 Hours
Mount Cesima, Italy

The goat herder was tired. He had not had much sleep the past few weeks, and now he had to take two teenage boys with guns onto the mountain. Still, he was being fed, which was more than many of his countrymen could claim.

When he had been roused from his tent two hours before by one of Major MacMahon's men, he had been brought to the saddle ridge again and introduced to the boys. One was short, with glasses and a scarred face. He looked impossibly young to be a soldier, but he carried the heavy American rifle, the one the Americans called the Garand, with ease and confidence. His companion was taller and slim, with sandy blond hair and a German sur-name. He carried a bolt-action rifle with a scope, and he seemed just as confident as his partner.

Major MacMahon didn't seem impressed with either, though, and MacMahon's translator told the goat herder that MacMahon thought the boys were wasting their time. They would be of no use to Captain Berger from Mount Cesima, but the boys were emphatic that those were their orders. So be it. If the Americans wanted to pay him to take some teenagers on a sightseeing tour of Mount Cesima, that was fine by him.

1240 Hours
Mount Cesima, Italy

"Did you see the mustache on that son of a bitch?" As someone who shaved weekly, whether he needed to or not, Private First Class Edwin Kulis was impressed with Major MacMahon's uninhibited flouting of regulations.

"Hell yeah. Only an officer can have a mustache like that," Private First Class Roscoe Pfadenhauer groused. Pfadenhauer also only had a passing acquaintance with a razor, but he, too, admired the major's lack of adherence to the army's standards of personal hygiene. "That reminds me: when the war's over, I'm gonna become a Fuller Brush salesman."

Kulis grinned and said, "Is that a fact? And why on earth would you wanna do that?"

"Because those sons-a-bitches get more action than they can handle. That's why. Just think about it: A woman's home alone with nothin' to do all day, then along comes Fuller Brush salesman, Roscoe D. Pfadenhauer, war hero . . . ."

"I don't know if you meet the classical definition of a hero yet. Maybe you might wanna do somethin' in the war first. Let's see . . . what are your military accomplishments so far? Oh, don't bother answering, it's a short list. Ya didn't even fire your rifle this morning, so that don't help much, but uh . . . let's see . . . you got the tanker at Paestum, and everyone agrees that was an OK shot. Of course, that was two months ago. And then . . . let's see . . . oh, not resting on your laurels, you caught the clap in Naples . . . ."

"I did not!"

"And you were so indiscreet as to write your brother back home and tell him about it, and your brother was so indiscreet as to tell your mom, and then your mom writes General Walker to complain. 'What kind of division are you running over there, General?' And, 'what are you doing to my boy?'" Kulis said in a falsetto, and then laughed at his own wit. "Were those the heroics you had in mind?"

"I told you, it weren't the clap. The doc said it was a 'non-specific' somethin' or other. At least he didn't give me the ream and scream. And I didn't tell my brother about that neither . . . Mom wrote the general 'cause I said 'butt fuck' in a letter to my brother." Private Pfaden-hauer shook his head, appalled at the memory. "Artie had to explain to her what it meant, and he said she cried for two days straight. Brother, am I gonna catch hell for that when I get home—she's gonna wash my mouth out with soap."

"That don't seem like fair treatment for a war hero," Kulis observed.

"No, it don't. And I didn't shoot this mornin' 'cause I'm a sniper. Precise application of death is my business. None of this shoot-into-the-smoke crap for me. So, what are your accomplishments, Eddie? Don't answer, it's a shorter list. Let's see, you've killed a half-dozen wounded men, includin' one more last night, and you lost your vir-ginity. Uh-huh . . . war hero my ass!"

Kulis grinned, "Hell, I look on those as the highlights of the Ed Kulis Story . . . so far. Shoot, in Paestum, I killed a wounded private. Last night I killed a wounded sergeant. Before the war's over, I plan to have worked my way up the ranks of the wounded to kill a general or a field marshal."

"You ain't supposed to kill the wounded, you know."

"All them sons-a-bitches were gonna die anyhow, I just helped move them along to the great Teutonic Reich in the sky. Except for that cocksucker who killed Corporal Pena. He might have lived."

"Yeah, and who the hell wounded him? Me."

"Well, we already covered your war record, remem-ber? We're talking about me now, and don't you think those are accomplishments? Certainly more noteworthy to write home about than catchin' the clap. You know, I'm puttin' them in the first chapter of my autobiography. Maybe in the prologue. Or the preface. Or the dedication: 'This book, about the war hero Ed Kulis, is dedicated to the wounded men he killed and the whore named Paula who took his cherry.'"

Pfadenhauer started laughing. "Leave it to you to dedicate a book to a whore."

"At least I know how to write. Besides, them whores're the nicest people I met in Italy so far." Kulis paused, looking around. "Do you really think you could hit somethin' from here?" Kulis was beginning to get a little worried that maybe the major was right, and they couldn't be much help from Mount Cesima.

"I don't know, Eddie. I think it's close on to half a mile. But you heard Lieutenant Bear. He said he'd beat us like circus monkeys if we went onto Mount Sammy."

"You really think they treat circus monkeys poorly?"

Pfadenhauer nodded sagely, "Oh, hell yeah. It's a rough life bein' a circus monkey."

"No kidding?"

"No kidding. There's a lady at my church in Comfort who was all up in arms about it. She was a free thinkin' do-gooder, and she said that if the monkeys can't ride a bike or drive a car or juggle bowlin' pins, the clowns take away their cigarettes and beat the hell out of 'em. Said it weren't Christian at all."

"No. I don't reckon it is." Kulis contemplated for a moment about free-thinkers and do-gooders and monkey-beating clowns, filed it away to puzzle over later, and asked, "Are you gettin' hungry?"

Private Pfadenhauer was, and Private Kulis put down the binoculars that he'd been staring through for the entire conversation about Pfadenhauer's post-war career aspirations and opened a can of C-ration hash. Kulis ate half while Pfadenhauer stared at the opposing mountainside through the scope of his Springfield, and then they switched. Pfadenhauer didn't have much of an appetite. Kulis turned to offer some to the herder, but he was curled up in a ball behind the two soldiers and gently snoring. "Snooze, ya lose," remarked Kulis to his comrade, who made no comment as he was feeling a little nauseated. Kulis picked up the binoculars again and went back to staring at the cave entrance and the area around it.

1255 Hours
Mount Sammucro, Italy

Perkin awoke with a start. He thought he heard voices, but he had been dreaming of a staff meeting with the division adjutant. *Good God,* he thought groggily, *what a terrible thing to waste a dream on.* He was cold and uncomfortable, but he had slept hard. What was the time? Just about 1300. He had slept for six hours—a luxury in wartime—but he had another four hours before dark.

There were other requirements of life that needed attending to, and he stiffly reached back and pulled out his canteen and took a deep drink, and then another. His pack was squeezed in beside him, and he fumbled it open and pulled out a can from a box of C-rations. Perkin had not looked at the box when he grabbed it from the mess tent, and he was extremely irritated to find that he grabbed a can of the experimental mutton stew with vegetables. In a mental retort to Liebniz and Pangloss, Perkin ruefully told himself that he had the worst of all possible meals— only Private Kulis seemed to genuinely like what was universally regarded as a failed experiment. As he opened the can up and sniffed tentatively and unappreciatively at the contents, he thought that the only thing the army could do worse to its soldiers was to replace this meal with the lima beans and ham dish that the soldiers had been told was in the works. *Lima beans—not even Superman would eat those,* he thought. *Well, maybe Clark—*

There were the voices again. Whispers below him. Perkin slowly set down the can of uneaten stew and reached for his pistol. His Thompson was beside him, but it was unwieldy in the confined space. Perkin rolled slowly to his left, unsnapped the flap on his holster and pulled out a newly-issued Colt .45. Only the day before he had seen a Fifth Army directive proscribing the carrying of captured enemy equipment, and Perkin had decided to ship his captured Luger home to Old Perkin before a senior officer made him turn the forbidden weapon in. A trusted supply sergeant said that he would get the Luger back to Texas for him for the low fee of a month's supply of cigarettes. As Perkin didn't smoke, it was an easy trade, but he did add the stipulation that payment would only be made upon confirmation of delivery in Portland.

There was already a chambered round, and Perkin covered the hammer with his left hand to mask the sound. He slowly pulled the hammer back two clicks with his right thumb. Holding his breath, he inched forward on his belly to the lip of the cave entrance and he peered through a gap in the rocks stacked by the goat herder. Two German helmets were below him—not close enough to touch, but close enough that he couldn't miss with the .45.

Perkin didn't have a clear view of the Germans. He could see their helmeted heads and the muzzles of their slung rifles. Both soldiers were carrying K98 Mausers, and they might be two soldiers on a patrol, which meant that there might be more enemy soldiers in the vicinity, or more likely, they were a scout-sniper team. The two Germans were having an animated conversation in hushed tones, which Perkin could neither hear clearly nor understand. He glanced at the sky and realized that they were fogged in, but the clouds seemed to be moving quickly.

The Germans turned and faced the mountain, and Perkin could clearly see their faces, although he hoped they could not see his. Both had dirty faces, but there the similarities ended. The soldier to Perkin's left, only ten feet away, was young and appeared confident and cocky. The other soldier, the older one, appeared deeply concerned. Perhaps scared. The older soldier stepped cautiously onto a rock, and Perkin saw the rank of a *feldwebel*—a staff sergeant. The sergeant pointed towards the crest of Mount Sammucro, directly over Perkin's head, and began counting: *"Eins, zwei, drei."* At *"drei,"* the sergeant pointed at their feet.

The other soldier shook his head. *"Nein. Zwei."* He also pointed at their feet. *"Zwei!"* he repeated in an emphatic whisper.

Perkin now understood what the argument was about. The Germans were lost. There were multiple paths running laterally across this face of Mount Sammucro, and the second and third paths converged closer to San Pietro. If they missed the path's fork in the fog, then they might have been on the lower trail when they needed to be on the upper, or vice versa. Although Perkin couldn't see their map, he was on the third trail from the top. He had chosen that route in order to be closer to the olive groves that dotted the lower slopes of the mountain. The old sergeant was right, but why was there fear in his eyes? Perhaps he wanted the higher path so as to be further away from American snipers. Perhaps he just preferred the higher ground.

A brief gust of wind lifted the cloud, and the sergeant pointed up the mountainside once again as if to say, "See, I told you so." The two Germans looked at each other, and the younger soldier briefly hung his head in self-disgust. When he looked up at his sergeant from under his helmet, he grinned, blew out a long breath, and mockingly wiped his brow in relief.

"*Mein Gott,* Hans," the sergeant also wiped his brow and looked back on the path to San Pietro. Relief had replaced the fear in his eyes. The sergeant grabbed the younger soldier's arm and nodded up the mountainside. They were climbing over the rocks at the upper path—straight over Perkin's cave.

1255 Hours
Mount Cesima, Italy

"So you know that Italian dame from Ugly-Assed Children?" Kulis asked, his eyes still glued to the binoculars and staring out into the fog.

"You ain't gonna start in on her again, are ya?" Pfadenhauer had been with Kulis when the beautiful Italian woman had chatted with the bespectacled private in the village of Ogliastro Cilento. Next to losing his virginity, talking to the beautiful woman and getting a clear, unobstructed view of her perfect cleavage was the sexual highlight of Kulis's young life and a topic of frequent conversation—very frequent conversation.

Ignoring his friend's comment, Kulis said, "Seein' as she might be Mrs. Edwin Kulis some day, I think it's appropriate to fixate on her . . . ."

"It might be appropriate for you to shut up about her. . . ."

"And I got a friend down on army staff, you know, Big Mike, who says he thinks he knows who she is. And she's in Caserta!"

"Now, how would he know that?" Pfadenhauer wasn't really listening, he was watching the terminus of a bank of clouds work across the mountain. Hopefully, they would be able to get eyes on the cave soon. Their view had been obstructed so many times by low-hanging clouds that they weren't even sure Captain Berger was still in the cave.

"He's in the CIC.* Remember? He said that they checked out a skirt who was bangin' a bunch of senior officers. She's a rich girl and her daddy's got lots of homes all over Italy, includin' Ugly-Assed Children and Caserta. He made the connection based on my story."

"No shit? That's impressive. Based on your description?"

"Yeah. I was tellin' him about the most beautiful woman I'd ever seen, and that she was arm-in-arm with some Fifth Army major when Cap'n Berger pulled over to talk to him." Kulis shivered at the memory. When then-Lieutenant Berger was talking to the major, the beautiful woman came over to his jeep and chatted with him. She was so beautiful it was almost hypnotic, and Pfadenhauer and the other soldiers were resentful that she talked solely to Kulis. It still rankled.

"She must be a whore. You know she was bangin' old what's-his-name . . . Ebbins . . . at regiment."

"I hope she's a whore!" Kulis said sincerely. "I don't have much chance otherwise. Although I ain't clear on why'd she'd be a whore if her daddy's rich. I swear . . .that Ebbins is an idiot. Did you ever hear him brag about being on the regimental staff? He made me dig his jeep out of the mud once, and the son of a bitch wouldn't shut up about staff life. I wouldn't mind bein' on a staff, but not while he's there. Too many Hitlers and not enough Nazis."

"Huh? What's that? Hitler's on the regimental staff?"

"No, dumbass. What I was sayin' was—hey, do you see that?"

---

* Counter Intelligence Corps

1300 Hours
Mount Sammucro, Italy

Eye contact was all but inevitable. Perkin simply couldn't move any farther back, and he had to hope that the Germans wouldn't see him. It was a forlorn hope. He felt instinctively that he should look out of his little cave with his peripheral vision, and perhaps the soldiers would not sense his presence. But he couldn't bring himself to look down, and then there they were: dark brown eyes widening in shock just inches from his own.

The German soldier screamed, and as he instinctively jumped backwards his footing gave way in the scree of the mountainside. Faster than he could have reacted on his own, his head dropped down below the lip of the cave. Perkin was so stunned that he lay still for the briefest of moments . . . during which time he realized he had not fired his weapon. Then he began to crawl for the entrance. He was not going to stay in the cave and allow the Germans to lob grenades in at their leisure.

Just as he was preparing to fire blindly out of the cave, he heard a *ziiiip* and a thud and the fading echo of a distant rifle. In disbelief, Perkin watched as the younger soldier fell over the cave entrance, his eyes staring into the cave as he rolled onto the path below. With his left hand, Perkin grasped the rim of his cave's entrance and he pulled himself to the edge. His heart pounding wildly, he peered out through the stones. The sergeant was not in sight.

Cautiously, Perkin stuck his head out and looked below him, his pistol ready. Nothing. Another zip, a bullet's impact on a stone twenty yards to Perkin's right, and the report of the rifle. It had to be an American sniper on Mount Cesima or further back on the mountain towards the saddle and American lines. Perkin craned around and looked to his right and left, but he still saw nothing. The soldier must be sprinting down the path towards the olive groves. Perkin came to an instant decision, and he began to kick, wiggle, and frantically pull himself out of the cave. As his torso came out, he reached back and grabbed the muzzle of his Thompson, and he allowed himself to awkwardly slide out of the slit of an entrance. With not enough room to get his feet under him, there was no graceful way out of the cave. In the inevitable way of nature, gravity took over. When the bulk of his body had exited the cave, Perkin dropped several feet onto his face and he slid down the mountainside on his belly, his left hand dragging under his body in the sharp rocks, his right hand frantically trying to push himself over onto his shoulder. It was to no avail, and when he came to rest on the path, his face was only two feet away from the body of the dead German soldier, the victim of the unseen American sniper.

Perkin's face felt like it was on fire. His fingers and hands were scraped horribly, and much of the skin on his left hand had been peeled back towards his wrist. Ignoring the blood that was dripping from his chin and a torn left nostril, Perkin scrambled to his knees, knelt, and fired the Thompson through watery eyes down the trail towards San Pietro—the only way the sergeant would have run. But Perkin could not see him—the fog was rolling in again, and soon his visibility would be measured in yards. Perkin's first inclination was to sprint after the fleeing German, but the fog made that suicidal. After listening for the sound of movement, he clumsily picked up and holstered his Colt. As they had several times before in battle, his hands were shaking from the adrenaline and fear—this time they hurt intensely as well. There were no broken bones that he could discern, but two nails had been torn off the fingers on his left hand. He wiped his right palm on the front of his jacket, trying to pull small shards of stone from his hand. He could get them later, he decided. With more grace than he had shown coming down, Perkin climbed up to the cave and quickly pulled out his pack and helmet, leaving the mutton stew behind. He had to move quickly if he were to hunt down and kill the sniper before the sniper killed him.

1305 Hours
Mount Cesima, Italy

"Get him!" Private Kulis screamed, although whether he was shouting at Private Pfadenhauer or the distant Captain Berger was unclear.

Pfadenhauer had in fact shot a second time and barely missed the fleeing German soldier. Together they watched in disbelief as Captain Berger launched himself from the cave and fired down the path with his Thompson.

The clouds moved in inexorably. First the distant slope of Mount Sammucro was lost to view. Then the narrow intervening valley was filled with the grey clouds that brought a cold drizzle.

"Did you see that? Mom can't wash my mouth out now . . . not after a shot like that." Pfadenhauer had a broad grin on his face. "That was 850 yards! I can't wait to tell Captain Spaulding and Lieutenant Taft!"

Kulis was excited too, but was worried about Captain Berger. As he pointed out their Italian guide, who was scuttling down the path towards the saddle ridge— the guide was already fifty yards away and putting good distance behind him—he asked, "Reckon we ought to go after him? Cap'n Berger, I mean."

Pfadenhauer lost the smile and said, "I dunno. What do you think, Eddie?"

"I think we wait here until near dusk, then if we don't see Cap'n Berger again, we hitch a ride back to the company. We can't get around to the other side without the Eye-tie, leastways not quickly, and I reckon he's long gone."

The two young men pulled out ponchos and then leaned against the rocks, looking for signs that the clouds might lift. As they settled in to an afternoon of ice-cold drizzling rain, they laughingly relived over and over the triumphant shot and the specter of their old comrade shooting from the mountainside.

1315 Hours
Mount Sammucro, Italy

Perkin knew that the German sergeant had retreated back towards his lines, but where would he go from there? Would he return to the safety of his quarters, lick his wounds, and come out to fight another day, or would he seek to complete his mission and kill infiltrating Americans? Would he suspect that Perkin was hunting him as well?

It was an easy assumption to make—that the German would attempt to reestablish a position in the rocks and be the distant eyes, ears, and defenses of the German Army. That's what he would do, Perkin decided, and he expected no less professionalism from the Wehrmacht. It thus became the analytical officer's working hypothesis: the German soldier was a sniper, that he would disregard the loss of his partner, and that he would attempt to establish a new sniping position.

It was apparent from the discussion that Perkin had partially overheard that the Germans intended to be higher in elevation. The second trail from the top was nearly two hundred yards higher than the one they were on, but it was unlikely that the sniper intended to establish a covert position on the trail, so Perkin decided he might try to split the difference and hunt for the sniper in the rocky debris between the goat paths.

Before he left, he quickly wrapped his left hand and the ends of his fingers with gauze bandages as best he could. The split on his chin was not severe and would eventually stop bleeding, although the tide of blood flowing from his nostril showed no sign of turning. Perkin's jacket was in terrible shape, having been ripped as he slid down the rocks. The dirt and grime from the cave floor was now mixing with his blood. It certainly would look worse than it was, but it also felt pretty bad to Perkin. He shrugged to himself and decided he'd wasted enough time.

His plan was to climb straight up to his chosen elevation and then work his way laterally over the rocks. Being in the fog, he had no way to measure relative distances, so he decided that he would try to count his body length in distance over and over again as he climbed. His first waypoint was his cave. Perkin at first grinned at himself, thinking that the American sniper must still be laughing at the unknown soldier who ejected himself from the mountainside, and then he almost laughed out loud thinking of how amused Sam would be when he heard. As Perkin went higher, he found that the going was challenging but not impossible. The mountainside alternated between large boulders, scree, and the occasional patches of grass and vegetation. There was a steep slope, but it wasn't vertical. He could climb it.

The temperature was only slightly above freezing at his altitude, and Perkin suspected that there might be snow or ice by the morning. The clouds had set in firmly again, and the cool, wet blanket it provided would have brought a bone-shaking chill had he not been climbing the rocks. As it was, the cool mist felt good on his shredded face. Of a more immediate concern than the likelihood of precipitation, the fog greatly distorted the echoes upon echoes of sounds in the mountains. An intense artillery duel was underway, and German rounds screamed over Perkin's head en route to targets in the valley. When he looked upwards, he found the noise and the closeness of the clouds caused a vertigo that he had never experienced before. When he kept his head down, the dizziness disappeared. The truth was that he was grateful for the artillery firing—no one would notice a little popgun like his Thompson amid all the echoes and explosions in the valley.

The masking of sounds had mirrored his argument for the mission to take place at all as he delivered it to his superiors, first to Lieutenant Colonel Walker and then to Major General Walker. It had taken nearly twenty minutes of persistent reasoning to get Lieutenant Colonel Walker to even contemplate such a mission. Even after he had been won over, the G-3 had insisted on having the commanding officer's approval. As he walked into General Walker's office in the farmhouse, Perkin wondered for the hundredth time whether it was possible to have a foolhardy and an essential mission wrapped into one.

The notion had come to him two mornings before as he watched the 3rd Ranger Battalion march bravely towards San Pietro. In that reconnaissance in force, eleven Rangers had been killed and nineteen more had been injured, yet the forces which had so grievously harmed the Rangers had been unseen German artillery sited further back in the hills. Little knowledge had been gained about San Pietro itself. But that didn't mean that the purpose of the mission was unimportant. Perkin understood General Keye's pressing need to have an appreciation of German defenses in San Pietro, as the Fifth Army could not advance into the Liri valley until it passed San Pietro, and that village would have to be taken or reduced before the advance could resume.

What eluded hundreds of Rangers and numerous aerial reconnaissance missions could be accomplished by a single man, Perkin had argued. It wasn't necessary to enter the village, it was just necessary to get close enough to observe and then report back. A Ranger battalion could not infiltrate in force along the slopes of Mount Sammucro, yet a single man could—or as they said back home in Texas, he might could. General Walker was initially no more inclined than his son was, yet he remained open-minded as Perkin outlined a plan that would take him two to three days to complete. Any longer than that, and he would risk being in the village when the assault began.

"Why not send one of your troops?" General Walker had asked.

Perkin had anticipated the question and had replied in a rush, "Because they're all committed along our line, sir. Besides, I can't ask them to do something like this—I know this isn't what you're suggesting, but I would hate to give the appearance that it's OK to risk an enlisted man and not an officer. I'll no longer be employed anyway, General, and I understand that you believe that I would make a good intel officer—this is a chance to find out!"

The general had coughed and replied dryly, "Well, I've always known that intelligence officers and intelligent officers aren't necessarily the same thing. Go over your plan again."

At that point, Perkin had known that he had won the commanding officer over. There was nothing ingenuous about his plan: work his way through the German defenses through the most inhospitable territory, and do so primarily at night. Let the rocky, mountainous terrain provide his cover. As he had argued, the German defenses were more porous in the mountains. There wasn't a coherent line per se, but rather isolated outposts of defenders. And unlike nearly every linear foot across the floor of the valley, the rocky mountainside was difficult to mine.

Perkin stopped, frozen in his climb up the mountain. His line of reasoning about the absence of mines had rung true—which made the shin-high steel wire glistening with little beads of moisture rather ironic in Perkin's opinion. The trap stretched across a small gap between the rocks and was attached to two hidden S-mines. One step more and the irony would have been lost on him.

1340 Hours
Mount Sammucro, Italy

There was a natural gap between the two boulders, and the German soldiers who had set the booby trap had done a good job. The mines were well-concealed, the thin steel wire nearly impossible to see in any light. Any soldier moving laterally through this part of the mountain would gravitate to a gap such as this as opposed to going over the rocks. The gap provided cover and concealment, while climbing the boulders brought exposure to enemy fire.

The S-mine was also known to the Americans as the "Bouncing Betty." When activated, the mine fired a small powder charge that ejected a canister containing the main charge and more than three hundred steel balls. The main charge would then detonate at two to four feet above the ground, and the steel balls would scream out indiscriminately for upwards of a hundred yards. The mine itself was frequently non-lethal, but it instead inflicted severe damage on legs and genitals—leading the soldiers to call it the "castrator" mine.

Perkin had seen hundreds of the mines before, was very familiar with the disarming procedures, and had, in fact, disarmed live mines in training and on the battlefield at Salerno. Like most soldiers, it was a task he did not relish. The S-mine was not complicated, and disarming it was relatively simple, but it took time and was dangerous.

In the case of a mine or mines set by a trip wire as opposed to burial, the wire itself could be cut and the immediate danger neutralized. But the mine remained armed and would be deadly if actuated. Perkin could've easily left the mine in place with a mental justification that his mission could not afford the time or risk required to disarm the mine, but the thought that another Texan might some day be patrolling through this little cut in the rock pushed him to retrieve his wire cutters from his pack. Perkin toyed with the idea of trying to set a small trap by detonating the mine and seeing if he could bag the sniper if he came to investigate, but decided he might attract more than a single soldier. The sniper, in all likelihood, would not give away his position, but Perkin certainly would with such an act, so he quickly passed on the notion.

Crouching behind the protection of the boulder, he carefully snipped the wire and ducked behind the rocks. Fortunately, the tripwire was itself not boobytrapped as reports indicated they sometimes were, and Perkin carefully removed the sensor and the percussion cap of each mine to render them safe.

He stepped away from the booby trapped passage and backtracked down the mountain for several yards, then worked his way through the rocks towards the American lines for an equal distance. Stepping only on rocky surfaces, he began to climb the mountain again, parallel to his original track and careful to keep his profile low against the rocks. A quick climb of twenty yards and he had found what he was looking for—a path through the rocks that wouldn't require much exposure if he kept low.

Perkin resumed his lateral movement across the slope of Mount Sammucro. The wind picked up considerably and then it began to rain—an ice-cold rain driven by the winds coming down from the mountaintop. It was a rain that whipped in horizontally, drenching his clothes and trickling down his neck despite the rubber poncho he pulled on. Unlike the gentle mist of earlier, Perkin didn't find this precipitation refreshing. This would make life miserable, but as a consolation to Perkin, he understood that it would make life miserable for German sentries and snipers as well.

Perkin increased his speed moving through and over the rocks, and the olive groves on the mountainside were just barely visible in the rain. The slope of Mount Sammucro flattened out in front of him, became shallower and less rocky, and revealed land where Italian farmers had terraced the mountainside and cultivated olive trees for generations.

The olive groves were his first objectives, and he understood that there were plusses and minuses to leaving the rock-strewn part of the hill. Olive trees are evergreens, and they offered better cover than the rocks—particularly from a sharp-eyed sentry or sniper on the mountain. The terraces were relatively flat and they offered Perkin the opportunity to advance more quickly across the mountainside. On the other hand, he thought, the cover might apply to German outposts as well, and the relatively flat terraces perhaps offered enough soil for German mining.

Perkin was looking for a place to wait out the remaining daylight, a perch where he could look for the escaped sniper, and he saw a warren of rocks and crawled into it. The vantage wasn't ideal. He had little visibility directly below his position on the slope unless he lifted himself onto the rock. Being in a little depression, he had some relief from the sound of fierce combat in the valley, but the artillery still ripped overhead. Perkin could also hear the drone of aircraft. He had no idea where they might be headed, but there was no visibility to speak of on the slope. Friend or foe, he thought, he was safe from above.

Perkin's stomach was growling, and he pulled his canteen out and took a drink of water, then unwrapped and ate an emergency ration chocolate bar. It wasn't very tasty, but it had much-needed calories. The bar was no substitute for a meal, and he was even beginning to regret leaving the mutton stew behind. He had another C-ration kit, but decided to hold it for his return. He would have to make do with the chocolate bar.

After Perkin had finished with his little meal, he took stock of his own physical state. His chin and his nose had quit bleeding, but his face hurt abominably. His hands were even worse, particularly his left hand, which throbbed painfully. Perkin considered unwrapping his bandages and applying sulfa powder to the wounds, but it was pointless in the rain.

It was time to take a look outside of his rock palace and see if he could identify any pickets or traps between his position and the first olive grove. Perkin pulled his German field glasses out of the leather box on his web belt—he had decided to keep those—and he tightened his collar around his neck to keep the freezing rain from trickling down his back. He lay on his stomach and began creeping to a large boulder. The best way to scout from a rocky position was to look from under a rock's edge if possible or from its side if necessary, and he was fortunate to be able to view most of the slope down to the olive grove.

He slowly and systematically began to scan the hillside. Over the course of twenty minutes, he looked at every rock and bush that was within his sight. Nothing. It was as if he were the sole person on the slope of Mount Sammucro. He began to push back from his position—he decided to try to make it to the grove in the rainstorm—when he heard a sharp explosion below him on the slope. Steel balls went whirring over his head, and the terrible screaming below him chilled his bones worse than any cold rain ever could.

1445 Hours
Mount Rotondo Spur, Italy

Sam marveled once again at the miracle of the American experience. Here he was, he thought, fighting a war on the distant shores of another continent, and the American military was able to get mail to him that was postmarked less than a month ago.

He had received the letter from Margaret a day before, but in their frantic preparations to move out, he had not found the opportunity to read it. It was ironic that he was on the front line now and he found he had a moment or two to spare between rain showers.

The German counterattack of that morning had been the sole attempt of the day to push the Texans off of their newly won possessions. *Well*, he thought, *the sole* armored *attempt of the day*. There had been several infantry thrusts on Mount Lungo since then, and the artillery pounding was nearly ceaseless, but that too was primarily directed at the defenders of southern Mount Lungo. The spur had been shelled several times, but it was clear that the spur was secondary to the mount in the eyes of the Germans.

In the aftermath of the counterattack, Sam had done a quick muster of his platoon. Several minor casualties, but no fatalities, thank God. Even if his bazooka team was still shaking from their experience, everyone seemed as upbeat as soldiers could be in these miserable conditions. More than a few soldiers had made the point to come shake his hand. Some would look at the ground as if he were a stern uncle, rather than a young man their own age, and shyly mumble things like "We sure showed them, Lieutenant." Others, particularly the grizzled old hands that Sam had known since before the Louisiana maneuvers, showed great familiarity to the officer and slapped him on the back and just grinned. He couldn't help but grin back—he understood what they meant.

Not all the soldiers were tough and grizzled. Most weren't, in fact. Most were steady, earnest young men who didn't want to fight, but would; who didn't want to be in Europe, but made the best of it; and who didn't want to fulfill the thousand exhausting duties of a soldier, but did so without *serious* complaint. Sam had a few malingerers—rotten apples that would shirk their duties, complain vociferously, and go to sick call for a runny nose—but today they were quiet. It was a pleasant surprise.

He pulled the letter from his coat pocket and looked at the skies. It would rain again soon, but he had some time. Sam opened the letter and began reading:

Taft Ranch, Texas
October 31, 1943

Hey Baby,
 By the time you get this letter, it will be a whole year since I've seen you. I can't say that the time is flying away, because it isn't—it's just

hard to imagine a year without you in my life. Yet I look around and I see you everywhere—when I look at those nasty deer heads on your study wall or when I walk by the stables or ride along the fences. Sometimes I go to the closet and smell your shirts, or I look at your boots or your hat and just start bawling like a little girl. Enough of that! But I do wish I could see you in person. At least it's true that absence makes the heart grow fonder. I miss you so much that I almost can't sleep at night—sometimes I go into town to stay at Mother's, or with Old Perkin and Anna, just to be in a house with family.

Please tell Perkin that I'm very happy he's found an Italian girlfriend. Gianina sounds very nice, and I've always thought that he needs a feminine touch in his life—I just hope she knows what she's in for. You don't need to tell me that she's not as pretty as me (although I appreciate the thought); I'm not the insecure or jealous type, and I know you're forever wrapped around my little finger.

Sam felt bad. Margaret still hadn't heard about Gianina's death, and he knew that it'd be a shock when she learned of how she died. He grinned though when he read her comment on jealousy—while she would deny it, Margaret was precisely the jealous type.

We're excited to hear any news about the division (I know that you can't say much), but the paper said that it was touch and go at Salerno. And yet all you could find to write about was the bad food, your athlete's foot (and scratchy t----t paper). Ha ha. While amusing, I expect better re-

*porting from the front! I want to know what my
Little Bear is up to!*

*I've got good news and bad news for you.
The good news is that everyone is doing well.
The weather is lovely. Sunshine every day and a
beautiful cool breeze off the bay. Hurricane sea-
son ends today, and there were only two storms
in the Gulf all summer. One went ashore near
Houston in July, and another blew past us and
went up into Louisiana about a month ago. So
while you were being shot at, Alice and I were
watching some lovely waves on Mustang Island.
She's still pretty down, but there's something electrifying about the waves on that beach. It doesn't
matter how low you feel when you go, you always leave feeling uplifted. We sat and watched
a flight of pelicans cruise along the shoreline, and
they flew with more precision than any of the
navy pilots from Corpus that are always over the
ranch. I know it's not fair that we were enjoy-
ing our day at the beach while you were working
so hard, but we didn't know the division was in
combat then.*

Alice was a friend of Margaret's from Rockport. She
had dated Perkin some years before but had not seemed
inclined to wait for him to settle down, and she had married a Rockport car salesman named Fred in the summer of 1941. Margaret had been Alice's maid of honor,
and Sam had taken leave and attended the wedding. He
thought that Fred, Alice's husband, was a fun and ener-
getic man and like Perkin, he had a long list of very funny
Aggie jokes which he loved to tell. Fred enlisted in the
navy a week after Pearl Harbor; reported to his first ship,
USS Cushing, in San Francisco in August 1942; and died

with seventy-one of his shipmates when *Cushing* was sunk off of Savo Island on November 13 of that year.

Sam didn't know how he'd be able to make it through the day if something happened to Maggie, and he had felt terrible for Alice, who was a bright, vivacious girl. *But Maggie's right. There's no substitute for a day on the water to lift your spirits. I could use a day on the beach right about now,* Sam thought, then added dryly, *a beach where no one's shooting at me.*

When he was in high school, Sam and Perkin would cut class, get a cooler of Shiner beer, and spend the day playing and fishing in the surf. Even with the inevitable certainty that they would catch hell when they got home, it was always worth it. As if Margaret were reading his mind over time and distance, her next sentence made him smile:

> *Yesterday, Old Perkin and I went fishing, and I out-caught him seven trout to five. Ha ha. He got so grumpy from being beaten by a girl that maybe I shouldn't do my victory dance around him any more . . . .*

Sam laughed out loud. Margaret was highly competitive and the most patient fisherman he'd ever seen, and she'd frequently beat Sam. However, she was no better a winner than Old Perkin was a loser, and Sam was sure that the old man found her victory dance as irritating as Sam did.

> *There is some bad news, and I don't know how to break it to you other than to just say it: we had to put Old Igor down.*

Instantly, Sam's throat tightened. Igor was a champion bull, one of the best Santa Gertrudis bulls that he'd

ever seen, and to add to his sorrow, the old bull had belonged to his father. Certainly, he was a cantankerous old
thing who would challenge anyone—including Sam. Perkin particularly had always given Igor a wide berth. While
Perkin felt the bull's animus towards him was unfair—he
had named Igor as a calf, after all—discretion remained
the better part of valor.

> *We don't know how it happened, but his
> hind left leg (driver's side) got broken. It tore
> my heart up to see him limp so, and the vet said
> he couldn't do anything, so I decided to put him
> down. I know he's wasn't a pet or anything, but
> you always seemed fond of the beast, so I'm very
> sorry. I don't know if it was the right thing to do,
> but I decided to have ~~his pelt~~ his hide tanned and
> saved for you. Maybe you can take down some
> of those horrible old deer heads and hang him in
> your study. I hate to say it, and I mean no offense
> to Old Igor, but his brisket was extraordinarily
> tough, and the steaks were even worse. I donated
> what was left of the old brute to the Presbyte-
> rian School for Mexican Girls in town, and they
> made a tolerable guisada out of his loins.*

Sam reread the last paragraph and didn't know
whether to laugh or cry. On the one hand, he was pretty
fond of the creature, but he never would have wasted the
money to have his hide specially tanned and mounted. On
the other hand, it was kind of shocking to think of eating
his champion bull, and he could have told Margaret that
there was nothing, absolutely nothing, on Igor that was
tender. Even though guisada was not one of his favorite
dishes, the mention of it made his stomach growl.

> *Mr. Bob of the King Ranch delivered two bulls to us this week. One's a calf; the other a year old. The calf was a personal present to you, and Mr. Bob said to tell you that the one-year-old is a descendant of Monkey. I hope that's good because he charged a pretty penny for him, but he's a fine-looking bull in any case. Given your circumstances, I named him Salerno (I think it sounds better than Paestum) and the calf I named Octavius. He has the potential to grow up to be an emperor. Get it? He came from the King Ranch, ha, ha, and if he grows into his potential, then I'll call him Augustus.*

Sam wasn't sure what she meant and why one would change the name of a bull calf, but he didn't care. He was delighted that Margaret was taking an active interest in the ranch, and with the help of a very good foreman, seemed to be doing a good job in its day-to-day operations. She was as smart as anyone he knew, including Perkin, and was plenty tough. Sam knew that running a ranch was fine with Maggie as long as he was there to do it with, but this was not the path that she had wanted to take. She had told him that she wanted children and wanted them quickly. *Well,* he thought, *that one's gonna have to wait.*

It began to drizzle, and Sam quickly skimmed through the remainder of the letter. It was mostly ranch business and small stuff, and it broke his heart to read it. That was the life he wanted for himself—running the ranch with Margaret. He should be in Texas, not sitting in a mud-filled foxhole in the Italian mountains. *I'd kill to go fishing with Maggie. My God, just a quick walk from Old Perkin's house, wade out a hundred yards into the bay, and cast out for the trout. Reel 'em in as fast as I can and maybe take the fish home to the ranch for a fry; drink a beer or two with Maggie and watch the sun go down and the stars come out together.*

1450 Hours
Mount Sammucro, Italy

Despite the screaming, Perkin did not move for a long time. He resumed his lookout over the slope and waited to see if there was any reaction to the mine detonation—for that surely was what had happened.

The screams for help were in German, although they oddly sounded English—a holdover from the English language's Anglo-Saxon ancestors. The cries, "*Hilfe! Hilfe!*" were getting weaker, and Perkin decided that no one had noticed the explosion in the downpour. Although he hated to move now, he thought he would see if he could discretely check out the situation. There was always the possibility that a ruse similar to the one he had contemplated was being tried on him, and if help was on the way, he was loathe to give away his presence by helping a wounded German soldier. But a soldier was wounded, German or not, and he thought he would at least look.

As he descended down the slope towards where he believed the mine had exploded, he moved slower and more cautiously than ever—his senses on alert for sound or movement. But outside of the continuing downpour, and the little streams that had appeared from nowhere, there was neither sound nor movement on the mountain.

The German was in a little hollow in the rocks, much like the one Perkin had just left. It was only thirty yards from his position, and the soldier had obviously been preparing a sniping position when he tripped the mine. When Perkin first glanced over a rock into the little hollow, he thought that the German soldier was dead, but then he saw movement of the man's chest. The rock walls had magnified the damage from the mine, and Perkin was shocked to see a band of blood and flesh sprayed in a nearly perfect semi-circle on the rocks. The rain was already washing it away, and before long, there would be no geologic record of what had happened to this soldier.

With his Thompson ready, Perkin walked crouching along the rocks until he could kneel next to the German soldier. It was the *feldwebel* sniper that he had seen before. The soldier had pulled himself up to a sitting position, and Perkin could see that his right leg was nearly severed below the knee. It remained attached to the German's body by a single ligament and strips of lacerated skin, and Perkin watched mutely as each heartbeat pulsed more of the German's life into the water and mud in the hollow. The soldier had made a tourniquet around his thigh with his rifle strap, but Perkin knew that it was a hopeless gesture—a prolonging of the inevitable—as there were more holes in the soldier's body than even a team of medics could hope to patch. The sergeant's eyes were closed, but he was groaning and mumbling to himself. He opened his eyes as Perkin knelt beside him, and the German watched as Perkin removed the dagger from the soldier's belt— there was no holster for a pistol, and his shattered rifle lay several feet away.

"Afraid that I was going to put up a fight?" The German's English was spoken with a thick accent, but he was understandable.

Perkin smiled at the soldier, a kind smile reserved for a brave adversary in a hopeless situation. "Well, some of you boys are pretty tough hombres. I wouldn't put it past you."

"*Ach* . . . I think my fighting days have ended. Were you in the cave?" The sergeant's hands were trembling uncontrollably, and his teeth were gritted, but it was apparent that he was grateful for the companionship of someone, anyone—even an enemy soldier. It was a terrible thing to die alone.

Perkin nodded.

"In four years of war, you scared me like I was never scared before. I was setting up here to kill you when you passed." The sergeant offered a shrug as if to say, "Don't take it personally."

Perkin understood. It had been his plans as well to kill the other soldier on the mountainside, but the circumstances had oddly changed. "Can I do something for you, Sergeant?"

The German sighed and considered for a second before nodding, but when he spoke he asked, "Am I going to live, Captain? Please, the truth."

"No. You ain't. I can't fix you up myself, and by the time I carried you to either your lines or mine, I reckon you'd be gone."

"*Ach* . . . I thought so. Then, yes. You can do some things for me, *und vielleicht*, uh, maybe we can exchange." The German grimaced as a spasm of pain passed through his body, then he controlled his expression.

"Well partner, I don't know that we're in a position to swap belt buckles or nothin', but what'd ya have in mind?"

The German smiled weakly, and said, "You are welcome to my belt buckle. I don't think I'll need it, but I would like some morphine. On my belt is a first aid kit. Please hurry."

Perkin pulled away the German's greatcoat, exposing a bloody tunic. On the sergeant's belt were several pouches for ammunition, binoculars, and his first aid kit. From the last pouch he pulled out a box that he was familiar with—a box of five American-issued ER Squibb morphine syrettes. He raised an eyebrow at the German who shrugged wearily.

"I took it from an American prisoner at Salerno. I was hoping not to need it."

Perkin pulled open the sergeant's tunic and undershirt, pulled the cover off a syrette, and pushed the wire plunger down through the needle and into the foil, exposing the morphine to the needle. He discarded the wire and pushed the syrette into the soldier's armpit and squeezed the morphine through the needle. Out of habit, Perkin hung the empty syrette on the German's uniform by bending the needle through the greatcoat's lapel, and then he pulled the overcoat together. Perkin looked through the soldier's light pack and pulled out a gray woolen blanket, tucking it around the soldier's body.

"Thank you, Captain. It won't be long now. Can you do two things more for me? *Bitte?*" Although it would take several minutes for the morphine to take full effect, the soldier began to relax, the pain eased somewhat from his pinched white face, and his rapid breathing began to slow.

"Yes, of course."

"First, will you pray with me? I would like to let the Almighty know I'm coming." The German coughed, then groaned weakly. "I guess I should ask: do you believe in God?"

"Mostly." It was a question that Perkin grappled with himself, and while he would have answered "of course" to an American chaplain or even to Sam, he felt a dying man deserved an honest answer, and "mostly" was the best he could do.

"Ah . . . you wonder why God would allow this war? Maybe the things you've seen make you question your faith?"

"It ain't that simple, but you're right. We have a phrase in our army, 'there are no atheists in a foxhole—'"

The German interrupted Perkin, "We say the same."

"And in those times, I pray for salvation, and I pray for guidance and help and safety, and just about everything else I can think of. But when I have time to think about these things, I wonder about God, and how a good loving Father could allow this wholesale slaughter of generations of His children, and I'm afraid that free will isn't a sufficient answer. I wonder why He would create a man like Hitler—no offense, Sergeant—or even allow wars to start."

"He also created Bach, I think. And Mozart and Luther. And Goethe. As for the Führer, we both know where he will spend eternity. You aren't Catholic, are you?" This was said with a very faint smile.

"No, Presbyterian. Why?"

"Most Catholics in Germany don't see Martin Luther as one of His crowning achievements. But I do. I'm from Kehl, which is a little pocket of Lutherans near Catholic Strasbourg. Lovely cathedral over there—a beautiful monument to God. I could see the spire from my house." The German soldier was beginning to drift a little, and his arm jerked as if he were falling asleep.

"I've heard that it is. Maybe when the war is over, I'll go see it," Perkin said gently. The German's last moments were drawing close.

"I'm so very glad to hear it. That is my other favor. I have a letter to my wife and sons in my pocket. Would you please post it with the Red Cross, or even take it to Kehl if it is convenient? *Meine Frau* will make you *Schnitzel und Bratkartoffeln*, oh, *mein Gott*, what a cook . . . ."

The sergeant stopped and swallowed hard, then looked at Perkin with the slightest touch of despair as silent tears mixed with the rain on his face. He said, "My comrades may not have the opportunity to recover my body, and I want her to have this. I think we will not win this war, and if that is God's will, then so be it. Captain, I pray your armies will be more merciful than our own have been, so please show me this mercy and do as I ask. Tell Sofie that I died as a man, not as *ein Soldat*. Now, we had better pray, good captain, then I shall do something for you. Do you know the Lord's Prayer? Will you say it with me?" The German offered a hand covered in blood.

Perkin nodded and grasped the German's hand. In a voice so soft Perkin could barely hear it, the soldier began in German, and Perkin whispered the familiar words in English:

> *Vater unser, der Du bist im Himmel,*
> *Our Father, which art in heaven*
> *Geheiligt werde Dein Name,*
> *Hallowed be thy name,*
> *Dein Reich komme.*
> *Thy kingdom come,*
> *Dein Wille geschehe,*
> *Thy will be done,*
> *Wie im Himmel, also auch auf Erden.*
> *In earth, as it is in heaven*
> *Unser täglich Brot gieb uns heute,*
> *Give us this day, our daily bread*
> *Und vergeib uns unsere Schuld,*
> *And forgive us our debts*
> *As wir vergieben unsern Schuldigern.*
> *As we forgive our debtors.*
> *Und führe uns nicht in Versuchung,*
> *And lead us not into temptation,*
> *Sondern erlöse uns von dem Übel.*
> *But deliver us from evil*
> *Denn Dein ist das Reich und die Kraft*
> *For thine is the kingdom and the power*
> *und die Herrlichkeit, in Ewigkeit.*
> *And the glory forever and ever.*
> *Amen.*

"*Vielen Dank.* Do you think that's good enough?"

"Good enough for what, partner?" Perkin looked at the German sergeant with something approaching awe. Even though the man had to be in terrible pain, and even in shock, the sergeant remained coherent. He had visibly relaxed, and the shaking had subsided. His breathing, however, had slowed to the point that Perkin feared that each breath would be his last.

"Good enough for heaven."

"I . . . I reckon that it is. Sergeant, what is your name?"

"Krieger. Wilhelm Krieger. I was named for the last emperor. He was half English, you know."

"He was half mad, you know."

Krieger laughed a short sharp bark, then gasped for breath. "That was the English half. Too much inbreeding. His grandmother married her first cousin. Consanguinity issues, yes? I was a horse breeder before the war, and was always more careful than the royalty of Europe. That's why my horses weren't idiots like they were." Krieger seemed ready to wrap things up. He said, "Well, my captain, for a man who I would have killed an hour ago, you have shown me great kindness and respect . . . I have some things for you. Reach into the pocket of my greatcoat."

Perkin did and pulled out a piece of paper. Using his body to shield it imperfectly from the rain, he saw that it was a hand-drawn mine chart of Mount Sammucro on one side and another chart of the valley between San Pietro and Mount Lungo on the other. Looking at the chart of Sammucro, Perkin noted that the third trail from the top was marked as extensively mined almost to his cave.

Perkin whistled and said, "That's why you were so worried on that trail."

Krieger nodded, "*Ja.* This will help you, but it is not perfect. Obviously. Damned pioneers thought they were being clever by mining a sniper's nest without informing the snipers most likely to use it. Damned fools have killed me." Krieger looked Perkin in the eyes and asked, "You are scouting, yes? Not going to kill today?"

Perkin considered his answer briefly, then nodded. "I'm just looking at defenses. We'll take San Pietro in a few days, and I thought we ought to know what we are up against. I don't plan to fight today."

"*Gut.* If it spares you the trip, all you will find there is the best army to ever march through this godforsaken valley." The German laughed weakly, but he was proud to be able to still laugh—weak or not.

Perkin joined in the quiet laughter. He liked the German's spirit and the challenge. "Thanks for the advice, Wilhelm. I see you still have a little piss and vinegar left in you."

"*Ja.* I am tough, but I will die soon, and you have helped me. So I will help you. Move at twilight. Stay *above* the upper path, don't drop down to the olive orchard. There are snipers there. Waiting for you."

Perkin laughed again, thinking this was another challenge from Sergeant Krieger. "Waiting for me, you say? Maybe I'll drop down and see them."

"*Nein!* I'm not joking, Captain. They are good snipers—not as good as the one who killed Hans though. *Mein Gott!* That must have been eight hundred meters and uphill—I would be proud of a shot like that. We were to have the upper path; they took the lower routes. We were waiting for you, Captain."

Perkin saw the earnestness on the German's face and felt a sudden chill. "What . . . what do you mean, waiting for me? Who do you think I am?"

"Captain Berger, an officer of the Texas Army. We heard you were coming this morning to scout out our defenses. No one took it too seriously. It seemed like nonsense—officers don't do these things—but I'm glad to see the Abwehr got something right for a change."

1810 Hours
Mount Rotondo Spur, Italy

For the tenth time that afternoon, Sam said a silent prayer for Gianina, and he thanked her for the warm sweater that he was wearing underneath his poncho and his jacket. It had rained all afternoon, and the temperature hovered a few degrees above freezing. Sam tried to stay active by walking back and forth along his platoon lines, but a German sniper had taken a shot at him in the early afternoon, and he was far more circumspect now.

The sniper had tried a long shot—Sam didn't even hear the sound of the rifle firing, but his hearing had yet to recover—and it had rained hard since then, so he doubted that the sniper was close enough to see him in the rain. But the sniper had only missed by inches before and Sam decided to take no chances, and he conscientiously remained as bent over as he could until he was in a defiladed position on the American side of the hill.

On Captain Spaulding's direction, Sam set up his command post in the lee of the hill. Any further back and he would be exposed in the open near the highway; any further forward, and he would be on the crest of the little spur. They had prepared defensive positions that they could occupy in minutes on the forward slope, and then they began to dig again on the American side—only a handful of well-dug-in troops remained on the far side of the spur. It was simply too dangerous, but the near side—the American side—offered scant protection as well. Even the defilade of the hill was susceptible to artillery fire and mortar fire from Mount Lungo.

Most of those mortars were engaged in the battle for the mount itself, but if an observer on the German side happened to spot activity on or near the spur, a mortar would shift fire and lob rounds at the offending activity for a few minutes. Most of those rounds had little effect as the troops remained in fighting positions most of the time, but it simply wasn't possible to remain in the mud and water indefinitely. Several of Sam's soldiers were pulled out of foxholes by squad mates—they were unable to move from the cold—and a few were sent back on jeeps, running a gauntlet of mortar fire, to a battalion aid station to be treated for hypothermia. It was a bone-chilling, soaking wetness under fire that never ended.

If the soldiers thought that the day couldn't get any more miserable, they were wrong. Artillery shifted back to the spur—this time in the form of air bursts. The shells exploded down on the troops in an unendurable rain of white hot fragments, the fragments themselves claiming more victims than the explosions.

Several soldiers leapt out of their foxholes to run to the rear, only to be cut down by the shrapnel, their cries for help lost in the terrible din of the explosions. American counter-battery fire attempted to bring the German batteries to bear, and it appeared to Sam for a moment that it was slackening, but then it began again. He and his soldiers had no choice but to bury themselves deeper into the freezing mud and ride the nightmare out.

2139 Hours
San Pietro, Italy

Perkin was finally close enough to the village that he could hit its church with a well-thrown rock if he wanted to. He was on the hillside above the town. Finally. The last part of his voyage—from the death site of Sergeant Krieger to the northern edge of the village—had taken him seven hours to finish. It was a distance less than a mile.

He had stretched Sergeant Krieger out on the ground, covering his body with the blanket, and had then returned to his own hollow in the rocks. Before he had sat down there again, though, he probed the area carefully with his knife, looking for mines. He found none, and he sat and thought about the events of the afternoon.

Sergeant Krieger had died like a man, and he had died like a soldier—regardless of how he wished to be remembered. Perkin was impressed with the soldier's fortitude and bravery when facing death, and he wondered if he would be able to be as calm as the German had been. That he liked Krieger was also an issue that he had thought about while waiting for twilight. He had been prepared to kill the man, and yet he came to find that he respected his courage deeply. Perkin wasn't the only soldier during countless generations of warfare to discover that he had more in common with his enemy than he cared to admit.

The shared prayer had also touched Perkin more than he thought possible, and while the words were different, the cadence of the prayer was familiar. It reminded Perkin that, as Abraham Lincoln had noted in his second inaugural address, he prayed to the same God as his enemy. Old Perkin had made him memorize the entire address when he was in high school, and there was a line dancing through the background of his memory that seemed appropriate to his musings. *What was it that Lincoln said? 'The prayers of both could not be answered; that of neither has been answered fully. The Almighty has his own purposes.' That's for damn sure,* Perkin thought. *I just wish He'd give me an insight now and then.*

Unfortunately, Sergeant Krieger had offered little insight on that subject before he went to meet his maker. In his last breaths, he told Perkin that an intelligence officer had personally called on Krieger's commanding officer and requested the immediate deployment of the snipers.

It seemed that Perkin had somehow come to the attention of German intelligence, although for the life of him,
Perkin could not divine how. There was no further light to
be shed from the sergeant, whose hand relaxed in Perkin's
as he simply stopped breathing.

Perkin realized as he crept up the mountain, past the
upper path, and then through the German razor wire in
the near dark, that although he was an impatient man
by temperament, that he could inch along, slow and me-
thodical, and enjoy himself. He tried to remain focused,
his senses attuned to danger as best he could. Thoughts of
Sam and the company crept in as it looked to Perkin like
the forward positions in the valley were taking a pounding, but Perkin found he could remain on task pretty
well—the fear of death or dismemberment was a remarkable tonic for flagging attention.

Twice he had passed outposts of German sentries. In
neither case had he come to their attention. There were no
dogs, for which he was grateful, although he was uncertain how sensitive their noses would be in the continuing
downpour. He was more grateful for Krieger's greatcoat.

Perkin had debated about taking the added risk of
wearing a German uniform coat over his own, and decided that the odds were good that he'd be shot if captured in
any case—German uniform or not. The downside, which
he thought of after the fact, was that he might have eliminated the mountain route home. Sooner or later, the German Army would send a team out to look for Krieger and
his partner. If they found his body, the Germans would
find Krieger laid out and tended to without a greatcoat
and helmet. Only time would tell if he had made an error,
but either way, the act was done. Krieger's coat was large
enough to fit over his own uniform, although the German
soldier's helmet rode absurdly low on his head. His fingers
were too cold and swollen to be able to adjust the leather

straps in the liner, so he shrugged and peered out from under the brim.

Now that he was at San Pietro, he was uncertain of what to do. The defenses, the guns and battlements, would be on the other side of the village—maybe a quarter of a mile from his position. He could just try walking through the village, but he was done for if he were challenged. The coat and helmet only helped at a distance or in the dark; his leggings and brown woolen pants would be a dead giveaway. Besides, his Thompson had a distinct shape, and he would look just as out of place without any weapon at all.

Perkin wanted a better vantage; either from elevation such as the church bell tower or perhaps a position from the front looking up. If he could get into a building in the village, he might be able to see the siting of the defenses, but how to do it? There was no easy answer, and he decided to stick with his original plan and cross behind the village, then come up from underneath on the German side of the valley—from the west-northwest. The aerial photos, and what little Perkin could see of the village through the fog and smoke of war, showed plenty of remaining foliage for cover. There were also reports of ancient caves to the northwest of San Pietro, so perhaps that would be a good place to scout first.

Perkin would take two or three steps in the dark and then pause to listen. Movement in the dark was especially tricky in hills and mountains, and he walked as he was trained—with the weight on his back foot and his forward foot tentatively seeking *terra firma*. Using this method, he could make slow but steady progress over the uneven ground behind the village. After a short distance, no more than a hundred yards, the terrain began to descend rapidly. Perkin realized that he was heading into the gullies on the far side of San Pietro, and after a terrifying slide on loose rock, where he just barely managed to keep his footing in the dark, he sat down. After the pounding of his heart returned to normal, he carefully slid down the hill on his backside.

In the dark it was hard to say how far his elevation had dropped—anywhere from twenty to two hundred feet—because the pitch black night and the rain played tricks on his imagination, and echoing artillery and small arms fire added to the surreal nature of his position. Several times, he thought he saw figures standing in the dark only to have tree branches brush his face when he reached out to the figures.

His panic rose several times, and he felt the odd sensation of claustrophobia—even though he was in the open, an eerie sense that he risked being crushed by the mountain weighed on his mind. Walking along the floor of the gully, he tripped and fell. He had fallen many times, but this time he landed on a mound of fresh dirt—mud, really. A few steps more and he stepped in another mound of mud. Then another. His feet slipped out from under him, and Perkin landed next to yet another mound. As his hands and feet served to outline the shape of the mound, he came to the horrifying realization that he was in a graveyard, and he was face to face with a grave.

Another panic, and a bolt of adrenaline shot through his body. He jumped to his feet and walked rapidly backwards away from the grave, only to trip over another mound of dirt. This time he landed hard on his back, the wind knocked out of him. Stunned, Perkin lay among the dead. Through sheer force of will, he began to calm himself—the only other option was running panicked through the dark, and he had already seen what that might bring.

Slowly, his heart rate returned to normal, and his breathing slowed down. As the rain fell onto his face, he thought of Sam's ranch, and the memory brought first calmness and then, several minutes later, a rueful self-mocking smile in the dark. Perkin and Sam could have walked the length and breadth of his huge estate blindfolded with never a worry about a consequence more severe than stepping in a pile of manure. No cliffs to run over, no soldiers to fight, no unmarked graves—just honest-to-God flat Texas ranch land. While Perkin almost never pined for Texas like Sam did, he silently wished for home this time.

After the mocking smile faded, Perkin's intellect took over, and he began to take stock of his situation. As he washed the mud off his hands and face in the rain, he thought about the graveyard. He wasn't in a neat, orderly, family plot in a churchyard—he was surrounded by recent burial sites that seemed to be haphazardly laid out. *They wouldn't be German graves, not here,* he thought. *Graves for the Italian villagers? Not mass graves, thank God, but why so many fresh gravesites? What's going on here? Starvation? Disease? Executions?*

He stood carefully and began to work his way back to the gully wall. He discovered several more graves with the toe of his boot, and carefully stepped over them until he ran into the rock wall. Perkin began to work his way down the slope again, trailing his hand along the rock wall, step after infinitely slow step. Then the wall disappeared from the touch of his left hand. There was a sharp bend in the gully, it seemed, and as he turned to continue his trace of the wall he heard voices. Whispered voices.

Perkin froze and slowly brought his Thompson up. He took another step. Then another. The dim glow of a fire emerged from the darkness of the night and rain, and it seemed to be flickering from a hole in the rocks. As he got closer, he could see the light reflecting off the wall of a cave, and he could smell the smoke of the fire. The Idols of the Cave came to Perkin's mind for no logical reason at all, and setting aside Sir Francis Bacon for the moment, Perkin knelt to the cave entrance to listen to the voices. Female voices, speaking in Italian. *Of course, dumbass*, he said to himself, *what other language would they be speaking?*

Would they be willing to help? Could they help? The thoughts ran through Perkin's mind. He remembered vividly that not all Italians supported the Allies—only a few months before, a betrayal of his patrol by an Italian policeman had led to the deaths of three of his soldiers. Yet most Italians had been delighted to help him in any way that they could. The rewards were possibly great—a guide or perhaps a demobilized Italian soldier who was familiar with the German defenses—versus the risk of betrayal.

2314 Hours
San Pietro, Italy

   Perkin slipped off his German greatcoat and helmet, and laid them quietly at the entrance. He slung his Thompson, pulled his pistol, and crept into the cave entrance. The walls were smoother than he expected—maybe they weren't natural caves—and there was a small corridor leading into a chamber.

   Perkin crept closer and listened. His Italian was not close to fluent, but he had learned some of the language in his few months in Italy. He found that it was similar to Spanish with many key cognates, and as he had told Sam before Gianina's death, "There's no better way to learn a language than havin' a native girlfriend, a glass or two of wine, and a lack of normal inhibition."

   The conversation was ordinary, although whispered in intense tones. As far as he could make out, it was about who would talk to the Germans about food. Suddenly, the whispered conversation dropped off and Perkin leaned forward towards the end of the corridor. His face was down, pointed to the floor of the cave, in the manner of people trying to focus on hearing, so at the last second he heard, but didn't see, the shovel that was swung at his head.

2340 Hours
Mount Rotondo Spur, Italy

When Sam withdrew most of his troops from the far slope of the spur, he had left pickets with a field telephone line back to his command post—half of Italy was covered with telephone wires like some incomprehensible spider's web.

Once darkness fell, his outpost had reported movement on the far side of wire the Texans had strung during a lull in the shelling, and Sam had silently moved a squad back into position on the other slope. When no attack materialized, he called for star shells—flares—to illuminate the valley, and they had caught a German patrol cutting their razor wire. Three enemy soldiers had been killed, but one unharmed grenadier had surrendered and been taken prisoner.

The rain was turning to sleet, and although Sam had put his soldiers on fifty-fifty—half on alert and half sleeping—only the oldest campaigners were able to get much in the way of shut-eye. Sergeant Kenton was one. Sam and Kenton were splitting duties and Kenton was snoring away calmly, wrapped in a blanket under a poncho. He wasn't laying down, at least, not horizontally. Instead, he had found a smooth incline at the base of the spur and dug a little trench around it to channel the streams of water around him. He lay down on his side at an angle of forty-five degrees from head to toe and was asleep in minutes. Periodically he would slide down the hill, grunt and wake up, and reestablish his position. Sam was jealous. He doubted he would get much sleep—and his waking counter was at forty-two hours and running.

Compounding the soldiers' difficulties, most of the men had begun to experience cramping and diarrhea during the afternoon hours. Among the enlisted soldiers, it was nearly universal within the company. The officers, who had dined as the guests of the regimental commander, had no symptoms and Sam suspected that the troops' last cooked meal before leaving the line of departure a full day before had been contaminated. The exception to the officers had been the duty officer, Lieutenant Beams, who ate with the troops—and he was affected as well. Sam was meeting with Captain Spaulding earlier when he heard a groan in the bushes on the other side of Victory Road. A white-faced Lieutenant Beams emerged, offered a rueful grin, and groaned out, "Bowels: Green and Evacuating," before jogging gingerly and doubled-over back to his platoon.

It was a moment to savor, the humor nearly exquisite for soldiers, but neither Sam nor Bill could laugh. Two of the battalion's three rifle companies had been deployed in the taking of one little hill and half of another. The two companies were down nearly sixty men, the casualties growing by the hour. At Lieutenant Colonel Wranosky's direction, Frank McCarter's platoon had been deployed onto Mount Lungo and was now fighting under the tactical control of Charlie Company.

The battalion surgeon, a first lieutenant from San Antonio, had come through Sam's forward positions twice to check on the injured men. Some received adjustments to bandages, one soldier was pulled off the line and sent to an aid station, others just got a smile and a slap on the back from an officer they'd known from happier times.

Now the battalion surgeon was handing out bismuth tablets to the medics to dispense.

He jogged over to Sam and Bill, nodded to both and said cordially, "It's gonna be a long, shitty night—ha, ha. Your boys are gonna need to get warm and dry, but y'all already know that. I'm gonna see if I can drum up some hot soup and coffee for your boys . . . it won't help the diarrhea at all, but I'm more concerned about hypothermia. Your men won't feel like eatin' because of the runs, but they absolutely need the calories as hard as some of 'em are shaking. Make sure they drink and replace their socks when they get a chance—they can wrap the wet ones around their bodies to dry them out. Sam, Bill—y'all alright? Need any tablets?"

"We're OK for now, Doc. If we need some, we can get 'em from the medics. No worries here." Bill answered for them both.

"Okie-doke. If nothing else happens, I'll be back through at daylight to check on y'all. You gentlemen have a wonderful evening."

"Thanks Doc, you too." As the doctor and two assistants headed back to the battalion aid station several hundred yards to the rear, Bill turned to Sam and said, "Don't know about you, but I hate the feel of wet socks around my waist. Alright Sam, I'll check on you later. Keep your head down."

2357 Hours
San Pietro, Italy

It was the slap in the face that brought Perkin back to consciousness. Not a friendly tap that someone might use to revive a drunken friend, but a hard, businesslike slap— a slap reserved for cheating husbands or enemy soldiers who have been taken prisoner by angry Italian women who have been evicted from their homes and forced to live in caves for weeks.

"Oh, Jesus, that hurt." Perkin mumbled in English. His left eye was completely closed, the rip in his nostril had been reopened, and he had the worst throbbing headache of his life. He was seated in a room of the cave, and his hands were bound together by strips of torn red-checked cloth—not that he could discern colors very well at the moment—and the pain in his hands was agonizing.

"We told the commander that if any more of his men tried to rape us again, we would cut their balls off. He said we were welcome to try." The speaker was a kneeling middle-aged woman with black hair, black clothes, and a murderous look in her black eyes. She was surrounded by a half dozen other women, each as angry looking as the one confronting Perkin.

Perkin didn't quite understand every word, but the tone was unmistakable. The knife that was pointing towards his groin was equally unambiguous as well. Perkin looked at her with his one good eye, an action that provoked another slap on his tender left side.

"Hey, sister! Knock that shit off! I'm an American! *Soy americano, soy americano!* No that ain't right," he corrected himself. "*Sono americano,* for Christ's sake."

That failed to have the desired effect. The woman turned and picked something off the floor and threw it in his lap. It was the German greatcoat. She spat in Perkin's face and hissed, "German pig!"

"I ain't German, you crazy bitches! Look at my flag. My flag!" Perkin twisted and showed the women the sleeve of his uniform, where he had sewn on a Lone Star flag.

That too led to an unsuccessful outcome, as a young girl identified the flag as Chilean, which then provoked a conversation that Perkin concluded was over why would a German pose as a Chilean.

"I ain't from Chile, honey. I'm from Texas. Texas! Does anyone speak English? Where are the men? *Dónde están los hombres?*"

The last question, posed in Spanish, seemed to confirm, to some of the women at least, that he was not German—although suspicions remained that he might be Chilean. His personal guard, however, was not convinced. She pointed the knife at his groin once more.

"Sister, I'd rather you not do that. For the love of God, does anyone here speak English?" Struggling to remember one of the first phrases he had learned in Italian, he implored, "*Parla inglese?*"

"English? You are English?" It was a male voice.

Perkin looked up and could barely see an older, stooped man walking through another entrance into the cave room. A young girl, maybe eight or nine, was leading him by the hand and by the set of his head, Perkin guessed that he was blind.

"No, I'm an American. An American soldier. Do you think you could explain that to the ladies before they cut away my reason for living?" Perkin gave a sigh of relief.

"Maybe. My granddaughter says that you are from Chile, and she tells me that the women think you are German. Can you explain this?"

The woman with the knife moved away and allowed the old man to sit in front of the Texan, but she and the knife stayed too close for Perkin's comfort. Perkin's suspicions about the old man were confirmed when he saw that his eyes were glazed over with cataracts.

"I'm an American. From Texas. The Texas flag kind of looks like the Chilean flag, except ours is all blue on one side, and theirs ain't. I speak Spanish, but not much Italian—so I thought I'd give that a try."

"What about the German uniform?"

"I took it off a German soldier who died on the mountain. I thought it would help me get closer to San Pietro."

"What are you doing here?"

The old man may have been blind, but he seemed very sharp—his English was excellent—but Perkin was getting tired of the questions. He wanted his hands untied, he wanted some medical attention, and he was beginning to think he wanted out of the cave.

"What do you think, partner? I came to look at the local pottery."

At this the old man laughed and used a very American aphorism in reply, "You may be disappointed. The Germans are like bulls in a china shop. What they don't break, they shit on. What is the American army going to do? Take San Pietro and save our pottery?"

"Sir, can you have my hands untied? They're killing me. Is there a doctor that can take a look at me? I can't see at all out of one of my eyes, and I can't really see well outta the other one, either."

At this the old man cackled, "We have a doctor, but he can't look at you. It's me, and I can't see out of either eye."

Chapter Eight

December 3, 1943
0015 Hours
Mount Rotondo Spur

The report was whispered in the darkness. The artillery had died off and for the moment, the front was quiet. The sleet had worsened and was beginning to accumulate. It piled on the rifles and helmets of the living in muddy foxholes and on the rifles and helmets of the dead on the battlefield.

Although Private Kulis was the younger and more junior of the two PFCs sitting with Lieutenant Taft, he gave the report. Neither the officer nor Private Pfadenhauer found anything odd about it—the young soldier was becoming more confident and authoritative by the day.

" . . . So he leaps out of the cave—maybe falls out is more accurate, sir—and slides about ten feet on his belly to this trail. When he got to his knees, he fired a magazine down the path towards San Pietro, but I doubt that he hit nothin'. That's when the clouds passed over, and we lost sight of him. We thought for a second that he was goin' straight off the cliff, sir, but I think he grabbed a-holt of the dead Kraut, and that stopped him."

"What do you think he did then?" Sam shivered thinking about his cousin going off the mountainside.

"Well, sir, you understand we couldn't see but . . . well, knowin' Cap'n Berger, I reckon he took off after the other Kraut. When we got back to the 143rd's outpost, we talked to a Cap'n Waskow, and Cap'n Berger hadn't passed through there. We waited there after dark another two or three hours then hitched a ride back here. Our chickenshit driver wouldn't bring us all the way, so we had to march the last couple miles along the highway, and Roscoe's got the scours and kept—"

"Shut up, Eddie!"

"—havin' to jump into the bushes. Relatively speakin', sir, 'cause there ain't many of them anymore."

"Don't worry about it, Howie. Everyone's got the scours. You don't, Kulis?" Sam was happy the soldiers were back. He had doubted they would have anything to report on Perkin, and while what they did have to say raised his anxiety for Perkin even higher, he told himself that his cousin was at least alive at last report.

"No sir. Never felt better."

"Alright. You boys get yourself some coffee or soup over there, and then report to Sergeant Kenton. We could use some more rifles."

0030 Hours
San Pietro, Italy

Perkin had been moved to a room much deeper into the cave through a maze of passages. He had been astounded by how extensive the cave system seemed to be. He was sitting in a chair, one of the few that had been hauled to the caves by the displaced residents of San Pietro, and it was a seat of honor.

The doctor, whose name was Bonucci, had asked one last question of Perkin before having his restraints taken off, and Perkin's answer had him laughing still. The question: "Who won the Stanley Cup in 1938?" was met with the somewhat surly reply of "How the hell should I know? We don't have ice in Texas."

Doctor Bonucci was a well-traveled and erudite physician, but he was one of the few remaining men. All of the able-bodied males over the age of thirteen had been taken by the Germans and placed into labor battalions. While the men and boys were only five miles away building the winter line at Monte Cassino, the wives and mothers had not seen them for over a month.

A dreadfully thin woman—the doctor's daughter and the mother of the young girl—was awakened and brought in to look at Perkin. Her name was Angela, and she was a nurse. Her husband was the current town doctor, but he had been taken away as well, and the medical duties were now split between Angela and her father. Under her father's direction, she competently stitched Perkin's chin and put two extraordinarily painful stitches in his nostril. They had no anesthetics—all medications had been confiscated by the German Army. She rewrapped his left hand and was shocked at the damage to his fingers. She carefully bandaged those up, as well as using a liberal application of Perkin's sulfa powder.

Dr. Bonucci had sworn the women in the room to secrecy, and Perkin was moved quietly to his current room without awakening others in the underground village. Bonucci told him that it was unlikely that there were informers in the caves, but it was better to be careful. The woman who had hit him in the face with the shovel and later threatened him with the knife, was very apologetic, but it seemed that while the women who were still awake were curious and helpful, they still remained a little cool towards him.

Perkin's uniform—all his clothes in fact—had been taken from him and were being dried over a fire in another room, and he was wrapped in the blanket from his pack. While Maria, the would-be manhood-carver, rubbed his feet for him and Angela tended to his various cuts and abrasions, Perkin talked to Dr. Bonucci.

The doctor's questions were direct and troubling, but Perkin gave him straight answers as best he could.

"How long before the Americans come?"

"I don't know, sir. Soon."

"Is there any way to bypass San Pietro?"

"No sir. San Pietro looks out over the highway and the route to Rome. There's no way to go around it. Not if the town is defended."

"What will happen to the village?"

Perkin didn't answer. He didn't need to, and the old man simply nodded his head. But Angela, who spoke some English as well, asked, "Please, signore, what will happen to San Pietro?"

Dr. Bonucci spoke for him, "The Americans will destroy San Pietro because the Germans are here. The Germans are here because our beautiful little village looks out over the highway. There is no other way."

Angela shook her head angrily, "The Americans can go up the railway on the other side of Monte Lungo. It will take them out of this valley. They can go there, and we will be safe, can't they Papa?"

The old doctor looked at Perkin, although he couldn't see him, and Perkin answered, "I don't think so, ma'am, and before you ask, there ain't a thing I can do about it.

There just isn't enough room for a whole army to move through over there. I'm very sorry, Miss Angela, but there's nothing in the power of the United States that will compel the Germans to leave here except for force, and that's just a fact. I'm very sorry."

She nodded sadly. It was apparent that the Italian residents had had this conversation among themselves before, and the realists in the village had come to the same conclusion. This explained the coolness towards Perkin, and he really couldn't blame them. They might know deep down that the Germans were at fault, but surely in their hearts, he and the rest of the Allied armies were not guiltless either.

Angela nodded again and shrugged. "*Allora*. At least the Germans will be gone. What do you think that they will do with our men?"

"Oh, ma'am, I don't know," Perkin answered. "I hope that they release them as soon as their defensive lines are done." That was a hedged answer. The truth was that Perkin suspected that the Germans would keep the men of San Pietro as forced labor until the war was over. He had looked into the deep sorrow and despair reflected in the women's sunken black eyes, and he couldn't bring himself to explain that the Germans were unlikely to voluntarily release their unpaid labor—once they had committed themselves to slave labor, he believed, they didn't have enough goodness or altruism left in them to let the laborers go.

Another woman brought his clothes in, and Perkin dropped the blanket off his shoulders to put on his undershirt. Stefania, the little girl, saw Perkin's locket and asked to see it. He handed it to her, cautioning her to be careful. Delighted, she ran over to the kerosene lamp and opened it. When she saw the little painting of Saint Michael, she gasped and cried, "Mama, Mama! Saint Michael!"

To Perkin's bewilderment, all of the women in the room immediately ran over and looked at his locket, and Maria—who had so recently threatened to castrate Perkin—dropped to her knees and kissed his bandaged hand.

Immediately, there were questions in Italian which he could not understand, and finally Angela began to translate: "Where did he get the painting? Why did he wear the locket? Who gave it to him?" He patiently explained about Gianina—how he had met her in Naples, fallen in love, and how she had made the locket for his protection—but when he got to her death, he choked up and fell silent, staring mutely at the little painting. He was very tired, and didn't want to talk about Gianina anymore. "Why is this of interest to you?" Perkin asked amid a torrent of excited babble.

"Because of the village's connection to Saint Michael," answered Dr. Bonucci calmly. "Our church is dedicated to him. He is our patron saint. The women take it as a good omen that you wear that locket, and that it was given to you by an Italian lady."

Leaving aside the women's superstition and what that implied for him, Perkin said, "I would have thought that the village saint would have been Peter. Why Michael?" Perkin passed around the locket for the ladies to look at, and he just managed to stop Maria from trying to clean the tiny glasses off of Saint Michael with spit and her skirt.

"That's a very good question, young man, and I don't know that I have the exact answer for you. But I have a few possibilities for you." The old man rubbed his eyes and thought for a moment. "First, you should consider that this area was settled before Christ, and this village was founded in the Middle Ages. It's over a thousand years old, and many things have happened over the centuries, good and bad, since this lovely village graced this valley— plague, earthquakes, invasions, and now Germans. I'm a religious man, not superstitious, but you must understand that many rural Italians are—they don't look at bubonic plague as an infectious disease; nor do they understand that earthquakes are merely unstable geology; or that the invasions of Saracen or German soldiers serve some dictator's quest for territory. No, they see these events as portents that evil is about. Not evil, but *Evil*—that the Beast is on the march. They believe this because that is what the Church taught and promoted for centuries. Today I think we know better, but old beliefs die hard in the mountains of Italy. I think that virtually since the time of Christ's crucifixion at Golgotha, people have awaited the second coming and the apocalypse with a mixture of anticipation and dread—mostly dread, I suspect. In the frightening times that I mentioned, the people have believed that the end of days was upon them, and during, say, the plague, who could blame them for thinking so?

In their distress they turned to the Church, and often a particular saint for help. Saint Michael is a protector from evil, and yes, the village honors Saint Peter by bearing his name . . . but some time ago, for reasons I can only guess, the church was named in honor of Saint Michael. Perhaps the people believed they needed greater protection from evil. So, we have a church honoring Saint Michael in a village honoring Saint Peter."

The old man paused to light an old red meerschaum pipe with the carved face of Garibaldi. After a moment, Dr. Bonucci spoke again, "A second thought is that, as Saint Michael is the patron saint of soldiers, like yourself, perhaps this church was named thus to protect local knights traveling to the Holy Land during the Crusades. Many soldiers left Italy to throw the invaders out of Jerusalem, and maybe this church protected or comforted them—maybe it protects you, young man! Finally, and least likely—although I appreciate the symmetry of this—

consider that Peter was the founder of the Church. 'Upon this rock, I will build my church.' Yes? So that is the role of Peter—the first Pope. The beginning of the Church. But what is the office of Saint Michael? I think Revelation tells us the Archangel Michael is the soldier of God who commands God's army and defeats Satan in the final battle of good versus evil. Do you see what I'm saying?"

Perkin thought for a moment and answered, "Yes . . . I think so. By doing this, Peter and Michael are honored as the beginning and the end of the Church on earth. Is that what you mean?"

"Yes, there is great symbolism there, I think. But, I'll say again, I don't know. Father Masia would have been able to tell you . . . ."

"Who's that? The village priest?"

"Yes. He's gone now. The Germans took him away a month ago in the dead of the night—not for a labor battalion. He's just gone, and I suspect that he'll never come back. So, is it any wonder that some people believe we're in the time of tribulation? It's why they're excited about you and your locket."

Perkin came to the subject that had been troubling him since his locket was revealed. In a tired voice, he asked, "Doc, you aren't suggesting that they think this is going to help them, or that Saint Michael has shown up in the form of Perkin Berger, are you? Because the sad news is, Perk or Mike notwithstanding, the village comes down when General Clark is ready. I mean, my hands are torn up, but it's hardly stigmata—Doc, I'm sorry, but this doesn't change anything."

"I know, young man," the doctor said gently. "But it gives them hope . . . because it reminds them that God has not forgotten us."

Doctor Bonucci ordered the women from the room while Perkin dressed. Then they returned with a worn thin pillow and a thick blanket for him. After he laid down, Stefania, the little girl, and Angela tentatively came over to him. Stefania lifted up his blanket and crawled in next to him on his right side and put her small head on his chest, then Angela did the same on the other side.

0400 Hours
San Pietro, Italy

It was a distant rumbling, like far off thunder on a hot Texas summer day, but there were no breaks, no stops in the rumbling. Perkin heard the noise subconsciously, and it became incorporated into a dream he was having about the Crusades. In his dream, set in a hot, dry, ancient city, the Crusaders were laying siege to a walled Muslim fortress but were being thwarted their entrance to the city at every turn. A massive thunderstorm was building at sea behind Perkin's army, and it threatened to overwhelm the attacking force in minutes if they didn't get shelter. White-hot streaks of lightning crashed down from the skies, and the thunder shook the ground as the first drops of rain began to fall, and Perkin became desperate to find a way into the city.

He had started the dream as a foot soldier but then, in the manner of dreams, found himself promoted quickly to the commanding general of the assaulting armies. No matter what they tried, the Crusaders simply could not breach the walled city, and what had started as an interesting dream was beginning to frustrate the soldier in Perkin. In anger, the Crusader Perkin screamed at his commanders, "Find a way or make one! There are always passages, there must be. Send our spies out: talk to the people outside the wall, the merchants, the clerics—"

He awoke with a start. The noise wasn't thunder but artillery. More than Perkin had ever heard before, even at the height of Salerno, but it wasn't directed at San Pietro. It wasn't directed at Mount Sammucro either—maybe the Germans were hitting American or British positions, he thought. No, American artillery on Mount La Difensa. That made more sense. The 1st Special Service Force was going up the mountain at the position he had looked at in—he checked his watch—a couple of hours. The artillery was going to pound the hell out of the front slope of the mountain to draw German attention there, and then the Forcemen would take the mountain from the back. God, he hoped it worked.

Angela had rolled over with her back to Perkin, and he was grateful for the warmth. Stefania had not moved, and her head was nestled between his chest and shoulder. Perkin's arm was a little numb, but he didn't want to wake the girl. The contact with another human was reassuring in any case, and Perkin closed his eyes and tried to go back to sleep. He wanted to see how the dream ended. There was a theme there that was interesting, but he couldn't quite grasp what it was. Maybe it would come to him later, he thought, as he began to dream again of storms and sieges.

0415 Hours
Mount Rotondo Spur, Italy

"Jesus Christ Almighty, would you look at that!" The admiration was clear in Bill Spaulding's voice.

"I've never seen anything like it. I swear I'll remember this moment as long as I live—I wish Maggie could see this," Sam said, likewise in awe.

It was the largest Allied barrage in the war since El Alamein over a year before. Every available cannon, howitzer, and heavy mortar opened fire—some nine hundred British and American pieces in all—and were in the process of reducing the tops of Mounts Camino, Maggiore, and La Difensa. The connected peaks housed the defenders of the German 15th Panzer Grenadier Division, and although the rounds were landing on the German fortifications thousands of yards away, the force of the explosions could be felt through the echoes in the Italian mountains.

The 15th Panzer Grenadier Division was a relatively new unit formed in Sicily the summer before. But the *Siziliens* were veteran soldiers, and they had come from units of the storied *Afrika Korps* and from broken battalions and regiments salvaged from the Eastern Front. The 15th had retreated from Sicily, been thrown into battle at Salerno, and had fought fiercely during the German retreat to the winter lines. The division had been in the Cassino area of operations for over a month, and the *Siziliens* assigned to the Camino hill mass had dug extensive fortifications and prepared themselves well.

On and on it went, like a never-ending Fourth of July display. In the first second, tens of rounds pounded down on the German defenders in the mountains. In the first minute, hundreds of rounds. Thereafter, thousands and scores of thousands of rounds exploded in the rocks, sending shards of stones mixed with the deadly steel of the shrapnel. Most of the German soldiers ducked into the caves and bunkers, and for these fortunate soldiers it was terrifying. For the unlucky grenadiers unable to make it into shelter, it was an indescribable hell.

0545 Hours
San Pietro, Italy

The artillery had not ended nor even slowed down. Perkin guessed that hundreds of guns were firing. This had to be the heaviest barrage of the American war, he thought. There was an incredible fortune being expended to take these mountains, and Perkin hoped that it would prove worthwhile.

He had been awake for fifteen minutes. The artillery fire had awakened many in the caves, and several strangers had walked in with lanterns to see the American as he slept. The last one had been an old lady who had awakened Perkin so she could see the locket. *So much for Bonucci swearing the women to secrecy,* he thought. His time in San Pietro had to be short, or sooner or later he would be betrayed to the Germans. Not only that, but his presence in their caves put them at risk. He would have to leave today.

There was a problem—unforeseen to be sure, but still a problem. He couldn't see worth a damn. His left eye was still closed and very sore, and his face was swollen to the point that his right eye was nearly closed as well. Perkin wasn't sure that Maria hadn't left him with a concussion, although to be honest with himself, he knew he was so tired that the effects were likely the same.

Angela brought him a chamber pot to use, and after he had gratefully relieved himself, she wiped down his face and neck with a cloth soaked in rainwater—soap was a luxury, and there was none to spare.

With a concerned look on her face, Angela said, "Your face looks terrible. Maria nearly killed you last night."

"She almost did worse than that," Perkin replied.

Angela considered his answer for a moment, then her face broke out in a shy smile and an honest laugh.

"She would have, too." She stopped laughing, and her face darkened, "The Germans haven't been good neighbors."

"Has it been bad?" asked Perkin.

She nodded. "The people who could leave have left. There are about five hundred of us remaining, but we are losing several each week from illness and, well, starvation and malnutrition. We have little food, and the Germans have dumped dead sheep into our cisterns. Why? I don't know. To drive us off, maybe. To punish us for wanting a better life?"

Angela wiped a tear away with the heel of her palm. "Before the rains started and we were able to run rainwater into barrels, we had no water here. The Germans had forbidden the use of the fountain in the village, and we were desperate. Dying of thirst. Two girls went to get water anyway, and the Germans shot them for disobeying the rules. They were shot . . . ," Angela choked over the words, " . . . for getting water. Our water. Now . . . we don't go to the village much. We would leave here, but there's nowhere to go. Things aren't any better in the zone of occupation, and the Germans won't let us through the lines to the south."

"What about food?" Perkin had been thinking about breakfast.

"There's not enough. The Germans deliver food once per week. We are left to distribute it as best we can. Potatoes, flour, some oil. Occasionally rice. No meat, eggs, fresh milk. No vegetables, no sugar, coffee, or tea. It is about eight hundred calories per day, and the weekly shipment is two days overdue. We are expected to supplement what the Germans provide with our own stores and what we might earn in exchange for labor."

"What kind of labor?" Perkin asked.

"I treat some of the German wounded at the aid center here. Men hurt—like you. Those that are worse off are treated at a field hospital on the other side of Mount Trocchio—about eight kilometers from here. Some of the girls work in a laundry. Some make up the rooms for the officers, others cook. That's the best job—they're searched to make sure they don't steal food, but they can eat while they work."

"How many Germans are billeted in the village?"

Angela shrugged. "I don't know."

"Can you take a rough guess? How many meals are cooked? How many officers' beds are made every day?"

"Um, I think that they take care of five officers. They have each taken the nicest homes in San Pietro. The se-nior man is Captain Mueller, and I met him once when he visited the aid station."

"What's he like?"

She shrugged, "I don't know, but I think he's a hard man. It is said that he's fought in Poland, France, Russia, and now here. One of his men tried to rape a girl from the village, and when we complained, it is said that he got very angry at his men. He told us it wouldn't happen again, and it hasn't. But I think that maybe in truth he has no regard for us at all, and we are a distraction from his real business—maybe all he wants to think about is you Americans."

Perkin nodded. Mueller sounded like a tough sol-dier—businesslike, wouldn't countenance rape, focused on the enemy. Five officers, commanded by a captain, suggested to Perkin that the village was defended by a company—maybe 150–200 soldiers. In this case: panzer-grenadiers. Using the old rule of thumb of three troops on offense for every soldier on defense, Perkin figured that it might take an entire battalion to rout the defenders of San Pietro, depending on how well they were dug in—and that was just for the village. Counting the compa-nies and independent platoons and squads that would be dug in throughout the valley and back through the hills, it might take a regimental action to force the route past San Pietro. There weren't enough regiments to go around, Perkin knew, and if the Germans were dug in as well as he knew they would be—San Pietro would have to be destroyed before the gun club was sent in.

Perkin sighed silently, and asked, "When was the last time you ate?"

Angela lifted her head high and said, "I'm fine."

"OK, how about Stefania?"

Angela's pride evaporated, "She had a *brotchen* yesterday morning, a gift from a German soldier. Nothing the day before that."

Perkin reached for his pack and pulled out his remaining box of C-rations, unfortunately also mutton stew, and handed it to Angela. He gave her a summer sausage taken from Sergeant Krieger as well. Perkin was ravenous, but the villagers were starving. A few hundred calories a day in the late fall was a starvation diet, and the sooner the offensive began, the better it would be for these people— assuming that they lived through it.

0715 Hours
San Pietro, Italy

"I can get what you want, but I will be shot if I do. I'm sorry signore, but I won't help."

Perkin looked at the pretty Italian woman seated on the floor of the cave directly opposite him. Several other women and Doctor Bonucci were also present, and there was a lot of muttering and shaking of heads at the woman's pronouncement.

Angela looked at the woman in disgust. "The longer the Germans are here, the more we suffer. The Americans will save us, but don't we owe it to them to help? Can't we take some risks as well?"

"Don't talk to me like that, Angela Frattini! I am suffering as well. My husband is dead and my sons are taken—you still have your daughter at least—and I want to be alive when my sons come home. Is that wrong?"

Judging by the reactions of the women around him, Perkin decided that the woman was not winning converts to her defense. But he had asked a lot from Signora Moroni, and he wasn't surprised when she refused flat out.

"*Capitano*," Angela said, "Would you please leave us for a moment? We have some family business to conclude here. Please take Papa with you."

Perkin and the old man walked hunched over to another room, and Perkin asked the doctor, "What's going on?"

"They are going to kill her if she doesn't agree to help." The old man's tone was slightly nervous and concerned.

"Oh, dear. I can't have that." Perkin turned to head back, but the doctor grabbed his arm.

"No, she will come around. Well, probably. She's strong-willed like her mother was, and she may not speak to Angela for a month. But, yes, she will come around. Sisters are like that."

"Mrs. Moroni is your daughter too?"

"Yes, that's why I know she'll do the right thing—her older sister will make her. See? Family business."

"And the other women in the room?"

"Cousins."

"And you don't want to be in there?"

"Oh, no. Absolutely not. Better to leave it to the women to sort out."

The unhappy Signora Moroni worked for the German supply sergeant, and her task was to sort uniforms and boots of wounded and dead soldiers. Those that could be repaired were mended by Italian women working in a shop in the village, and those that couldn't were generally burned. Perkin and Angela were asking her to steal a complete German uniform—greatcoat, tunic, trousers, and boots. The greatcoat of Sergeant Krieger's that Perkin had taken was too badly damaged and would not stand close scrutiny. It was a tall order for what he had in mind.

"Doctor, while the women sort that out, may I ask you about the caves?"

"Of course."

Before Perkin could begin, Stefania ran up to the two men with a huge smile on her face. She curtseyed to Perkin and out came a stream of excited Italian.

Her grandfather translated, "She says to tell you, 'Thank you, *Capitano*, for the tinned stew. How I love mutton—and it was the best I've ever eaten! There was so much that Mama and I shared with two friends, and Mama gave me a whole sugar cube because I'm a good girl! What a treat!'"

1010 Hours
San Pietro, Italy

Perkin stood in the uniform of a German sergeant before Angela, "How do I look?"

"Like a despondent Texan in a German uniform."

"That's because of the black eye. With it droopy like that, it makes me look a little down on life. Seriously, how do I look? I can't see if my trousers are bloused right."

"Try to look a little more arrogant, make sure you strut, and you'll be fine." She smiled at Perkin, who smiled back painfully at her.

"OK, let's finish this up. I need to get movin' along," said Perkin.

"You are sure about this? *Capitano*, there must be a better way."

"Call me Perk. No. This is how we're gonna do it. Tell Maria and your sister that they made this possible. Go ahead and cut it." Perkin sat down in the chair, wrapped his blanket across his shoulders, and closed his eyes. He didn't want to see the scissors coming.

Angela tilted his head back and carefully snipped the stitches in his chin. Using a pair of tweezers, she pulled the stitches out and spread the cut open again. When she cut the stitches in his nostril, he pushed her away and sneezed violently four times in rapid succession, spraying blood over his blanket before allowing her to finish.

The nurse quickly and expertly wrapped his face up, leaving the black and bloody eye exposed, but half-covering Perkin's mouth with gauze. She carefully daubed blood on the outside of the gauze at the corner of his mouth, and ensured that blood soaked through the gauze covering his chin and his nose. She then took his wrapped hand and brushed it through the blood on his blanket. When she was done, Perkin looked like a German soldier injured in combat and fresh from the aid station.

1100 Hours
Mount Rotondo Spur, Italy

There had been two more counterattacks that morning, and the third was just getting underway. Tanks and armored assault vehicles had pushed hard against the Americans on Mount Lungo in the first assault. It had been repulsed, with heavy casualties on both sides. The second had been along Victory Road, straight up the middle, and it had ended poorly for the Germans.

Destroyed tanks and half-tracks littered the valley floor, and more than one German vehicle had been mired in the terrible mud only to be destroyed by deadly accurate artillery fire.

"Now I understand why armies used to go into winter quarters and wait for spring," noted Jim Lockridge to Sam as he pointed out a destroyed tank. He had been walking through the battalion positions with Lieutenant Colonel Wranosky and stopped to chat with Sam.

"I'll be damned if I want to wait. Let's get this over with." Sam's reply was overheard by his battalion commander who mistook his statement for enthusiasm, and Colonel Wranosky walked past, nodding his head in agreement.

Before they moved on to visit other units of the battalion along the line, Jim gave Sam a quick update on the progress of the battle.

"We're doing what we're supposed to do. We've fixed the Germans here at the gap into the valley, and we've wedged our foot firmly in the door. I don't think we have enough juice to take Lungo by ourselves, but the Germans don't know that we're only holding the door open for now. You know, not going through it for a while." Jim took a bite of a tasteless chocolate bar and continued, "The 142nd moved this morning against Mount Maggiore, and most of this artillery has been in support of them. German prisoners are indicating that the artillery hasn't done much damage yet, as they were able to get into bunkers, but it did tip them off that the attack was coming. The good news is that it tipped them off to the wrong attack. As the Krauts moved to defend against the 142nd on the right, the 1st Special Service Force scaled that mountain cliff last night and took the defenders by surprise from the left. Colonel Fredericks is reporting that the Forcemen have taken La Difensa and are already moving against the next hilltop, Rementea, while the Limeys are moving against Camino proper."

"How do you read it, Jim?"

"Well, the Fifth Army planners seem to think a day or two of fighting and a day of mopping up and the Germans scamper away. Then the western gate belongs to us. Now, by my lights, I figure that since the staff bubbas have underestimated Jerry every time, I'd say that five days to a week is probably more in line with reality."

Sam let out a long sigh. "Oh, Jesus," he groaned. "So, we have to wait in position here for a week for the 142nd and the Forcemen to tidy things up?" It was an unappealing prospect.

"No. We're gettin' hammered here—we can't make it a week at this pace. They're gonna relieve us in a day with an Italian brigade, and they should be able to take Lungo. Then we'll go into defense on Rotondo, or into reserve somewheres else."

Sam hesitated, then asked, "I know you couldn't say much, but any radio intercepts about Perkin? Any word at all?"

Jim laughed, his first humorous reflection of the day, "Oh, I'd tell ya if something came up. But it hasn't. I'm sure he's fine—that boy's got more lives than ten cats, and he's the luckiest son of a bitch I ever knew. In Austin, he'd drink his first beer in 1.3 seconds and then nurse ten more over the course of an evening. And he'd dance all night with the prettiest girl, then sleep with her and her sister, wake up without a hangover, and go get an A on his final the next day. Meanwhile, no one would dance with me— not even the ugly girl sittin' in the corner until she got so drunk that she puked when I put my arm around her." Jim laughed again at an obviously real, but distant, memory, then said, "I've never seen anyone get away with more shit than Perkin, and outside of Gianina, I think that war's just an extension of college for him. I know some things that happened have set him back a little, but I reckon he's havin' the time of his life in that village—drunk a gallon of Dago red, slept with at least two Italian beauties last night, woke up without a hangover, and is now hand-in-hand with the prettiest one on a pleasant stroll through the village."

Jim's words had comforted Sam some, but compounded by fatigue, Sam's anxiety was mounting by the hour. As he watched the third counterattack since daylight unfold and head towards Mount Lungo, he wondered where his cousin was and how he was doing.

1115 Hours
San Pietro, Italy

From the day that the Texas National Guard had been federalized for national service, Perkin had begun learning both German and Japanese—he deeply regretted not spending more time on Italian—and he had dropped Japanese from his studies when the division was sent to Africa a year before. He practiced frequently with Jim Lockridge, who had learned the language in college, and Roscoe Pfadenhauer, who spoke German at home. He had mastered the fundamentals, was close to a point of proficiency, but was nowhere near fluent. Even Pfadenhauer spoke the language with a Texas accent, and the German prisoners that he spoke to over the months remarked on his accent and outdated syntax. His antique grammar was not surprising, as the Pfadenhauers had lived in the Hill Country in an insular German community since 1850. Perkin was confident that he could follow a conversation relatively well, certainly better than in Italian, but he prayed he would not be called upon to speak to anyone.

His language skills were in danger of being tested in short order. He was in a dusty chamber of rock walls and underneath a table, his ear against a small wooden panel. On the other side of the panel was, he believed, a room in the church, and from there he hoped to gain entrance to the village.

The concealed corridor leading to this chamber had come to him during his dream of the Crusades—it was the piece of the puzzle that his subconscious mind had been working on. It was one thing to imagine being able to skirt around the village and take careful note of the German defenses, but it was something else altogether to do it in practice with only partial vision from his swollen face.

When practical, the medieval builders of the European churches often built hidden passages in case of attack by pirates or rogue knights, thieves, Moors, Normans, or any of the other countless invaders. The same passages were later used to flee the troops of Protestant princes, as well as those of Napoleon. As Perkin was well aware, the Church had developed a long list of enemies over the centuries, and a quick egress from the church had saved many a priest's life during turbulent times. But what could lead a priest out could lead an invader or a thief in, so the passages remained privileged information and were passed down quietly through the generations of priests.

Doctor Bonucci was not privy to the underground passages from the church of San Pietro. In fact, he had laughed at Perkin when he was asked. "No, young man. There are no secret tunnels leading from the church. That is the stuff of Hollywood movies."

Disappointed, Perkin was contemplating Plan B, or rather contemplating developing a Plan B, when Stefania spoke up, "But Grandpapa, the tunnel of the bones leads to the church, I am sure of it!" Although the girl spoke in

Italian, this was his first indication that she understood at least a little English.

Stefania had led Perkin down a maze of tunnel using a small candle for light. From her explanation to Doctor Bonucci, Perkin learned that the children of San Pietro knew the tunnels the best. Those rooms closest to the many cave entrances had been expanded most recently, but there were many unused tunnels and rooms in the cave complex. The connecting tunnels between the rooms that Perkin had seen had been smoothed by the work of many villagers with modern steel tools, but the older passages were rough and narrow.

As Stefania led him through the labyrinth, Perkin noted that many of the little passageways were dead ends. Perkin guessed that as a passage was dug, the workers would frequently find veins of hard rock and simply begin digging elsewhere. But Stefania showed him a passage that seemed to go nowhere only to terminate at a small hole that Stefania indicated had to be slid through on one's back. She went first while Perkin took off his German greatcoat. He passed it carefully through the hole to Stefania, and did the same with his pack, the Thompson, and a cane borrowed from Dr. Bonucci. On the other side of the hole in the wall, he emerged into yet another passage.

The children had been playing the ultimate game of hide-and-seek in the caves when Stefania found the hole. The new passage took them to a set of rough-cut stone stairs, which in turn led to another warren of tunnels at a much higher elevation. While Perkin shuddered to think of the children playing in the maze of caves, he was impressed at Stefania's bravery and cleverness. He was certain that she was right, and the upper passages led to the village. Even so, he felt slightly claustrophobic. Stefania did not, however, and guided him by the hand up the stairs.

One spur off the passage that the stairs had led to ended in a brick wall. At some point in history, it may have been an entrance to the caves, but had been covered over by the village of San Pietro. *Perhaps to keep the children out,* Perkin guessed dryly. The main passage ended at an intersection of another flight of stairs and a passage. The passage led to the left, the direction Stefania pointed, and when Perkin asked where the downward stairs led, she shook her head. The children hadn't explored them yet, but Perkin wondered if they led to another exit under Mount Sammucro.

The tunnel ended in a small rectangular room where the ceiling opened up to eight or ten feet high. In the flickering light of the candle, Perkin jumped backwards nearly to the point of falling over, and the tall Texan gasped in surprise as he saw what was in the room. When Stefania led him in by the hand, Perkin found himself face to face with scores, maybe hundreds, of skulls staring at him out of empty sockets. Simple wooden tables covered the length and breadth of the room, the tables pressed against walls, and the skulls were stacked one upon another to the ceiling. The space under the tables had neatly stacked bones from the remainder of the bodies—some tables had nothing but thigh bones under them while other tables housed ribs, and yet another table had hands and feet under it.

As Perkin looked around the room in the dim light of the candle, he noticed Stefania tugging on his coat and pointing to a bare spot on the wall. Painted on the smooth rock of the chamber was a winged angel with a sword held high above his head and his foot pinning Lucifer to the ground. Perkin was in an ossuary dedicated to Saint Michael.

1145 Hours
Mount Rotondo Spur, Italy

The third counterattack faltered. The Germans were finding that possessing all of Mount Lungo was a formidable task for them as well. From his foxhole on the spur and with mist-covered binoculars, Sam watched the battle disintegrate for the Germans as American artillery and anti-tank guns ripped through the attacking infantry and armor.

Through the smoke and fog, Sam caught sight of a German squad in the valley working back towards Mount Lungo. They were either relieving soldiers in outpost positions or had just been relieved themselves. In a few minutes, they would be behind the safety of a swell in the ground, and given the angle, Sam doubted that anyone else except for his platoon on the spur could see the enemy soldiers. He motioned to Sergeant Kenton and pointed out the soldiers. Immediately Kenton ran forward to one of the machine guns assigned to the 1st Platoon sector and began firing at the fleeing soldiers.

Sam estimated that the range to be at least six hundred yards, and as Sam watched, two soldiers dropped instantly. They were casualties. The other soldiers dove to the ground and began crawling to safety, but Sam wasn't inclined to let them off so easily.

He grabbed his handset, requested artillery onto the slowly retreating soldiers, and was told that no support was available. He motioned over to Sergeant Kenton and issued a string of orders. When Sergeant Kenton ran back towards Victory Road, Sam turned to his radio operator and said, "Get to Cap'n Spaulding and see if we can get a heavy machine gun brought forward. Find me Froman."

Sam had directed mortar fire near the soldiers, but not right on top of them. Within seconds of hearing the first thunk of the mortar, rounds began to drop in the path of the soldier's retreat. They froze—afraid to move forward and afraid to stay put. Like a herd of gazelles chased by a lion, they instinctively shifted crawling to their left, towards the safety of Mount Lungo.

"Block 'em. Don't let the sons-a-bitches get to the hill." The soldiers of the platoon continued to fire at the crawling soldiers without much effect except to keep them down, but Sergeant Kenton had the mortar team adjust fire quickly to block the Germans. This time they stayed put in the smallest of hollows, and Sam knew they were waiting for smoke or fog to be their savior.

As Sam's soldiers looked to him for instructions, as if to say, "Are we gonna finish these bastards off?" a huffing heavy weapons team ran up the hill to its small crest. "Keep firing! Keep 'em pinned!" Sam yelled. "Froman!"

One of Sam's soldiers materialized in front of him.

"Yes sir?" The soldier was a private named David Froman, a butcher's son from Chicago. He was a sniper who had been next to Sam at the defense of the bridge at Mount San Chirico, and although Sam had always known the young man was a bit of a scam artist, on that day, he had earned Sam's undying trust and affection.

"Don't kill all of 'em. Just one."

Although Froman didn't understand the purpose of the order, he nodded, found a limb on an otherwise bare tree, and laid his Springfield on it. Froman followed Sam's finger, found the hollow, and saw the helmets or boots of several soldiers. It looked as if they had rolled a dead soldier in front of them to use as a small bulwark. Froman went back and forth until he saw what he was looking for, and he scoped in a terrified private from Darmstadt laying flat with his hands over his head. Private Froman calmly let out his breath and gently squeezed the trigger. The rifle kicked hard against his shoulder, and a split-second later, the butcher's son from Chicago accurately put a 30.06 round through the neck of the postman's son from Darmstadt.

"Got one, sir."

"Alright. No more unless I tell you." Sam was very pleased. It was a good shot—over six hundred yards—made on a grey, drizzling day.

"Where do you need us, sir?" The leader of the machine gun section was a very young-looking, confident corporal, and he pointed to a small mound of dirt on the crest of the spur. "How 'bout here?"

Sam nodded and told the corporal his plan.

The corporal grinned, and his team quickly set up the M2 Browning .50 caliber machine gun on a tall tripod. Moving quickly and without asking permission, two privates began taking sandbags from Sam's little command post, moving them to the gunner's position. They began weighing down the tripod and building a small wall around the M2.

Sam turned his attention back to the German soldiers. They were still pinned.

"Inch it in a little closer, Sergeant." This was to Sergeant Kenton, who was now on the field telephone with the mortar team.

A mortar round landed within ten yards of the pinned Germans, and several of Sam's soldiers grinned at each other, thinking his intent was to play a murderous game of teasing cat-and-mouse. After being on the receiving end of German fire without much opportunity to shoot back for the better part of the day, well, that would be just fine with them.

Finally, the Germans could stand it no more. A sergeant of the pinned troops, a veteran soldier of the 29th Panzer Grenadiers and a survivor of Stalingrad, leapt to his feet and began waving wildly back towards the German lines. Although dozens of rounds were fired at him, he miraculously escaped injury, and the sergeant dropped back to the ground as soon as he saw what he wanted to see.

It was the same thing Sam had been waiting for.

1145 Hours
San Pietro, Italy

"Where is the entrance? *Dove è l'entrata?*" Perkin mumbled, mostly to himself.

"Signore . . . here." Stefania knelt next to a corner table that had leg bones stacked like cordwood under the tower of skulls built on the tabletop. When she moved next to the bones on the floor, her candle flickered.

Perkin took the candle from the girl and walked around the room. Stefania's corner was the only place where such a draft seemed evident, and Perkin knelt next to Stefania again. The candle flickered once more, and Perkin handed it to the little girl to hold. As he began moving bones from under the table, he noticed there was no reaction from the girl—she didn't cross herself, nor showed fear or nervousness at all. *Curious*, he thought.

"You hide here?" Perkin asked with a smile.

"Si, signore. Luisa is afraid to look in here. It's a good place to hide."

"The bones don't bother you?"

"Of course not, silly. Papa and grandpapa are doctors."

That settled it. Behind the stack of bones was a wood panel. The panel was not rough-cut like a door, but smooth like one created by a woodworker, an artisan. Perkin leaned in and pressed his ear to the panel. Nothing. He pressed on the panel. Again, nothing. He felt for a latch or a lock, but there was nothing he could find. Perkin reached for his knife to pry it open, but Stefania grabbed his arm.

"You're not doing it right. Let me." Evidently strong-willed women ran in the Bonucci line. Perkin climbed out of the way, and Stefania crawled into the little space. "It pulls out. See?"

"Ah, yes," Perkin whispered. Stefania moved out of the way and Perkin cautiously crawled though the narrow space. The room was completely black, no windows, and he turned on his flashlight and looked around. It was the church office—a desk, bookcases, an open filing cabinet, a lamp. There were papers strewn across the floor, and many books had been scattered as well. The room had been ransacked and left as it was.

There was a heavy wooden door out of the room, and Perkin asked Stefania, "Do you know where this goes?"

She shook her head, and Perkin realized that it was time for the girl to leave. He left his Thompson and pack in the ossuary, thanked Stefania, and helped her put the panel back in place. The light and sound disappeared instantly from the other side.

Perkin tried the lamp. It didn't work, so he sat the flashlight on the table and got ready to go. Fearful of being discovered, his heart pounding, Perkin quickly brushed the dirt from his German uniform and wiped down his boots. His right arm went into a sling, along with his .45, and his bad arm went through the sleeve while he struggled to get the coat on and buttoned. When he was done, he knew what the effect would be: a wounded soldier just from combat, and the empty sleeve suggesting that he couldn't even salute. Signora Moroni had stolen a garrison cap, and he wore that instead of a helmet.

Perkin put his ear to the door, heard nothing, and opened it gently. It opened into a small library. No one was there, and he walked out and quickly closed the door behind him. The stone building was cold and damp, and there was a strong draft running through the library.

The door out of the library led to flight of stairs into a hallway, which in turn led into the nave. As Perkin peeked into the nave, he saw a few people were sitting at pews—two soldiers and one Italian—and when he walked into the church, none showed any interest in Perkin. The nave itself was beautiful, and Perkin's soul wept for what he knew would happen. Arched ceilings topped tall walls, and Perkin saw the reason for the drafts—the windows were gone. Looking around, he saw *Gott Mit Uns* scraped on a wall—God with us—the same motto stamped on Sergeant Krieger's belt buckle. *We'll see,* thought Perkin.

He walked slowly with a limp, with Dr. Bonucci's cane a welcome prop. He wanted an excuse to walk slowly through areas, and a reason to stop periodically. Perkin moved slowly up past the altar to the end of the church, and he joined a German soldier looking out of a window facing to the south.

The German looked at him, nodded, and his attention went back to observing two separate battles. Closest to the village of San Pietro was the battle for Mount Lungo, and the two soldiers, American and German, watched silently together as American artillery plastered the northwest half of the hill and a small skirmish took place near the gap. Sporadic machine gun fire punctuated the gaps between the fall of the heavy rounds, and it was impossible to make much sense of it from where they were.

Almost directly over the smoke from Mount Lungo, another battle was taking place on Mount La Difensa, and yet another battle was being waged to the right, on Mount Maggiore. Again, concentrated artillery fire pounded on the mountaintops, but it was impossible to gauge how the fight was going.

Without looking at Perkin, the German soldier—a corporal—said, "The Amis have scaled Monte La Difensa from the back. They have taken the crest, but will not hold it long. Damn big balls on those Amis, have you seen that mountain?" He looked at Perkin for confirmation of his opinion, and Perkin merely nodded. That sufficed for the other soldier, who gathered that the tall sergeant wasn't interested in conversation. After a minute or two of silent contemplation of the distant battles, the corporal nodded and walked off.

Perkin moved around the windows and looked around the church and what parts of the village he could see. His orientation to the south and the east from the nave was perfect—it was the face of the church directly opposite the Allied lines. Although Perkin had known that there was significant elevation to San Pietro, he was still amazed at how the village climbed the mountain. The roads and walkways were steep, and instead of sidewalks, steps provided the thoroughfare from the lower village all the way to the church.

The buildings were stone and mortar, just like every other village he had seen in Italy, and the rooftops were a dark red tile made seemingly darker by the endless rain. The raindrops hit and bounced, and the day outside was not fit for man or beast, yet countless thousands of soldiers were battling the elements in addition to the enemy.

Looking through the church windows onto the town and valley below, Perkin wished that they were on the defense instead of the Germans. What a defensible position this was, he thought, and perhaps the Germans should have put their winter line here instead of at Monte Cassino. He shuddered involuntarily at the thought of the Gustav line—*if the Germans think it's better than this, what the hell is that line like?*

His soldier's mind envisioned the coming battle, and it was ugly. From this village, all the movements of the Allies through the valley were easily viewed, and perhaps he had been too harsh in his judgment of the Ranger commander. There was simply no way across the valley except under fire, and the high ground gave the Germans an inestimable advantage. Perkin wondered if the German commander here appreciated this great ground like General Buford did at Gettysburg, and he then decided that the Germans likely had a battle or two of their own to look back on for inspiration and guidance.

Perkin turned and walked to the other side of the nave and looked briefly up at Mount Sammucro. The mountain towered over the church. He walked back and stared hard at Mount Lungo.

An infantry assault across the valley would be very costly if Mount Lungo weren't taken first. The assaulting forces' flanks would be exposed—it was that simple—and an armored assault would be difficult as well. Perkin suspected there were anti-tank guns deployed as part of the village defenses and on Mount Lungo, and German armor might be in the village as well. The steep slopes and the olives groves would make passage for the tracked vehicles difficult except on the road, which would be mined and covered by anti-tank guns in any case. A tough nut to crack.

1245 Hours
Mount Rotondo Spur, Italy

On a good day Sam might have heard the half-tracks before he saw them, but his hearing was shot. He had stuffed toilet paper in his ears, but he was still half deafened. Sam yawned and then wiggled his ears with his finger, even though that had never helped before.

He was back in the muddy foxhole. They all were, except for the gunner on Ma Deuce.* The corporal had

---

* Ma Deuce is the nickname for the Browning M2 .50 caliber machine gun.

brought a tall dual-purpose tripod that supported ground fire as well as anti-aircraft fire, which left him standing. The corporal and his team had quickly brought brush over and camouflaged the gun as best they could, but Sam knew that once Ma Deuce began firing, they would attract attention very quickly.

Sam hadn't been sure that his little trap would work. He still wasn't, and he was afraid that if it didn't, then he would have tormented the German soldiers for nothing. *Either way, they're dead,* he thought, *but no need to be cruel to the poor sons-a-bitches.*

The two German halftracks, lightly armored personnel carriers, were taking a huge risk. Their speed wasn't fast—they could do no more than thirty miles per hour off-road—but regardless, the soldiers in the field were comrades and friends. With luck and a little daring, perhaps they could be in and out quickly while the gunners suppressed the Amis.

Sam let them come. "Hold your fire! Hold your fire!" he yelled at his riflemen.

When the halftracks were thirty yards from the trapped soldiers, they both opened fire with mounted MG-34s. As the half-tracks were bouncing along the valley floor, the German rounds went wildly over Sam's head one moment, then ripped down the hillside before returning back up again.

Heedless of the German fire, Sam pulled himself out of the muddy foxhole and ran forwards two steps. He turned to Kenton and shouted, "Now! Drop right on 'em!" and Sergeant Kenton relayed the order to the mortarmen who made their incremental adjustments. To his riflemen, he shouted, "Wait for it! Wait!"

The halftracks had pulled slightly ahead of the soldiers on the ground. They had clamshell doors in the back that crewmen opened as they screamed for their men to hurry. There was no delay. The men sprang from the ground—some with rifles, others without—and dove into the waiting vehicles. It could not have been accomplished quicker.

As the halftracks each made a turn—one going left, the other going right—Sam yelled, "Now! Pour it on them! Give 'em hell!"

Instantly two dozen rifles opened fire on the turning halftracks, but their range was extreme for the Garands—over six hundred yards—and the few rounds that found the targets bounced off the armor-plating of the halftracks. But the range was not extreme for Ma Deuce.

The heavy machine gun opened fire, and the young gunner from San Antonio, grinning wildly, tracked the tracer rounds of his fire up and into the personnel compartment of the half-track. On Sam's orders, he had loaded the heavy machine gun with armor-piercing rounds, and they screamed through the thin armor of the clam-shell doors like a .22 round passing through a cardboard box. One single round ripped through an aft door and passed through the bodies of two panzer grenadiers before passing through another metal sheet and into the body of the driver. While all were grievously wounded, only the driver died instantly.

As soon as the gunner saw the first half-track slew, he re-trained Ma Deuce quickly to the other vehicle. It was accelerating rapidly and heading for a small rise—hoping against hope to get to a defiladed position, any slight shelter from the death on the other side. Sam was bouncing on his toes, watching the tracer rounds track inexorably into the back of the halftrack when it suddenly exploded.

Sam watched, shocked, as the entire vehicle burst into flames and slowly rolled to a stop. Two soldiers pushed open the clam doors and fell burning out of the halftrack.

Several of his soldiers were screaming taunts at the burning Germans over the distance, and Sam looked at the gunner.

His wild grin was gone. He looked stunned and he shook his head sadly at Sam. "That's fucked up, sir."

Sam shook his head, stunned as well at what he had brought about, and half-shouted, "It wasn't you! Diesel wouldn't just go up like that. Not even from your rounds. He must've hit an anti-tank mine."

The gunner had targeted the first halftrack again and was still pouring rounds into it as the mortars shells started falling accurately on it. When it too burst into flames, he stopped firing, and looked over at Sam. The grin was back. "I know, sir. That's why it's fucked up."

1245 Hours
San Pietro, Italy

Captain Gerschoffer stood on a stone wall in the lower third of the village and looked out on the valley. Although the walls had been built to keep the mountain from sliding out from underneath the village, they served as admirable ramparts for the defenders.

He had walked past interlocking machine guns and grunted his approval. Anti-aircraft artillery was strategically placed around the village, and the 40 millimeter guns could be trained against vehicles or even personnel. Many could be used against targets advancing in the valley. Gerschoffer was not a fighting soldier due to the needs of the service, but there were many times that he wished he was a lowly grenadier fighting the hard fight.

Not against the Americans, of course, but he wouldn't object to killing British, French, Indians, Moroccans, Kiwis, or any other nationality represented in the Allies' polyglot armies in Italy. Of course, if it came to it, and it had, he would fight the Americans—he would just rather be somewhere else.

His two nationalities were slaughtering each other only a mile or so from his position in San Pietro. The fighting was sporadic on Mount Lungo—the American drive had been contained, although the counterattacks had not been successful—but reports were coming back from Mount La Difensa, and the news wasn't good. The Canadian-American force had completely surprised the mountain defenders and taken the mountaintop. They were stubbornly fighting to hold what they had taken that morning, and Gerschoffer doubted that the army would be able to dislodge the Forcemen.

The Abwehr had taken some heat for the events of the day. "Why didn't you know the Americans were going to attack there?" he was asked. "Because our sources in the American camp didn't know," he would answer calmly. Inside though, he was irritated. He had nothing but disdain for the army's dual outcome for every problem: an operational success or an intelligence failure. It irked him that they were not getting credit for the good work they had done and the extent to which American operations had been compromised.

He was not alone on the ramparts, despite the cold rain. There was a tall sergeant of the 29th Panzer Grenadiers to his left who was staring out at the valley—a shockingly wounded soldier looking to see how the battle was progressing. Interestingly, the soldier who leaned on a cane was tapping his toe, obviously playing a tune in his mind. Gerschoffer walked behind the sergeant and listened to him hum a song to himself. When the sergeant got to the end, he simply started over, as it was one of those songs.

"Charlie Barnet, *Unterfeldwebel?*"

The sergeant started, then turned stiffly to face the officer. Gerschoffer was taken aback and saddened by the damage to the sergeant's face. His left eye was completely closed and blood was oozing through the bandages that wrapped his face. His other eye, an intensely blue eye, was partially closed and Gerschoffer had the sense from the sergeant's tilt of his head that he couldn't see too well out of that one either. As the sergeant snapped to attention and an arm under his coat instinctively moved to salute, Gerschoffer put his arm on the soldier's shoulder and said, "At ease, Sergeant. You can salute me twice tomorrow."

Gerschoffer noticed a twitch of a smile on the corner of the tall sergeant's mouth that was not covered by gauze, smiled in return and said, "'Commanche War Dance,' yes?"

The sergeant nodded, but said nothing.

Gerschoffer turned back to the battle and said, "I saw Charlie Barnet in Los Angeles before the war. It was quite the party. Do you speak English, by any chance?"

The captain was amused by the widening of the sergeant's sole good eye, and switching to English, he said in a southern accent, "It ain't a crime. Yet. Yeah, I spent some time there. Would have liked to have seen old Charlie in Athens, that's in Georgia—a state in the south—but he had niggers in his band and wasn't really welcomed. Too bad. I saw Count Basie in LA as well when I was out there in '38 with my parents. My father can't tolerate niggers, so he didn't go, but I saw 'em. D'ya like Basie?"

The sergeant nodded again. Truthfully.

"Me, too. Goddamn, that band can play. I like Glen Miller, Tommy Dorsey, and Artie Shaw of course, but they don't hold a candle to the nigger bands. Above all, I wanted to see Bennie Moten, but he died before I ever got the chance."

The sergeant nodded in agreement, and Gerschoffer could tell that the soldier was a Moten fan as well. There were more than a few jazz and blues aficionados in the army, but as even music was seen by some through a racial and nationalist lens, it was best to keep quiet. Today was different for some reason, and Gerschoffer didn't care. *Ach, I would kill to go back to the States just to see some good bands again—just like the old days*, he thought.

1300 Hours
San Pietro, Italy

The last thing that Perkin had wanted to do that day was engage a German officer in conversation, but this was getting interesting. He was delighted and relieved when his wounds weren't questioned, and it appeared that no one expected him to talk; and when the German officer began speaking in English, in an American southern accent, the conversation became fascinating. To his great bemusement, Perkin had also found a German who liked American jazz as much as he did.

The German officer was not particularly tall, maybe two or more inches shorter than Perkin, but much heavier and wider. He was built more like Sam, although unlike Sam this officer tended more to fat than muscle.

"Benny Goodman." Perkin spoke without moving his lips, and he croaked the words out.

"What's that, Sergeant?"

"I also like Benny Goodman. 'Sing, Sing, Sing' is my favorite." Perkin spoke very slowly, in what he hoped was a German accent, and he winced as though talking was terribly painful. In truth, it was.

"Me, too. The first time I heard it was just electrifying. First the drums, then the horns, the woodwinds, then the drums again, then horns and woodwinds. But it was the drums that I liked. When I lived in the States, I saved all my money and bought an old Victrola, and I listened to that song over and over. Did you ever live in the States, *Kamerad?*"

"No, *mein Herr*. I visited England once though."

"You seem to understand the language well. Yes?"

Perkin nodded. "Yes, *mein Herr*. It is a pleasure to speak it again. I don't get much practice except with prisoners."

"Do you speak any other languages, Sergeant?"

"Yes, *mein Herr*. Spanish. My Italian is coming along. No Russian."

Perkin noted that the German officer was looking at him with interest, and the German's next question was not a surprise, "No need to speak Russian here, although you might need it some day. What do you do?"

"*Schütze, mein Herr.*"* Perkin began to think through the regiments of the 29th that he knew were engaged in the battle, as that was likely to be the next question.

He was wrong. "What happened to you, then?"

Perkin nodded with his head towards Mount Lungo. "Our counterattack. Hand to hand. Then, *Dachschaden.*† Hit in the face by an Ami shovel. I was sent to the aid station here."

"What happened to the Ami?"

"I hit him back so hard it killed his whole family."

Gerschoffer laughed heartily and looked at Perkin's face. "*Mein Gott!* I think I can see the outline of the shovel!"

Perkin couldn't help but grin, but it hurt to do so. Then he laughed as well.

Gerschoffer grinned back, "It may hurt to laugh, Sergeant, but at least you can still do it. I must return to

---

* A rifleman.
† Literally "roof damage"—head wounds.

Cassino, can I give you a lift somewhere? I have a car. We can talk some more about jazz and big bands."

"*Danke, mein Herr.* That would be wonderful. I've had my fill of this rain." Perkin answered without hesitation. "Do you like 'Big Noise from Winnetka'?"

1320 Hours
San Pietro, Italy

The slow, limping, walk to the *Kübelwagen** was uneventful, taken up by a discussion about American music that Perkin enjoyed, even as his mind raced through his courses of action. He unbuttoned his greatcoat, and explaining that he could not keep his arm in the sling for a moment longer, he stiffly ran it through the sleeve, and while Gerschoffer sat down in the driver's seat, Perkin moved the .45 from the sling to his pocket.

As the German captain started the car, Perkin asked, "What is it that you do, Captain?"

Gerschoffer shrugged and said, "I do analyses."

"Intelligence?"

"*Ja.* As I have an understanding of the Amis, I use that. Have you tested for intelligence work?"

Perkin gave a small laugh. "No. I came into the infantry, and I expect I will go out in the infantry." He paused for a second, his heart pounding. "I had a friend in the Pioneers who said he worked with *Auslandsdeutsche* in *Neapel.*† Was that you?"

Gerschoffer gave Perkin a hard look, "Your friend is indiscreet. Tell him to keep his mouth shut."

---

* The Kübelwagen was the German two-wheel drive equivalent to the American jeep.
† Naples

"He was killed on the Volturno, *mein Herr*." Perkin said smoothly.

"*Ach*. Sorry. We don't advertise ourselves. Too many detractors."

Gerschoffer wiped the water from his face, put the German jeep into gear, and they lurched and slid down a recently bulldozed and graveled road leading to the northwest—the existing road from Highway 6 leading into San Pietro was under observation and artillery fire. "I hate the fucking rain, and I'm ready to leave Italy as well and just go home. No rest for the weary, I guess. Where can I take you?"

"My unit is on Monte Lungo. Perhaps the base of the hill, and I can find it from there."

When the Kübelwagen reached a fork in the road, the route to the left headed to Mount Lungo and the road to the right to Cassino. They had only gone a few hundred yards down the left fork when Perkin ordered in a strong, clear voice, "Pull over here!"

In German, Captain Gerschoffer sputtered, "Who the hell are you to—" Gerschoffer noticed the .45 pointing at his ribs for the first time.

"Shut up and pull over!"

Gerschoffer had gone white—either with anger or fear, Perkin couldn't be sure—and he uncertainly steered the Kübelwagen to the side of the road.

"Into the trees!" The German officer drove the car into a small grove of olive trees. "Get out of the car!" Perkin ordered.

"I will not!"

"Do as I say, goddammit!"

"I will not!" Gerschoffer shook his head emphatically, and his right hand dropped to his holster, scrabbling for his service pistol.

Perkin dropped the nose of the Colt down and shot Captain Gerschoffer through the right thigh—the heavy slug shattered the femur, passing through Gerschoffer's leg and the vehicle's wooden floorboard. Following a split second behind the deafening noise of the Colt, the German soldier screamed and, unexpectedly, lunged across the car at Perkin—his outstretched fingers reaching for Perkin's face.

Perkin twisted to his left and let him come, swiftly wrapping his damaged left hand around Gerschoffer's head and pulling the German even closer to him. Before the German captain could regain his balance, Perkin struck the German hard in the face with the barrel of the heavy Colt, then again, then a third time. Perkin slammed the hot barrel into the eye of Captain Gerschoffer, who quit struggling and recoiled from the Colt.

As Perkin backed out of the car, Gerschoffer raised his hands in surrender, his face pinched tight with pain. Perkin shoved the Colt into his belt, grabbed Gerschoffer by the collar of his greatcoat, and with all of his strength pulled the stunned officer across to the passenger side of the car. The German dropped his hands and pushed up onto the passenger seat as he tried to make room for his shattered leg to cross the gearshift, but as the shattered fragments of his thigh bone grated together roughly, Gerschoffer screamed again. Perkin let go of the coat and pulled his pistol again. He quickly flipped it over in his hand and savagely hit Gerschoffer on the bridge of his nose with the butt of the pistol.

"Be quiet!" he snarled.

Gerschoffer screamed in rage and pain, lashed out with his huge fist, and hit Perkin in the thigh, next to his groin. The German pushed on the far door of the car with his good leg and clawed across the seats trying to reach the American. Perkin dodged another hard swing, calmly stepped back and then kicked Gerschoffer hard in the head. Still, the German didn't give up. He frantically rolled over onto his back, his body stretched across the car, his broken right leg wedged between the seat and the gearshift. As his hand reached for his pistol, Perkin kicked him in the head once more, then stepped up to the car and slammed his knee onto the throat of the upturned Captain Gerschoffer. Perkin lifted the Colt once more, but there was no need to hit the German again. He was unconscious.

Breathing hard, Perkin reached down and deftly took Gerschoffer's pistol and tucked it into his own belt. He felt around the Abwehr officer's belt for a dagger and found none. There was no reaction from Gerschoffer.

Perkin pushed and pulled the limp body, intending to get it upright, but the broken leg was wedged too tightly, and Perkin had to go to the driver's side and turn the leg until it released. He winced as he felt the bones shift in the leg of the unconscious officer, but he continued prodding and pulling until Gerschoffer was sitting in the passenger seat in a relatively normal posture.

Looking to see if there had been any reaction to the pistol shot, and there was none, Perkin walked to the front of the German jeep and unwrapped a length of heavy rope that was looped onto the steel bumper. He walked back, checked the wound in Gerschoffer's leg— it was bleeding profusely, but not pulsing blood—and then wrapped the heavy rope around the unconscious man's torso and the metal seat of the Kübelwagen. As he did so, he noticed blood dripping onto the car and Captain Gerschoffer. His own wounds had opened up again and his bandages had been torn from his face. It was odd, as he could not recall Captain Gerschoffer even touching him.

1340 Hours
Mount Rotondo Spur, Italy

Sam was tired, and he was having a hard time focusing. He had gotten no sleep at all the night before and he wondered several times whether he had gotten his days mixed up. *Could it be just yesterday that we took the little farmhouse?*

Sam sat on a rock partially covered by a few remaining scraps of an evergreen tree. After seeing that his troops were fed, Sam sat down and ate some hot food. Someone in the rear had shipped forward huge kettles of hot beans with an unidentified meat stirred in. Stale rolls supplemented the meal, and Sam washed it all down with hot coffee sweetened with his four remaining sugar cubes. Although he would not have thought twice about it on any other day, on this cold wet day, the meal seemed as good as Margaret's cooking back on the ranch.

To a man as big as Sam, food had always played an important role in his life. He had grown up on a south Texas smorgasbord of southern cuisine, Mexican food, Texas barbeque—which was clearly superior to the barbeque of the southeastern states—and fresh seafood. As he ate the huge helping of beans and mystery meat, he mused about what he would eat first when he got home. Maybe all of them in one meal, he thought. He shared Perkin's taste in C–rations, and Sam had long ago vowed that he would certainly never eat mutton stew after the army. Like any good Texas rancher, he had no use whatsoever for sheep in any case.

Sam did intend to take some culinary tidbits away from his time in the army in general and in Italy in particular. He had looked carefully at a stone pizza oven in Naples once, and thought that pizza might have to be incorporated into his diet. Sam loved the Italian tomatoes and couldn't understand why they were better than what he grew in his private garden on the ranch, but as agriculture had been his minor at Texas A&M, he thought he could get to the bottom of it before leaving Italy. He didn't think much of Italian bread, but he loved the small purple Gaeta olives, and he saw no reason why olive trees wouldn't work in south Texas. Olive oil had an interesting taste to Sam, but it was ridiculous to think that it would ever replace lard for cooking.

Outside of the food, Italy held little interest for Sam. The mountains were beautiful, but they were less appealing when Germans were shooting at you from them. He had certainly liked Gianina immensely, but had yet to meet another Italian that struck him as worthy of his blood and toil, and he had seen very few indications that the Italians were prepared to spill their own blood for their country.

His thoughts roamed back to Texas, and he thought about what Maggie would be doing at the same time. Sam could never keep it straight whether there was six hours' difference or seven, but in any case, she was already awake. She woke up at six o'clock every morning, and Sam was sure that she had already had her first cup of coffee for the day. Margaret liked it strong and black, and Sam was sure that she would approve of the Italian coffee and espresso.

They had never had much of a stable family life on the ranch—only a few weeks while on leave nearly two years before. Other than that, they had lived in a small house in Brownwood while the division was at Camp Bowie, and then she had followed Sam as the division moved to Florida, Virginia, and Massachusetts before he deployed overseas. But Sam had a notion of what normal married life was like, and he despaired every time he thought that the war might continue to 1946 or even 1948, as some soldiers thought.

In his daydreams, post-war life was an extension of the idyllic three weeks of leave he took in 1942. He and Margaret would get up, have a cup of coffee together, and go for a ride on the ranch before it got too hot or maybe take the sailboat out on the bay. She would tend to the house while he managed the thousands of things that needed to be done on a 16,000-acre ranch. *Bigger than that, now,* Sam thought, *Maggie's bought another thousand acres west of Portland.*

Sam had nearly leaped out of his uniform when he read the letter announcing the purchase. He had always wanted the land which was adjacent to his own ranch, but had felt that the price was too steep. The land had been sold when the rancher, an old friend of Sam's father, had passed away. The rancher's widow had no use for the land but was openly delighted to sell it to a woman. Maggie had negotiated a good deal, and she had explained in her letter that even with the high market value of the land, that they would make it up in oil revenues within five years, and, yes, she had acquired all the mineral rights.

Margaret had made several aggressive business decisions that made the conservative Sam nervous, but she had been right in every one so far. He already had more money than he thought possible to spend in a lifetime—land interested him much more than money—and he was getting richer every day through the war. Although Sam had never had intentions of getting rich over the misery of others, he had two commodities that the government desperately wanted: oil and cattle.

Sam wasn't the only millionaire in the army, nor even in the division, but he was one of very few multi-millionaires serving in combat units. Perkin knew what Sam's worth was, and a few of his close friends knew that he was well-off, but Sam was careful to keep his wealth to himself. Likewise, he was careful to never trade on his name. As the great-nephew of a former president who also served as the Chief Justice of the Supreme Court, Sam knew the Taft name would open doors for him, but Sam saw no good purpose in exploiting it.

As he gnawed on the last of his stale rolls, Sam re-lived the skirmish of an hour before. He'd not had a clear idea what would happen if he pinned those soldiers down, but he had assumed that the soldiers of their company would attempt to rescue them. In retrospect, he didn't know what he would have done had the Germans sent out medics, but they hadn't. As it was, Sam was disgusted that he had played on a human foible like the ties of brotherhood in order to kill his fellow man, but every Nazi son of a bitch he killed now was one he wouldn't have to kill later. *By God, if I have to kill every bastard in the whole German Army in order to make it home, then bring 'em on.*

He was darkly contemplating that thought when Sergeant Kenton whistled from the left crest of the spur, "Hey, sir! Looks like they might be sending another team out to the wrecked halftracks."

1340 Hours
San Pietro, Italy

Perkin sat in the driver's seat, twisted until he faced Captain Gerschoffer, and then slapped the German hard on the face.

"Wake up!"

The German officer moaned, and his head moved slightly. Perkin slapped him again.

"Come on now, Cap'n. Wake up."

"No," the large German officer groaned.

"Yeah, come on, partner. Wake up now." Perkin slapped him again, and Gerschoffer's eyes fluttered. "There ya go. Come on."

"*Was?* What's going on?"

"You're my prisoner, Cap'n. The war's over for you. Pay attention and wake up!"

"Who are you?" Gerschoffer asked. His faculties were slowly returning to him, but he was still confused and in a great deal of pain.

"You know who I am. I'm Cap'n Berger. Weren't you expecting me?"

"I need to get to a doctor." For the first time, Gerschoffer realized he was bound. He struggled until he was slapped again.

"Stop that shit and answer my questions! You were expecting me?"

Silence.

"Who's your source on the American side?"

Nothing.

"You orchestrated the bombings in Naples?"

Gerschoffer stared stonily ahead.

On a hunch, Perkin asked, "How did Sam Taft come to your attention at Paestum?"

The German officer said nothing but his jaw tensed.

"Answer me, or I'll kill you now and leave you to rot in this fucking mud!"

"Gerschoffer, Mark H., Captain, German Army . . . ."

"Shut up! For Christ's sake, I don't have time for that." Perkin put the car into gear and as he let out the clutch he said, "Gerschoffer? Hey! You played for Georgia, didn't you? Well. Well. A football hero and a soldier of the Reich." Surprising Gerschoffer, Perkin's tone had turned to acid. "Fucking traitor. Murderer. Enjoy the hangman."

Recovering somewhat, Gerschoffer snorted, "Hang me for what? I'm a German officer, not an American citizen. You captured me in uniform. You can't hang me for being a traitor or shoot me for being a spy."

"I meant for Naples. They'll hang you for Naples. For the post office."

A note of distain entered Gerschoffer's voice, "I was just following orders. No . . . I think they won't hang me."

There was a long silence, then Perkin nodded and said, "You're right. They won't."

1345 Hours
Mount Rotondo Spur, Italy

"Right there, sir!" Sergeant Kenton pointed to a Kübelwagen that was tearing through the valley, apparently on a beeline to the two still-smoking halftracks.

"Froman!" Sam called out to his sniper.

"Sir?"

"Give me your rifle. I'm gonna kill this son of a bitch myself before he comes into sight of the other platoon."

Private Froman nodded and handed the rifle to his platoon leader. "There's a round chambered now, sir."

"Got it. Everyone hold your fire! Christian!" This was to Sam's radioman. "Tell company to hold their fire. This one's mine!"

As Private Christian raised the company commander on the walkie-talkie, Sam slid the Springfield over the same branch that Private Froman had used only an hour before. When Sam moved up to place his cheek on the stock, all of a sudden his world narrowed to a singular focus: killing the Germans in the Kübelwagen. Rather than the constant accompanying sounds of the combat in the hills and mountains, all Sam could hear was the sound of his own breathing, slow and calm. When he looked through the scope, everything seemed to slow down—the

German jeep was still speeding through the valley, but it appeared through the scope as if it were moving in slow motion. As it got closer, Sam could begin to make out occupants in the vehicle. There were two of them, and Sam could barely discern the field gray of their uniforms.

Sam was an extraordinary marksman, and had been one long before joining the National Guard. It was easy for him, particularly with the use of the limb, to track the Kübelwagen. He set the crosshairs on the driver, and began to gently squeeze the trigger. He would wait a few seconds, but part of him wanted to make the longer shot—for fun.

Through the scope, Sam thought he saw the driver struggling to take off his tunic and it seemed as if the car had slowed and was steering erratically. It was extremely difficult to tell—the vehicle was bouncing over the valley floor and the distance was still great. The Kübelwagen drove without stopping past the two halftracks and Sam thought he saw a tunic fly out of the window. He inwardly shrugged and applied more pressure on the trigger. Almost there.

Suddenly, Sam heard the distant popping of rifle fire and without taking his eye from the scope, he snarled, "Goddammit Christian, tell them to hold their fire!"

"Ain't us, L.T. The Kraut outposts are shootin' at that jeep."

Sam jerked his head up, the vision of the driver lost from the scope. A white flag, maybe an undershirt, was fluttering from the window.

"Hold your fire!" Sam bellowed. "If the Krauts want this fella dead, then we want him alive! Christian, make sure Cap'n Spaulding knows what we're seeing. Sergeant, call for smoke!"

He tossed the Springfield back to Private Froman and picked up his Garand. Sam began running to his left

towards the gap between the spur and Mount Lungo—
trying to get to the obvious destination of the German
jeep. Sam wanted to make sure that the soldiers on his left
flank, those in contact with the remainder of the company,
didn't fire on the vehicle.

Seeing the undershirt flap in the wind rushing past
the car, Sam was reminded of a Lone Star flag that Perkin's platoon had planted on the beach at Paestum two
months before. He had thought then, *Only Perkin would
think to do such a thing*, and the very same thought crossed
his mind now. With absolute illogical certainty, Sam knew
who was in the Kübelwagen, and his blood turned cold.

"Don't shoot! Don't shoot!"

His soldiers watched in surprise as the massive lieutenant tore through the woods across the hilltop and past
their position. They were even more surprised as he called
out across the distance to his company commander, "It's
Perkin! Don't shoot! It's Perkin!"

Sam watched as Captain Spaulding wheeled around
and shouted at his soldiers, and he was gratified to see
several rifles drop slightly. Perkin was almost home safely.
Just seconds now and Perkin would roll over a little crest
and could coast into the American roadblock on Victory
Road.

The Kübelwagen was getting closer, only two hundred yards. As smoke rounds from the Able Company
mortars began dropping in the vicinity of the burned out
halftracks, a machine gun opened fire from the base of
Mount Lungo at the right rear quarter of the fleeing Kübelwagen.

It was a hidden site—one that the Texans had not
noted before. Unlike the American gunner an hour earlier,
this site fired no tracer rounds, but the German gunner was
good, and had honed his skills in Poland, France, Yugoslavia, and now Italy. A moving vehicle, even a vehicle hun-

dreds of yards away, was no particular challenge. He fired a short burst, evaluated where the rounds impacted in the mud, adjusted his weapon, and fired another short burst.

The driver of the Kübelwagen was seemingly oblivious to the machine gunner to his rear until the canvas top of the German jeep ripped open in a dozen places. He ducked his head, gunned the engine, and as the Kübelwagen topped the small crest, the car went airborne. For a sickening second, Sam was afraid that the car was more exposed to gunfire as it seemed to hang in the air like a punted football. Then the vehicle came down, the nose of the Kübelwagen slamming hard into the mud, and the driver lost control.

The Kübelwagen began sliding, and the last of its kinetic energy was spent spinning in the mud towards the American lines, and Sam's heart stopped as the passenger's side lifted as the driver's side wheels struck a long and low oval-shaped rock. Surely it would tip over, he thought, but it didn't. The car dropped down on all four wheels and came to a halt fifty yards short of the American roadblock. Whether it was due to counterfire by the company machine-gunners, the smoke, or providence, Sam would never know, but the German MG-42 was now silent. As Sam came out of the relative safety of the tree line and ran the last hundred yards to the car, he watched as the shirtless driver pushed open his door and slid out into the mud of the valley.

Breathing heavily, Sam slid to a stop next to the car and knelt in the limited protection of the car's body. It was Perkin. Sam wasn't sure how he drove—one badly bruised eye was closed and the other one wasn't far behind it.

Sam heard running footsteps in the water and the mud, and he spun around with his Garand ready. He lowered his rifle as Private Kulis dropped and slid into the rock as easily as a base runner sliding into third.

As the young rifleman crouched with his rifle by the rear wheel of the car and looked carefully back into the valley, he said, "Thought you might need some help, sir. I saw some grenadiers moving up behind them halftracks through the smoke. We need to get moving, sir."

"Hey, Sam! Is that you, Eddie?" It was apparent that Perkin was having a hard time forming words. His face was badly swollen, and he had blood pouring from his nose and his chin.

Without answering, Sam quickly lifted his cousin up to a sitting position and looked for bullet wounds. Despite terrible scrapes and cuts on Perkin's arms, he saw nothing life-threatening.

"Kulis. Check on the other guy."

"Yes sir." A quick glance into the Kübelwagen and Private Kulis saw that the passenger, a German officer, was dead. The interior of the car was covered in blood, and a bullet hole in the German's left temple told the Texan that he needed to waste no time on the officer in the car. Kulis whistled softly and said, "He's deader than Sam Houston, sir."

"Hey, Perk," Sam finally said, tears in his eyes, and he effortlessly picked his cousin up and tossed him over his shoulder. Kulis picked up the lieutenant's rifle, and he and Sam jogged the fifty yards over another small crest to safety and a gathering crowd of friends.

1420 Hours
Mount Rotondo Spur, Italy

"I wouldn't think that I'd say these words to you again, not after Paestum, but you're the dumbest son of a bitch I ever met." The speaker was Lieutenant Colonel Wranosky, and he was shaking his head in wonder and amusement.

"Well, sir, I'm beginnin' to come around to your way of thinkin'." Perkin said with a grin. Although his body was in terrible shape, he had never felt so exhilarated. He had come through an impossible mission alive and had concrete intelligence to report to General Walker. Besides that, and maybe more important, Perkin had enjoyed almost every minute of the past two days, and he was one step closer to completely avenging Gianina.

Perkin was sitting on a large rock next to Sam. They were in the shadow of the spur, and Perkin had two blankets wrapped around his shoulders and a canteen cup of steaming hot coffee in his hands. A soldier had been sent to the quartermaster to get another uniform and pack for Perkin, and he would carry an M-1 carbine until he had the chance to recover his Thompson from the ossuary in San Pietro. He had told his story first to Sam and Bill Spaulding, with Kulis in attendance. Then he told it a second time to his old battalion commander, who had personally driven up in a jeep as word of Perkin's return spread.

After Perkin had given a condensed version of his voyage, he asked his battalion commander, "Where's Cap'n Lockridge, sir? I really need to talk to him before I report to General Walker."

"He's getting ready for a 1430 briefing with the regimental commander. I need to get ready as well. One last thing: tell me about the Kraut officer." Wranosky was taken aback by Perkin's condition and felt that young captain needed to see the battalion surgeon, but he wanted to make sure that he had a clear understanding of the events so he could brief Colonel Jamison.

"Yes sir. His name was Captain Mark Gerschoffer. A German intelligence officer in a group of *Auslands-deutsche*—German nationals who were raised outside of the Reich. He was involved in the bombing campaign in Naples, including the post office bombing."

Wranosky looked hard at Perkin. "You're sure of that?"

"Yes sir. He told me."

"Why would he do that?" asked a puzzled Colonel Wranosky.

"I think he was in shock, sir, and maybe had a bit of a concussion." Perkin hoped that the questions ended there, but they didn't.

"Alright, Perk. And why was he in shock with a concussion?" Wranosky's impatience was beginning to show.

"Well, it's like this sir . . . we, uh . . . we had a bit of a fallin' out, and uh . . . well, I shot him in the thigh. And, um, hit him in the head with my Colt."

"How many times?"

Perkin looked out at the ground and blew his breath out while he stiffly shook his head. "Hard to say, sir. Somewheres between five and fifteen, I'd guess."

Wranosky looked into Perkin's good eye, which was staring dispassionately at him through his bruised face, and the colonel shivered involuntarily as he reached a personal conclusion about the fate of the German captain. "How did Gerschoffer die, Captain Berger?"

Perkin noted the shift from his first name to the more formal Captain Berger. He shrugged, "Sir, I . . . ."

Private Kulis had noted the change in the colonel's tone as well. He coughed and interrupted the captain, "I beg your pardon, sir. I looked at the body while I was out there. That son of a bitch must have been hit by German fire while they were escaping. He was killed by a rifle round."

Lieutenant Colonel Wranosky wasn't entirely satisfied. "And just how would you know that, Private?"

The young rifleman looked his battalion commander in the eyes and said calmly, "Because the Kraut officer looked just like every one of the Krauts I've killed with a rifle. The one I kilt with a grenade looked different. I suppose I know what it looks like, sir."

Lieutenant Colonel Wranosky looked back at the private, and saw a dogged stubbornness begin to set in. It was a look that he'd seen many times before in soldiers—a look which said, *Fuck your rank—I know I'm right.* It was, however, very similar to the look which said, *If I don't get away with this whopper I'm telling, I'm a dead man.*

Wranosky wasn't sure which look he was seeing, and he turned his attention to Sam and raised his eyebrows. The cold stare that he got from the officer in return was just as dogged. "Well, Sam?"

Sam shook his head and replied truthfully, "I didn't see the cocksucker, but I don't give two shits how he died . . . sir."

Unconsciously, Captain Spaulding stepped behind Perkin and put his hand on his shoulder, and Sam stood up and towered over all of them. The battalion commander sighed to himself, and decided to revisit the issue at another time—maybe when they'd had the opportunity to examine the dead German's body after the 36th controlled no-man's-land. He wouldn't tolerate vigilantism in his command.

Wranosky offered a thin smile to Private Kulis and said, "I hear you, Private. I'm sure you're right. Lieutenant Taft, thank you." He turned back to Perkin, nodded, and said, "Good work, Perkin. Jim'll be done about 1500. He's over in that smokehouse yonder." Wranosky squinted at the smokehouse, then said, "Ah shit, I bet that's Colonel Jamison. God save me from early colonels."

With that, Wranosky put his jeep in gear and started the three hundred yard drive back to the smokehouse. When he was gone, Captain Spaulding dismissed Private Kulis. When the private was out of earshot, he said, "What's the straight skinny here, Perk? Did you shoot that son of a bitch?"

"Come on, boys. What'd ya—"

The three officers ducked involuntarily as inbound artillery screamed overhead. The Germans were having another go at the little farm. A German forward observer must have seen the two jeeps headed in the same direction from different angles, drawn the right conclusions about a headquarters or command post, and called in a strike.

The farmhouse and most of the outlying buildings were long destroyed, as the Germans had mercilessly shelled it the night before. But that certainly wouldn't have prevented the Americans from using the farm grounds, where for all the Germans knew, there may remain some intact shelter as well as potable well water—so they shelled it again.

The first round fell short of the farm. It was a ground burst fired from a 155 millimeter tube tucked up against the mountains in the Liri valley. The gunners could not see their targets, and could not have known whether they hit or missed. They simply received a fire order, prepared their weapon, and fired.

It burst twenty yards from Lieutenant Colonel Wranosky's jeep atop a small outcropping of rock. Searing hot metal and rock fragments went every conceivable direction in conjunction with a strong blast wave, and the rock and metal shrapnel ripped through Wranosky's jeep. One fragment tore through the canvas top of his jeep and embedded itself into Wranosky's helmet. Another fragment sliced through his chin as it whirled past, only to bury itself deeply into his shoulder. The front passenger tire blew from another fragment, and in his panic, Wranosky over-steered the jeep and it flipped onto its side and slid through the Italian mud. Wranosky was thrown from the vehicle and lay motionless.

The German call for artillery was for area fire in the vicinity of the farm, meaning that no particular building was the target. The goal was to spread the fragmentation and blast over as large an area as possible and try to kill or injure any personnel caught out in the open. The first shot had preceded a battery salvo, and that salvo was dead on target in arriving, and the rounds fell among the destroyed farmhouse and its outlying buildings.

One round, from the same 155 millimeter battery, scored a direct hit on Colonel Jamison's unoccupied jeep. It seemingly evaporated, but in truth the vehicle exploded. The metal, glass, wood, and rubber found on the jeep was added to the metal fragmentation, and a soldier thirty yards from the explosion had his collarbone broken from the whirling steering wheel flung from the jeep.

The most devastating round landed directly on the small smokehouse. The round penetrated through the roof of the building before detonating a fraction of a second later and instantly killing Colonel Jamison—the commander of the 141st Regiment; Major Howarth—the battalion executive officer; Major Turner—the battalion G-3; and Captain Jim Lockridge—the battalion intelligence officer.

Chapter Nine

December 4, 1943
0100 Hours
Victory Road, No-Man's-Land, Italy

The two soldiers moved silently through the night. For once, the artillery had died off, and the sounds of battle had diminished. Occasionally a rifle shot was heard from the mountaintops as small individual battles continued to be fought for control of an outcropping of rocks or for a ledge or a crest. Unheard in the darkness and distance to the valley floor were the cries of the wounded as they were carried down the mountains by stretcher, and the moans of soldiers having nightmares in their sleep.

As they knelt next to the German Kübelwagen in no-man's-land, Private Pfadenhauer whispered to his best friend, "Tell me again why we're doin' this?"

"That weren't no rifle shot." Private Kulis whispered back calmly.

"Yeah, you told me that. Why are we doin' *this?*"

"I don't want anybody to come out here and see what I saw. Look, we didn't save the captain's ass on the beach, and at the monastery, and on the mountain just to let some staff pussies charge him for killin' the enemy in wartime. Right?"

As Pfadenhauer readied the satchel charge, he whispered to Kulis, who was climbing into the Kübelwagen, "Don't you think that the right thing would've been to keep this fucker alive and interrogate him?"

Kulis turned on a flashlight with a red lens—it gave out very little light and was visible for only a few yards away. He rapidly looked over the dead German captain and around the vehicle, and he saw what he expected to see. Kulis bent over, picked them up off the floorboard, and put them in his pocket.

The normally calm and stoic Kulis shivered, turned off the light, backed out of the car, and knelt next to his friend. "You want me to do this?"

"Are you kidding me? Hell, no, I wanna do it. Maybe I'll put this in *my* memoirs: 'This book, about the war hero Roscoe Pfadenhauer, is dedicated to the already-dead Kraut officer he blew up in the middle of the fuckin' night, out in the middle of fuckin' nowhere.'" Pfadenhauer grinned in the dark. "How's that for a dedication?"

"Surprisingly literate." Kulis whispered. "Set the fuse and let's go."

Pfadenhauer pulled a cord coming out of the satchel, grabbed Kulis, and the two soldiers ran away. It was an improvised satchel charge, one definitely not one sanctioned by the army, that consisted of four American grenades and two captured German stick grenades stuffed into Kulis's gasmask bag—the gasmask itself having been casually dropped on the roadside months before as an unnecessary weight. With the help of a cousin, an armorer

assigned to the division's engineers, Pfadenhauer had de-
vised a slow-burning fuse to a small detonating charge,
and he had told Kulis that he expected the fuse to give
them five minutes to return to their shared foxhole.

With the aid of Private Vince Fratelli, they were back
through the wire and into their positions without challenge in four minutes. Fratelli didn't say a word—he just
gripped Kulis's shoulder and then disappeared back to his
foxhole.

"Hey." Pfadenhauer's heart rate was beginning to return to normal, and he finally felt he could whisper again
without sounding afraid.

"Yeah?" Kulis's heart rate hadn't changed all night.

"You didn't answer me. Wouldn't it have been better
had the cap'n just kept him alive and turned the fucker
over to interrogators?"

As Kulis debated telling his friend that he suspected
that Captain Berger had gotten the information that he
wanted before he killed the German officer, the satchel
charge detonated at four minutes and thirty-seven seconds after ignition.

Immediately and according to plan, Kulis and
Pfadenhauer began to shout "Germans! Krauts on the
wire!" and all of no-man's-land lit up like the Fourth of
July as a bright brief spiral of flame roared from the fuel
tank of the Kübelwagen and tracer rounds screamed back
and forth across the valley. After a few seconds, Kulis quit
firing himself and sat back and watched his handiwork
with great satisfaction. There was no doubt in his mind
that even his own command would assume now that the
charge was set by the Germans.

In the excitement of the explosion and firing into the
darkness at nothing, Private Pfadenhauer forgot about his
question. But when things died back down, Kulis reached
into his pocket and pulled put the five empty .45 casings

that he had picked up from the floorboard of the Kübel-wagen. Private Kulis dropped them on the ground and pushed them into the mud of his foxhole with his boot.

1245 Hours
Caserta, Italy

The small major stamped out a cigarette and looked across the small table and deep into the dark black eyes of his beautiful companion. It was not a lover's gaze, but a desperate look trying to divine the woman's soul. It was a questing look for the truth, and Major Grossmann knew that he'd never know for sure if he'd found it.

"You're sure Mark's dead?"

Antoniette Bernardi nodded. She was bored with the discussion and was thinking of shopping for shoes. She disliked strong emotions that weren't related to her or her work, and she reached across the table to take one of Major Grossmann's cigarettes. Bernardi was mildly surprised when he fiercely grabbed her wrist and glared angrily at her.

"Take your hand off me, Douglas," she said calmly, her boredom evident. "As I told you, apparently Captain Berger captured Gerschoffer in San Pietro, tortured him, and murdered him. There's nothing more to say."

Her actual understanding of Captain's Gerschoffer's death was that he had been captured by the American officer, and was shot by friendly rifle fire when Berger had made his escape. The notion that Gerschoffer had been tortured and murdered had come to her while she was sharing cornetti earlier in the day with Ronald Ebbins. She despised Ebbins, was bored with Caserta, and wished to return to Rome, and she thought that perhaps these little additions to the story might serve her interests.

"Oh, dear God. How has this happened?" Grossmann was saddened at the loss of his friend, but war was war. His evident concern was that his operation had been compromised—and by extension, so had he and Bernardi.

"Well, Douglas . . . ," Bernardi inhaled deeply of the cigarette and blew the smoke into Major Grossmann's face. After seeing the irritation in his eyes and the grim, pinched look on his face, she decided to push just a little harder for sport. "I did tell you to kill this man, did I not? And you've failed. Again, I believe. My contact says that Berger is smart and capable, which is why I suspect he dislikes him so, but I certainly can't imagine that he is smarter and more capable than you." The last was said in a slightly mocking tone. She would have said more, but there was a murderous look in Major Grossmann's eyes. *Better not to push him too far*, she thought, *after all, I had taken Mark as a lover to protect me from Grossmann if the need arose. And now he's dead . . . and the shops close for reposo in a few minutes.* She sighed.

Grossmann drank a glass of wine. He leaned back in his chair and thought in silence for several minutes. His agitation was clearly melting away, and was being replaced by his usual cool, analytical demeanor.

"We have to assume that we're compromised. We need to get to Naples today, lay low at the safe house for awhile, and then we'll use our contacts in the Camorra to catch a fishing boat to Gaeta and from there to Rome." Grossmann was staring at his wine while he talked, and so he missed the brief flash of triumph in her eyes. He thought that perhaps it would be best to leave immediately from Naples, but he wanted an opportunity to report back to Abwehr command at Cassino and confirm Gerschoffer's absence.

Excellent news. She could shop in Naples before going home to Rome. "Oh, Douglas. Must we? Our work here is just beginning to bear fruit."

"I know. I know! Damn it! But we need to depart immediately. Don't return to your apartment, you have clothes in Naples."

She shrugged. *Allora.* At least she would be free of the idiot Ebbins. She toyed with the notion of leaving him a note, perhaps claiming to be pregnant, but she decided that his anguish would be far worse if she just left without a word. *The stupid fool actually believes I love him.*

1945 Hours
1st Battalion Aid Station, South of Mount Lungo, Italy

The two officers stared at each other. One was a bull-necked officer wearing the clean eagles of a freshly appointed full colonel. He was lying on his back in a cot with a bandage around his head and his arm in a sling. The other was a tall captain who had stopped at the aid station to have his bandages replaced and to have a word with the new regimental commander.

"This might surprise you, Perkin, but I tried to do two very contradictory things regarding you in the past twenty-four hours. First, I talked to the divisional provost about having an investigation begun on you. To be frank with you, I suspect that you executed that German officer. But . . . as the Krauts conveniently blew up the officer's remains last night, and as you were here with me when it happened, I was told that division has no interest in proceeding with an investigation. By the way, I understand that division was very happy with the information that you provided on San Pietro. Not that it'll do 'em much good. Second, and you might find this odd given the first piece of news that I just shared with you, I tried hard to convince the general to put you onto my

regimental staff." Colonel Wranosky gave him a tired
smile and said, "While I think that you're a loose cannon
with near suicidal and homicidal tendencies, you seem
to get things done. I need people like that. But . . . I was
told that you've already *picked* a new billet, and I can't say
that I disagree with the choice. *Major* Spaulding's gonna
need a good intelligence officer on his staff. Don't let
him down. Now, I'm gonna ask you a question, and you
don't have to answer, but you have my word that it's off
the record."

Perkin nodded, knowing the question to come.

"You killed that traitor, didn't you?"

Perkin didn't answer.

"Did you get the information that you wanted?"

"Yes sir."

"Are there more of them? American-Germans working for the Nazis, I mean."

"Yes sir. There are. And I got a name and a location.
A German officer. There's also a girl, but he wouldn't give
me her name." Perkin grimaced at the memory. He had
put two more slugs into Gerschoffer's leg to get the information about Major Grossmann. The German officer had
screamed and cursed and struggled mightily against his
bindings, and had only been silenced when Perkin hit him
across the face with the pistol again. Perkin didn't know
what hold the girl had over Gerschoffer, but Perkin could
read in the German's eyes that he wouldn't betray her.

"Are you going to kill this officer, too?"

Perkin didn't answer, just a slight, almost imperceptible nod.

"Pass what you know to counterintelligence immediately. That's an order. Then, if you need to look into this
further, take your cousin and the little rifleman as soon as
the battalion's pulled off the line. Not before. I'll let Major
Spaulding know."

"Thank you, sir."

Wranosky was surprised at his mix of emotions concerning the young officer before him. He'd always been a by-the-book officer, and he had been quite willing to court-martial Perkin earlier in the day. But he had spent the hours on the cot staring at the sodden roof of the tent and thinking about the war and his lost friends, and while the philosophers might write that it was a new kind of warfare—absolute war—Wranosky knew that it was the oldest kind. *Maybe the book doesn't have all the answers*, he thought. *And maybe there's a need in this war for the Captain Bergers of the world after all.*

"Did he say anything else?"

Perkin thought of how Gerschoffer begged for his life. How he offered information to prove his worth. "Yes sir. Have you heard about a sickness in the port of Bari?"

Wranosky shook his head no.

"Based on an operation they're running against the Fifth Army staff, Gerschoffer's team provided the intelligence to bomb a US freighter in Bari. It was carrying the US stockpile of mustard gas, our strategic deterrent in-theater. Seems thousands of people are now dying in southern Italy after this shit blew downwind into the port—Axis Sally was bragging about us gassing our allies today on the radio. Guess there's something to it."

"Good Christ! Did you get the name of the leak on army staff?"

A fourth round through Gerschoffer's leg. "He didn't know."

They set in silence for several minutes—Wranosky sat in stunned shock of the news of Bari and the penetration of the Fifth Army staff, while Perkin's thoughts were of Gianina. She never would've forgiven him for the actions he'd taken in her name and, spiritually, he'd probably just bought a one-way ticket to perdition. Yet even as Perkin was thinking of how to atone for his sins, another part of his mind was figuring out how to kill Major Grossmann.

Finally, Colonel Wranosky cleared his throat. "Perk, I wanted to say that I'm sorry about Jim. I know he was a close friend. He was my go-to bubba in the battalion, and a fine young man. I'm sure gonna miss him."

Perkin groaned, "Oh Jesus, sir. I'm gonna miss him, too. I've known Jim since we were freshmen at UT, and outside of Sam, I never had a better friend. What a sorry pair of Exes we were." He wanted to say more about Jim—about how he was the first resident of Kermit to get a college degree, let alone a doctorate; how he was always shot down by the girls but kept trying; how he was quietly a Republican and whenever the President did something he didn't approve of, he would just shake his head and say, "Oh, Roosevelt"; and about how Jim preferred Pearl to Shiner and blues to jazz—but he couldn't bring himself to talk about his friend anymore.

Perkin's head dropped lower, and then he suddenly put his face in his hands and sobbed unashamedly. He cried for Gianina, he cried for Jim, and he cried most of all for himself. When he couldn't stand the self-pity any longer, he stood up, saluted Colonel Wranosky, and walked out into the cold rain where no one would notice his tears.

Epilogue

December 18, 1943
0830 Hours
San Pietro, Italy

Perkin pushed through the rubble of Saint Michael's church in San Pietro. There was very little of it left. The nave was completely open to the sky, and more than half of the once-beautiful church was destroyed. Completely reduced to rubble. Only the bell tower remained oddly intact.

The office to the church was also open to the elements, and the fierce cold wind had blown in rain and debris from around the village. Fallen stones were blocking access to the paneled wall where he had emerged in the village two weeks before. It would take at least half an hour to clear it away by himself, so he set to moving the stones one by one away from the wall. As he worked, Perkin reflected on the past two weeks—and what a hard ball-busting two weeks it'd been.

The Allies had taken San Pietro, but it was such a heartbreaking affair that he couldn't see how it was worth it. They had remained on the spur for several days longer than anticipated, and the battalion suffered greatly. Hundreds of soldiers had been wounded in mind and body, and scores of Texans from the 1st Battalion alone had been killed. The grind of combat had been so severe that replacement soldiers had been ordered into the company only to have been killed or wounded themselves before they even knew their officers' names. It was a terrible way to run a war.

On December 7, the second anniversary of Pearl Harbor, the battalion had been relieved by an Italian motorized brigade. Perkin had watched them deploy proudly to their positions wearing funny little feathered caps—the sight reminded him of the young man in the Caravaggio painting—knowing that such an anachronism symbolically spelled doom for the soldiers facing the battle-hardened 29th Panzer Grenadiers. He had been right. The Italians had been routed in their first attack as American allies, and only concentrated air and artillery strikes kept the Germans from occupying all of Mount Lungo again and possibly moving back into the Mignano valley.

Only when the 142nd Regimental Combat Team had cleared the Germans from the western mountain range and had been relieved by British forces could General Walker pour sufficient troops into the taking and holding of Mount Lungo. While the already decimated 142nd was taking Lungo, the soldiers of the 143rd fought what was perhaps the worst battle of all in the taking of San Pietro—the battle of Mount Sammucro.

It was the worst fight that Perkin had ever seen, and after his experience traversing it on his way to San Pietro, he had hoped to never set foot on that mountain again. The soldiers of the 143rd had no choice. In sleet and snow that continued day upon day, the soldiers had fought for every rock and every crevice on that godforsaken mountain. Sam had volunteered to help on the mountainside, and every day he had carried ammunition up and the wounded back down. Sam had worked like an animal, carrying twice as much ammunition up as any other soldier and gently carrying down the wounded—or sometimes respectfully carrying down the dead. Surprising Sam, the army had scoured the peninsula and bought every available mule in southern Italy to take supplies where even the indomitable jeeps could not go, and some days he would walk along holding onto a mule's tail and allowing it to pull him up the mountainside while he recharged for a moment. Other days, it would take Sam's great strength and patience with animals to coax and push the exhausted and recalcitrant beasts into making another round trip through the constant smell of death.

Perkin knew that Sam had amazing reserves of energy and strength, but even he was astounded at how hard his cousin had worked. Almost as if by a formula, Sam's boots—three-quarter shoes actually—had to be replaced every third trip from the walk up the mountain and the cautious sliding back down. Perkin watched in amazement as Sam almost melted away in front of his eyes—he had never seen his cousin so lean, and he guessed that Sam had lost more than twenty pounds in two weeks' time. But Sam's drive to finish the fight was stubbornly inspirational and Perkin had to work hard to keep up the one time he had gone up the mountain with his cousin.

His duties as the intelligence officer for the 1st Battalion took precedence over helping out the 143rd. The battalion staff had to be recreated almost from scratch, and Perkin and Bill Spaulding worked to hold the battalion together for its remaining days on Mount Lungo and the spur, and would work equally hard to rebuild it after being placed in reserve on Mount Rotondo.

They had both hoped that Sam would keep Able Company, but it was not to be. He was informed that a captain from elsewhere in the division would receive the command—Sam seemed content, however, as long as they made progress. It was not until they had made a trip to Caserta that they discovered who Spaulding's replacement was to be.

Counterintelligence had at first run into dead ends on the search for Major Grossmann. Extensive interviews in Caserta had identified a colonel on the Fifth Army staff as the source of information on the mustard gas stockpile. Before being dismissed from the staff and being remanded in custody to await court-martial, he had discussed his relationship with Antoniette Bernardi, whom he had known only as Teresa.

A clever CIC investigator began to connect the dots between Perkin's report, the colonel's confession about his relationship with Teresa, and a preliminary file on Antoniette Bernardi. An investigation had been in late November on Bernardi due to her contacts with so many officers. The lead CIC investigator had noted in her file that she was likely a prostitute and the investigation had been shelved.

When investigators went to the apartment that Antoniette reportedly maintained in the town, they found clothes, wine, and a powerful narcotic next to an eyedropper. That information would later be used in the colonel's defense, and it would be a sufficiently mitigating circumstance to keep the colonel out of prison. It was not, however, good enough to keep his commission.

Perkin, Sam, and Private Kulis had gone to Caserta two days before to follow up with counterintelligence. At Perkin's request, Private Kulis had been transferred to the battalion staff and now worked for Perkin again. Sam went along to Caserta mostly to keep his cousin company—he had resisted going, but had been told by his battalion commander that he *would* go, and to make sure he got a good meal and a drink while he was there.

While Private Kulis guarded the jeep, Sam and Perkin had walked into the apartment building that had been identified as the one belonging to the woman called Teresa. As Sam walked in through the building door, he collided with another officer—Captain Ronald Ebbins. The past encounters with Ebbins had been invariably unpleasant, and while he was obviously unhappy to see the cousins, he simply nodded and stood aside for Sam and Perkin to come in.

"Mornin', Ronald," Perkin said brightly enough. He was very intrigued to see the officer in the apartment building.

"Berger. Taft. What are you doing here?"

"We're lookin' for a girl named Teresa. Is that the name of your friend that lives here?" Perkin asked on a hunch.

"No, my girl's Antoniette." Ebbins seemed troubled but he answered without his normal distain. "I don't know where—hey, Lieutenant Taft . . . um, I'm actually glad to see you. I just found out that I was appointed to the command of Able Company. I know there's been some bad blood between us, but I can't be at constant odds with my senior platoon leader. If you agree, I think we ought to bury the hatchet." As if he was almost afraid that it would be rejected, he tentatively put out his hand.

Sam had a much deeper well of forgiveness than Perkin, and without hesitating, he had accepted the outstretched hand of Captain Ebbins. "Absolutely . . . and congratulations, sir. It's a great company and some real good boys. I'll meet with you at your convenience to begin turning the company over to you."

"Thank you, Sam. I'd appreciate it. Do you fellas want to get a cup of coffee or something? I know a café near here." The troubled look had not lifted from Captain Ebbin's face, and he had the air of a man who needed a friend.

Perkin answered for both of them, "We'd be happy to, Ronald. I just want to see what I can find out about this girl Teresa."

"Is she a whore?" Ebbins asked. It was a matter-of-fact question, not intended to offend.

"No, Ron." No offense was taken. "A spy. She was sleepin' with a Fifth Army colonel and pumping him for information."

"Oh." Ebbins was aware that Perkin had recently become an intelligence officer. "Hope you catch the bitch."

"Me, too. Wait one while I try her apartment." Perkin bounded up the stairs to the next floor and pounded on the door of the apartment belonging to Teresa. No answer. He then knocked on the neighboring doors hoping to talk to the spy's neighbors, but there was no answer there either. When he came back down, he found Sam alone. "Where'd your buddy go?"

"When you started beatin' on that door, he got kinda sickly-lookin' and said he'd forgotten somethin' at Fifth Army headquarters. Hey, couldn't you knock any louder? I think you woke the whole building."

"They should be at work anyway. Never rebuild this country with the hours the Italians keep."

Sam nodded; it was a sentiment he shared. "Anyway, Ronald said he'd catch me up with me tomorrow. Wasn't that nice of him, though?"

"Maybe we'll see him at headquarters. That's where we're headed next."

They did not see Captain Ebbins at the Fifth Army headquarters. This time, Sam remained in the jeep with

Private Kulis while Perkin walked into the building used by the army intelligence staff. A naval officer sat at a corner desk stacked high with papers, smoking a cigarette and drinking a cup of coffee. Lieutenant Commander Jimmy Cardosi had been introduced to Perkin by Lieutenant Rose of the 1st Special Service Force. Cardosi had been in Italy for months—even before the landings at Salerno.

Cardosi's service dress blues seemed out of place in the army environment, and he had a frown on his face when Perkin walked up. "Hullo there, Captain." He stood up and pulled another chair over to the desk. "Let me guess. No one was there."

Perkin nodded, and the commander continued, "Well, I got some good news and some bad news. Good news is that we think we've identified the girl. Her name's—"

"Antoniette?" Perkin interrupted.

"—Yes, Antoniette. Antoniette Bernardi. How did you know?"

Perkin explained his encounter with Captain Ebbins and his impression that Ebbins was upset because Bernardi had left. Under questioning from the naval officer, Perkin explained his long relationship with Ebbins, ending with his opinion that Ebbins might be an idiot but was not a deliberate traitor.

The naval officer nodded thoughtfully and said, "Well, we'll talk to CIC in a minute and see what they want to do about it. Maybe they'll leave Ebbins be for now and see if she reestablishes contact, since he appears to have the most longstanding relationship with her. CIC had already been looking at Bernardi when this broke, so they have a preliminary background profile of her—she's from a wealthy fascist family in Rome. So . . . Bernardi and Grossmann leave Caserta, and they next pop up in Naples. Grossmann was identified there by a waiter in a trattoria. The waiter said he had seen the same man before in a German uniform, so he calls a cousin in the Camorra, who in turn works for me. He lets me know about Grossmann, or at least the guy I think is Grossmann, and I tell CIC, and they flood the area with Italian informers and Carabinieri. Next day, the waiter and his cousin find both of them in another restaurant near the port. CIC loses Bernardi and Grossmann's trail at this point, and the waiter was found dead a day later at his restaurant. His throat had been cut. Don't know if it's related, but I can guess that he'd been made by Grossmann. Anyway, it's said that Grossmann is a small slight man, blondish hair, wearing the uniform of a major assigned to the Fifth Army staff."

Perkin jumped out of his chair, "Jesus Christ! I think know who he is! I talked to the son of a bitch in . . . what was that village . . . Agropoli. No . . . Ogliastro in September. He was with a short, beautiful girl. I'll bet that was Bernardi!" And there, Perkin realized, was the connection to Sam: Perkin had known that Sam had gotten on the bad side of Ebbins's woman in his first week in Italy, and now he could guess that she had tried to use her connections to German intelligence to have him killed. The more he thought about it, the more the connection between German intelligence and himself emerged from the shadows. Ebbins must have mentioned his reconnaissance to the girl, who reported it to Grossmann and then to Gerschoffer. *Was that really possible?*

"Would you recognize him again if you saw him?"

"What? Yes sir . . . I think so," Perkin nodded.

The commander continued with his story. "That's good, because I talk to folks around here, on this staff, and there's no major on the staff that matches that description. But several people do seem to remember seeing someone like that in these halls, and in the officer's club, and about in town. They all thought he worked in a different department, and it makes me wonder if that son of a bitch actually penetrated this staff—talked to people, walked through rooms, maybe even attended meetings. No telling what damage he's done. What a snafu, shipmate."

Perkin shivered. "OK, so if that's the good news, what's the bad news . . . shipmate?"

"We're a day late and a dollar short. My sources say they were picked up by a Camorra-controlled fishing boat off of Mondragone—great mozzarella, but a mob town. They were probably taken to either Formia or Gaeta just a few miles up the coast and in the German zone. British sentries had reported a British officer, a Captain Drinkwater, and an Italian female passed through a checkpoint south of the town. Guess what? No Drinkwater in the Fifth Army." The naval officer shook his head sadly. "There's no stopping the coastal trade and smuggling between these Italian ports, even if one's in the Allied zone and the other's in occupied Italy. These local sailors have been avoiding customs and controls long before Mussolini, and it's just not possible for us to stop all fishing boats without starving the locals."

"And we don't control the Camorra?"

"Oh, hell no. No one controls the Camorra. Period. Not even themselves. It's not like the New York mob where there's a *capo di capi*, you know, a head motherfucker in charge. The Neapolitan mob is like a loose confederation of crime syndicates, which may or may not cooperate with one another depending on whether it's good for business. So if I say that I have an Eye-tie boss working for me from the Camorra, he doesn't represent the Neapolitan mob at large—no one does. It's as organized and fragrant a setup as Naples itself."

One last comment from the naval officer had stuck with Perkin: "You're gonna be a valuable commodity in the weeks to come, shipmate. Don't dick-dance around and get yourself killed. You're the only dogface in the US Army that can identify this son of a bitch—who, for my money, is the most dangerous intelligence officer that we've faced in Italy."

That evening the three soldiers had stayed overnight in Caserta. Sam and Perkin stayed in a hotel that was converted into a bachelor officer's quarters. Kulis stayed in a brothel. Perkin said nothing to Sam about Ebbins or the investigation. The decision had been made to leave Ebbins in place, a decision that Perkin did not concur with, to see if further contact would be made by Bernardi. Perkin had made the observation that as Bernardi was likely in Rome, contact was unlikely to happen. He was then informed by the senior CIC officer that the Fifth Army would manage any investigation, and he was not to discuss the matter further. Ever.

Perkin had been in a fairly black mood when they went out for a dinner and drinks. Sam, on the other hand, was the most relaxed and cheerful that Perkin had seen for over a month. There was nothing like even a brief relief from responsibility to lift a man's spirits, and so Sam lifted many spirits himself that evening. His good mood was infectious, and soon Sam and Perkin were singing bawdy songs with other officers at the bar's piano and telling jokes and swapping tall tales. Everyone in the club seemed to have a good time, even though men were still fighting and dying mere miles to the north, except for one table where two gentlemen, one in his thirties and one in his forties, were having a drink.

The older of the two men was pretty drunk but not wild, and the younger man was clearly trying to shepherd his friend through a hard night. Sam recognized the older man, and had said to Perkin, "You need to meet these fellas."

"Howdy boys," Sam said as they walked up to the table. The older man started to wave them away. He obviously didn't want company, but stopped when he saw the T-patch on their uniforms. The older man glared for a minute at Sam through squinting eyes, then his face lit up, and he pulled two chairs over from another table.

"Don, this is Sam Taft! I met him on the mountain while he was bringing down our men. Sam, this is Don Whitehead of the Associated Press." He looked at Perkin, stuck out his hand, and said, "Ernie Pyle."

"Perkin Berger. What're you fellas drinking?" Perkin looked at the near empty bottle on the table and motioned for a waitress to bring another. "It's a pleasure to meet you both. If you don't mind me sayin' so, I think y'all have a great feel for the boys. What're y'all workin' on now?"

Pyle hung his head and tried to focus on a few sheets of typewritten pages before him. "It's crap. I don't have any feel for the boys. I've lost my touch."

Whitehead leaned back where Pyle couldn't see his face, grinned, and rolled his eyes.

"I'm gonna go puke outsides. Pour me another one, would ya?" With that pronouncement, Pyle headed for the door with an artificially straight and upright posture.

"May I?" Perkin looked at the papers on the table, and while Sam chatted with Whitehead about his experiences in the war, Perkin looked at Pyle's article. It was entitled, "The Death of Captain Waskow," and the title saddened Perkin. He had just met Waskow a few weeks before.

He read through the words slowly—it was not so much about the death of Henry Waskow as it was about how his death impacted the soldiers in his command. It was a sad, touching tribute to a soft-spoken warrior and leader, and Perkin choked up as he read through it.

"He ain't lost his touch," Perkin said to Whitehead. "Tell him not to change a goddamned word. Not one. Sam, you ready to go? I want sleep more than booze."

Sam started to protest that they'd just bought a bottle of bourbon, but his protests died away at the sad look on Perkin's face. They shook hands with Whitehead, found Pyle outside, and steered him back to his seat, then made their own way back to the hotel.

Henry Waskow was on Perkin's mind as he cleared away the rubble in the church's office. He had only to walk a few steps into the nave of the church, and he could see where Waskow had died. Or, at least, he could see the same mountain.

San Pietro was in ruins. It was the worst destruction that he'd ever seen and far worse than he had expected. The village was completely devoid of a single habitable residence, and the villagers would have been better off staying in their caves than trying to reoccupy their homes. It didn't matter, as they had been evacuated to a displaced persons center established by the Italian government. There simply was nothing left to reoccupy, and he was already hearing that San Pietro might not even be rebuilt— just left alone as a reminder to future generations of the cost of war.

This battle had been bad for the division too, he knew. The casualty reports indicated that over a thousand boys from the 36th alone had been killed to take the village and clear the mountainsides and the path through this little valley, and those numbers would go up as more soldiers died in the hospitals. *Goddamn it all to hell.*

"Hey. Ain't you done yet?" Sam stepped carefully through a doorway that looked a little shaky.

"Almost. Give me a hand." Perkin was dirty and sweating from his labors, even though the temperatures were near freezing.

"Yeah, let's hurry. I just seen John Huston outside. He's reenacting some of the battle scenes for his film, and he says he wants us to be extras."

"Really? I hope it's in Technicolor—I'd hate to waste my good looks on black and white. That might work best for you, though." Perkin grinned at Sam, who just rolled his eyes.

Together they threw the stones and bricks out of the way until Perkin found the panel that he was looking for. He pushed, and the panel dropped past the wall and into the ossuary. Perkin didn't want to go back into the room of skulls, and Sam had no desire to see the bone collection for himself. Fortunately, they had no need go in. In a little space between the walls and a stack of thigh bones lay his gear. His uniform was cleaned and neatly folded, his boots had been cleaned and polished, and his leggings were cleaner than when they'd been issued to him. He pulled the clothes out and immediately put on his sweater from Gianina, a delighted look on his face. The rest of his clothes were set on the floor, and Perkin reached back into the ossuary. He found his Thompson, his father's trench knife, and his pack stacked neatly inside. On top of his pack lay a small envelope that he didn't recognize. He set it aside for the moment and opened his pack. It was still there—the letter that Sergeant Krieger had entrusted to Perkin's keeping. Perkin slid it into his coat pocket and patted it as if to make sure it was still there—he intended to keep his promise to the German soldier. Perkin looked at the other envelope.

It was addressed to *Capitano Berger* and was written in a young girl's handwriting. Perkin accepted Sam's hand, and when his cousin had pulled him up, Perkin opened the letter. They read it together.

*Capitano Berger, it was a pleasure mak-
ing your acquaintance. We wish to thank you for
your bravery, and for trying to save our village.
It was in God's hands and there was nothing you
could do. May Saint Michael protect you, and
always remember us, here and everywhere. Sincerely, Stefania Frattini.*

There was a small postscript under her signature.

*P.S. We live in the third house below the
church. Please visit when the war is over.*

Sam put his arm around Perkin's shoulder as he wiped
away a tear, and Perkin slid the small letter into his pocket
next to the one from Sergeant Krieger. Perkin patted his
pocket again and touched his locket as the two warriors
walked out of the destroyed church and past the rubble of
the third house.

Author's Note

The Battle for San Pietro occurred at a point in the Second World War when Americans had been fighting in the Pacific for over a year, but the European campaign was still in its infancy. The Allied governments had high expectations for their soldiers and their generals, and there was a desire for the Allied advance to be as dramatic and electrifying as, say, the German sweep through France.

Italy in 1943 simply wasn't the place for rapid maneuver warfare. Mountains dominated the geography, and the valleys between the ranges were narrow and defensible. The German Army was exceptionally good at defense, and the Germans had no qualms about impressing slave labor to build their fortifications. Mountain fighting in winter conditions made the battle nearly unbearable for the combatants of both sides, and the weather and terrain took a toll nearly as great as the enemy.

Victory Road is a narrow slice of the first fight against the Germans at the Winter Lines. San Pietro was part of the reduction of the Bernhardt Line by the Fifth Army, and it began on the shores of the Tyrrhenian Sea in the British X Corps sector and continued through II Corps into the VI Corps sector. Meanwhile, the Eighth Army was heavily engaged along the Italian shores of the Adriatic.

Many more units were engaged than just the 36th Division, the Rangers, and the First Special Service Force, and I regret that I couldn't do their stories justice and stay within the bounds of Perkin and Sam's story. I hope the veterans of the other divisions understand.

As in *The Texas Gun Club*, I tried to weave in some of the real pearls from history into the storyline of *Victory Road*. The German destruction of Naples was as bad, if not worse, than I described, and it compounded the destruction caused by the Allied bombing of Naples when Italy was still an enemy combatant. The time-delayed bomb in the Naples Post Office was the first of many to go off in the city, although it occurred earlier in real life (7 October 1943) than it did in my novel, and it killed or wounded seventy people—of whom nearly half were soldiers.

Although there's no indication I've seen that the Neapolitan venereal disease outbreak was the result of scheming German intelligence officers, it was as prevalent and as virulent as described. The bombing of the American stockpile of mustard gas on the liberty ship *John Harvey* is likewise factual, although it was more likely happenstance as opposed to a result of German intelligence collection. As the presence of the mustard gas was highly classified, thousands of sailors, soldiers, and civilians were sickened, and scores died because no one understood the true nature of the problem. The doctors simply didn't know what they were dealing with.

The citizens of San Pietro endured terrible hardships before, during, and after the battle. The able-bodied men and boys were taken from the village and sent to work on the German defenses on the Gustav line. The women, children, and elderly or infirm men retreated to the caves outside of San Pietro—they emerged after the battle to find their village utterly destroyed. Today, the original village of San Pietro Infine is a ghost town—a shattered monument to the war, its heroes, and its victims. The village was rebuilt several hundred yards from its original location, and the two San Pietros exist almost side by side.

With the exception of Fred Walker, Jr., John Huston, Ernie Pyle, and Henry Waskow, all characters below the rank of brigadier general are fictional. Some fictional characters are inspired by true-to-life historical figures, such as naval intelligence officers CDR C. Radcliff Haffendon and LT Tony Marsloe, who were the loose models for the character LCDR Jimmy Cardosi in *Victory Road.* Haffendon met with mob boss Lucky Luciano in a New York prison and arranged for waterfront mob cooperation with the war effort, and Marsloe (and others) conducted intelligence collection ashore at Sicily and Salerno in advance of the landings.

Henry Waskow's story was brilliantly captured by Ernie Pyle and Don Whitehead. His article, "The Death of Captain Waskow," greatly contributed to the body of work leading to Pyle's Pulitzer Prize in 1944. It is a touching tribute to a fallen warrior, and I highly recommend reading it.*

The Battle of San Pietro was immortalized by the great film director John Huston, who was embedded (to use a current phrase) with the 143rd Infantry Regiment of the 36th Division. Huston, who had Texas ties himself, shot some scenes of the documentary during combat and reportedly reenacted other scenes on the battlefield after the fact. His documentary, which showed the fighting on the slopes of Mount Sammucro and the olive groves outside of San Pietro, was considered too graphic by the War Department. The army brass told Huston that he had produced an anti-war film, and Huston was afraid that his whole effort in Italy would be tossed. According to Huston's autobiography, it wasn't until General George C. Marshall had personally screened the movie that it

---

* Pyle, Ernie. *Brave Men,* Lincoln: University of Nebraska Press, 2001.

was approved for viewing by a military audience.[†] As the American public became more desensitized to the scenes of violence seen on reels of combat footage from dozens of battlefields, *The Battle for San Pietro* was finally made public in 1945. Today, *The Battle for San Pietro* is considered one of the best documentaries on war ever made.

There was a great story for Huston to tell. San Pietro was one of the hardest-fought, most grueling battles of the war. Veteran soldiers, some of whom had been with the 36th for years, were killed, wounded, or taken prisoner and were replaced with green soldiers in the heat of the battle. The 143rd alone required more than one thousand replacements, and once more, the Texas character of the division was diluted.

As terrible a fight as San Pietro was, it pales in comparison to what's next for the Texas Gun Club—the Rapido River. I'm afraid that Sam and Perkin will be sorely tested by what lies before them.

CDR **Mark Bowlin**, USN (Ret.)
Flower Mound, Texas
September 2010

[†] Huston, John. *An Open Book*, New York: Da Capo Press, 1972.

About the Author

Commander Mark Bowlin, USN (Ret.) is a somewhat opinionated former naval intelligence officer who believes that the Dallas Cowboys will win this year's Super Bowl, that Texas is truly God's country, and that good Texas barbeque and a cold beer is superior to champagne and caviar in every respect.

Mark was a soldier in the Texas National Guard before being commissioned as an ensign in the United States Navy. Mark has lived in Wales, Japan, and Italy and served in a variety of billets ashore and afloat in the United States and overseas. Among other personal, unit, and campaign awards, Mark has earned the Legion of Merit and Defense Meritorious Service Medal.